RESCUING BROKEN

THE KANE BROTHERS

GINA AZZI

DISCLAIMER

Disclaimer: Rescuing Broken is a sweet, second-chance, military romance that includes sensitive issues regarding sexual harassment and assault and PTSD. It is intended for mature audiences.

1

EVIE

"I'm hurrying," I grumble to my ringing cell phone as I dash into my townhouse, kicking the door shut behind me. Turning around, I flip the locks and reach into my purse, searching for my cell. Of course, my fingers connect with the phone just as the ringing ceases.

"Shit." I already know I'm going to be late. I should probably cancel. I don't even feel like going out tonight.

The shrill ringing cuts the air again and I sigh. Dropping my purse on the console in the hallway, I head into my living room, collapsing onto the couch.

"Jenny," I answer, curling my feet up below me and resting my head back on the cushions. My eyes shut. "I'm not sure about tonight. I'm really not up for it and I've—"

"Save it. I don't care. You're coming. Miranda and I haven't seen you in forever, and I really need a night out. You owe me."

I smile in response to her tenacity, but refuse to give in that easily. "I don't know. It's been a really long—"

"Day, week, month for all of us, which is why we need to grab a drink. I know you're probably pouting on your couch at the moment, trying to think of an excuse to ditch us again, but

I'm not having it. Get your butt up, hop in the shower, pull on a pair of jeans and a sexy halter, and maybe, just maybe, if you cut the resting bitch face and smile a little, you'll even get laid tonight."

I manage to choke out a chuckle while a shudder runs down my spine, my eyes snapping open. "With a guy I meet at Raf's? Come on. We're lucky we don't contract STDs just from entering the place."

Jenny laughs, a girlish giggle she's had since high school. "Or needing a Tetanus shot from the hazardous bar."

I join in her laughter now, forcing myself to stand up. "Fine. I'll meet you girls there in an hour."

"We'll be sitting at the bar."

"Duh."

"There will be a Cosmo with your name on it so don't be late."

"No. Lenny makes the worst Cosmos ever. Just order a whisky sour or a gin and tonic, or something he can't mess up."

"A shot then. He should be able to handle that."

"See you there." Ending the call, I walk into my bathroom and toss my cell on the vanity.

Pinning up my hair since I know I won't have enough time to dry it, I take a quick shower and towel off in front of the mirror. Taking a moment to study myself, I note how my shoulders curve inward, as if they're trying to kiss. I can count my ribs, my boobs are nonexistent, and my arms hang awkwardly at my sides. Dark smudges from too many sleepless nights glare from underneath my eyes, exaggerated by the paleness of my skin. I look sallow, dejected, and exhausted.

I look like me.

* * *

Fifty-four minutes after confirming I am, in fact, the most unde-sirable human on the planet, I slide onto a bar stool at Raf's Bar and Grill and hesitantly accept the shot of tequila and lime chaser Miranda pushes in front of me.

"You look like shit," she greets me matter-of-factly as Jenny comes up to stand beside me, throwing an arm around my shoulders in a half-hug.

"Bad day?" Jenny asks gently.

I wave to a girl I used to work with who is sitting across the bar at a high-top table. She left Morris last year to go to graduate school and do something with her life.

Turning toward my friends, I smile it off. "Nah, just the usual run-in with a couple of tough guys at work. Nothing I can't handle."

"The same guys that have been giving you trouble?" A frown twists Jenny's lips as she peers down at me.

I shrug.

"That's bullshit." Miranda shakes her head. "You work at a physical therapy center for the goddamn military. You think they'd be able to control their own with all their talk of discipline and service and blah, blah, blah."

"It's not that simple," I say, my voice quiet. I focus on my hands.

"It is," Miranda counters, nodding as if to agree with herself. "You need to tell someone, Evie. Tell your boss or superior or commanding lieutenant or whatever the guy is called. Tell him you're being harassed. We saw it that day in the parking lot. They were awful!"

"Miranda's right." Jenny squeezes my shoulder. "We're just worried about you. You've been avoiding us."

"I've been busy."

Miranda's eyes widen.

"I have been." I sit straighter on the bar stool, defensive to the core. I wish they never saw what happened in the parking lot two weeks ago.

"I know," Jenny soothes. "We just miss you and want you to be

3

happy, Evie. That's all. You need to tell someone about what's been going on. It isn't right."

"I know. Thank you, guys. Look, I just, tonight, I just want to catch up with my best girlfriends and relax and have a good time, okay?" I gesture toward Lenny, who is walking toward us, a tray of shot glasses and mixed drinks balanced on his open palm. "Look, Lenny's bringing more shots."

Miranda's eyes brighten as Jenny nods. "Absolutely. We can definitely do that."

"Thank God." I smile at Lenny, accepting the gin and tonic he hands me and passing my shot glass off to Miranda.

"You're not going to have this?"

"It's all you, girl." I raise my gin and tonic in her direction. "Cheers, ladies!"

"To forgetting all the stupid things I do tonight." Jenny raises her shot.

"And forgetting whoever I do stupid things with," Miranda adds, a snort of laughter erupting from her nose as she clinks her shot against Jenny's.

I laugh along with them, taking a small sip of my G and T.

I wish it were that easy to forget.

I wish I could throw back a shot, dance in a crowd, and give myself just one moment to turn off my mind. Enjoy a night out with my girlfriends.

I wish a lot of things.

"I love this song," Jenny squeals, pulling Miranda off her barstool and swaying with her just to the left of where I sit.

"Dance with us." Miranda tries to pull my hand, but I shake my head, taking another tentative sip of my drink.

"I'm good. You girls are crazy." I sing along with the lyrics, trying to get into the good time mood. Trying.

"How've you been, Evie?" Lenny asks from across the bar, a welcome distraction from trying to fake having a good time with my friends.

"Same old, Lenny. What's going on by you?"

"Not too much. Kep's giving me more hours here, which is really helping. I'm hoping in another month or two, I'll be able to quit my job at the mini-mart and bartend here full time."

"No kidding? That's great, Len."

"I know. Then I can enroll back in school. I've only got one semester left 'til my BA, you know?"

I nod. I do know. I know because Lenny has always been focused on the future, even in high school. Even when things didn't work out the way he planned after graduation, he remained determined to get his college degree, to do more with his life than anyone else in his family.

I offer a smile because I'm proud of him, even as the reminder that I've yet to finish my own degree flashes through my mind. Taking courses on and off, in-person and online, has stretched my typical four-year degree into nearly eight years. If I take summer courses, I can complete my B.A. by July but then what? I'm studying Psychology. Who the hell would want me rooting around in their head?

Coming from a long line of accomplished, successful, determined soldiers, my family is all military. And I'm all sorts of disappointment.

"I hope it works out, Len."

"Thanks, Evie. You need anything?"

"Just water when you get a chance."

"You got it." He pulls a glass out from underneath the bar and fills it with water, setting it in front of me.

Once he's called away from the opposite side of the bar, I shift my focus back to my friends. Grinding against each other, giggling, throwing back their heads, they attract the attention of nearly every guy in Raf's.

I nurse my water and check my watch.

How long do I have to stay until it's acceptable to slip away? Closing my eyes, I think of my comfortable couch, the soft sleep pants I wear at night, and the oversized mug I like to drink my tea from.

Gah!

One night out won't kill me.

Plastering a bright smile on my face, I bop my head in beat with the music. I can do this. I'll be fine.

2

JAX

"**M**an, come on. You can't sit around all day and just play... hold up, is this *War Cry*? When did it release?" Denver drops onto the couch next to me, picking up a controller. "After this round, add me. I want in." He settles back against the lumpy cushions.

"All right," I agree, emptying my clip into an enemy and waiting for my kill count to increase. Once I've secured the area, I pause the game, saving my progress, and navigate back to the main menu, so I can play against my brother.

"You know, for someone who's been in a real war, you think you'd get tired of this shit," he mutters, scrolling through battle-field options before selecting a jungle in Vietnam.

Our setting and players load and the TV screen morphs into a war zone.

Reality shifts as memories and forgotten moments suddenly flood my mind.

A blur of onscreen bullets transports me to overwhelming heat and loud noises. Fear swells in my gut, eating at my stomach like acid, as I try to dodge real enemy fire. Ethan flickers before me, his blood seeping hot and angry from his chest and I open my mouth to call out just as Den curses beside me. Jumping in my seat at his voice, I swallow back the dread creeping up my throat and try to quiet my breathing. Ignoring Denver's concerned look, I shake my head to warn off his questions as onscreen me tosses a grenade.

We've only been playing a few minutes when Carter bounds through the door and presses power on the game console, ending our play and blacking out the television screen.

"What the fuck?" Denver tosses the controller onto the coffee table in front of us.

"Get up." Carter orders, kicking my feet off the coffee table and leveling Denver with a glare. "You've been home over a week." He turns his gaze back to me. "You can't just sit around all day and pretend to shoot fake people. You gotta get out and see your friends and act, I don't know, normal. This mopey shit is getting old."

"Man, I'm sorry, Carter. I didn't realize that my being here, settling back in, is so difficult for you to fucking handle." I jump to my feet, my posture defensive, tone full of sarcasm.

Denver heaves a sigh beside me. "Let's go get a beer," he suggests.

I laugh, but the sound is hard and jarring, not like a laugh at all.

"Fine," Carter agrees.

Under the scrutiny of both my big brothers' stares, I shrug, tugging hard on the back of my neck.

Following them out of the house and piling into Denver's old black SUV, I'm reminded by all the times we did exactly this: three brothers hanging out, driving around with the windows open and the radio blaring, searching for a good time. It used to be our norm, as customary as ordering pizza on Friday nights, eating the cold leftovers on Saturday mornings, and watching football on Sundays. But that was before.

Seven long years have passed, and I'm back now, feeling my way around a familiarity that is no longer comfortable.

Staring out the window, I watch the crummy shithole of a town I grew up in pass by. The houses are all the same—more worse for wear now, but still standing. I see the high school and football field and general store. The pharmacy and supermarket and old movie theater. Everything is exactly as it was when I left, but it feels different now, like it's a façade. It should have changed. How could seven years pass, how could the world be ripped apart and parts of it haphazardly sewn back together, how could a man like Ethan die in a land so far from his family, and my tiny hometown in Georgia remain constant?

"You know, she might be there tonight," Denver says. His voice is cautious.

"Who?"

Carter and Denver exchange a glance that is so obvious, I'd have to be blind to have missed it.

"Evie," Carter says clearly, an undercurrent to his tone.

I continue to stare out the window, the cool glass pressing against my forehead. Even this, the silence that stretches between us, feels forced. They watch me warily out of the corners of their eyes, gauging my reaction to things, testing me to see if I'll smile or snap.

"I just wanted you to know, so you're not caught off guard."

"Okay."

"Sometimes, she meets her friends for a drink. Jenny Bailey and Miranda Harris from high school, remember them?"

"Mm-hmm."

"Jenny's a nurse now."

I close my eyes, feigning disinterest but hanging on to every word Carter mumbles. I've only been back a week, and since the second I learned she was in town, I've picked up the phone more than a hundred times to press the buttons for the Maywood Residence. Absorbing as much information as I can from Carter's nervous rambling, I soak up every detail he offers about Evie Maywood. The general's daughter. The all-around good girl who was determined to change the world the last time I saw her.

"Did you keep in touch with her at all?" Denver's deep voice catches me off-guard.

"Evie?" I work a swallow, just saying her name causes a surge of feelings and memories to unfold in my mind. "I tried. I'm not sure what happened. I reached out a few times over that summer and things between us were okay, not great but not awful. I called her the weekend before she reported to West Point and she blew me off. Told me to let her go, to stop playing head games by keeping in touch. She asked me not to contact her again." I bang my forehead lightly against the window, a distraction from the pain of that conversation. Seven years ago it was devastating, today it's still pretty brutal. Guess that saying "time heals all wounds" is bullshit.

Denver whistles lowly but doesn't press for more details which is a relief but also irritates me. I miss talking about Evie. With the exception of Ethan, I never mentioned her to the other guys who were constantly bragging about the women they had waiting for them back stateside. One, because most of their brags were bullshit. And two, because Evie was never waiting for me. It's been a long time since I've said her name aloud and now that I have, I want to keep going. My brothers knew her, know her, almost as well as me.

"Miranda works at a daycare," Carter supplies randomly, continuing to fill the silence with life details of people we've gone to high school with.

The entire time, my thoughts are caught on Evie. The thump in my chest grows louder, ringing in my eardrums as we approach Raf's. Suddenly, I feel both desperate to lay eyes on her and to never see her again. Will she be here tonight? Do I want her to be? Will she be happy to see me?

Nervous energy builds in my limbs, anxious for a release. My left knee bounces up and down while my fingers tap out a beat on the side of the SUV door.

Carter and Denver exchange another look as Carter pulls into a parking space and kills the engine. I exhale, trying to expel some of the electricity jumping around in my veins.

We're here.

* * *

Raf's is a hole-in-the-wall bar that's been around since the inception of our town, way back in the late 1800s. Sure, it's changed a lot since then, but the general spirit is the same: old-timers bitching about new ways of life, has-beens and cougars trying to score a lay with the younger population, the usual military lot, and everyone in between who lives around here and hates it. But you can get a decent burger and fries, a pint, and, if the bartender likes you, a bourbon for eight bucks even. And even though it has been seven years, I'd bet my life that that hasn't changed. What's not to love?

Walking in, the heavy smell of peanuts, stale beer, and frying oil, of something distinctly Raf's, hits me square in the chest and floods me with snippets of memories I'd forgotten about. Some of them are of me and my brothers kicking it here when we had nowhere else to go. Others are of the guys on my old football team and how we'd end up here for burgers after tough practices to bitch about Coach. But most of them scrape at old wounds and I wish I could just forget. Most of them feature her.

We take a booth in the back, near the darts. A couple of guys shoot pool in the corner. The speakers belt out an old throwback tune I haven't heard in forever but somehow brings me back to high school. The corners of my mouth tick up as a swell of nostalgia grips me.

Denver drops into the booth. "Glad we came?"

I slide in across from him. "Yeah. It was a good idea."

"Told ya," Carter says, ambling off to the bar to grab a few beers.

I take a look around, breathing in the familiarity of the place. A place that once was as consistent and comforting to me as my own home. Raf's can be pretty rowdy at night but during the day, it's full of old-timers reminiscing, families grabbing a bite, and everyone capping their meals with a piece of cherry pie on the days that Gladys baked. Scanning the bar, my eyes sweep over people I remember now that they're before me, but haven't thought of once while I was gone: Petey from the tackle shop, Jack from the bank, Vivian who won homecoming queen Denver's senior year.

My eyes settle on a girl toward the end of the bar. Her back is to me, her hair down. I pause, narrowing my gaze. A natural pull keeps my eyes trained on her. A realization sweeps through me, causing my palms to break out in a sweat.

Denver shifts across from me, following my line of sight. He whistles under his breath. "She's here."

I can't believe it's her. Even with her back to me, I can tell. I know the outline of her body, the way her dark hair falls around her shoulders, the delicate curve of her neck. Eons could pass, and still I would know her.

My eyes narrow at her thin frame, note the way her shoulders poke through the fabric of her shirt. She turns toward me then and I realize her skin is two shades too pale and a heavy tiredness hugs her eyes. She's my Maywood, but not.

I feel bulldozed. As if the universe is playing a masterful trick on me. Is it really her? So much time and space are between us; we're different people than we once were, and still it's as if I'm transported back to high school, walking onto the football field. And instead of thinking about the next play, I'm trying to figure out how to approach and impress the beautiful girl that is so far out of my league, a ninety-yard Hail Mary couldn't bring her closer.

Her gaze sweeps over me suddenly, her eyes meeting mine as I stand, my focus zeroed in on her.

She freezes, her shoulders stiffening.

"You sure about this, Jax?"

I take another step, walking toward her. A flicker of uncertainty in her deep blue eyes has me pausing for just a second. Her face is impassive as she looks away. If it weren't for the clenching of her hands and her tight grip on the underside of the bar, I wouldn't think I affected her at all.

But I know I do.

I always have.

3

EVIE

Jenny and Miranda have moved on to sugary sweet, brightly-colored beverages that remind me of all-inclusive vacations to Mexico or the Caribbean. Completely out of place in Raf's, we can't stop joking over how ridiculous they are, but Lenny insisted as he's trying to improve his bartending skills. Still nursing my G and T, but drinking more of my water, I smile at my friends' antics, posing for a quick selfie.

I'm looking over Jenny's head, laughing at something she's saying, when my eyes fasten on his. A mirage. A shadow of my past still haunting my present, despite his absence from it.

It's the scar that causes me to falter, the sight of it, long and thin and pale, hooking around his left eyebrow like a jab. Like the ones he threw so many years ago on the football field. Back before I really knew him. Back before I fell in love with him.

Sometimes, it seems like yesterday and other times, another life completely. And yet staring at the man before me, tracing his scar with my eyes, it still takes a full minute for me to realize that it's him. Undeniably so.

Jaxon Kane has returned home.

And I've never left.

I swallow back a nervous giggle threatening to escape as I avert my gaze, my fingers moving to grip the underside of the bar for something to hold on to. Some of my drink sloshes over the rim of my glass when I knock it with my elbow, and I watch the little droplets as they form a sticky pool on the surface of the bar. I take a deep breath. Jax has always had this ability, to somehow knock me completely off balance while centering me at the same time.

"Is that..." Jenny's eyes flick over Jax's shorn hair, his broad shoulders, the soft blue Henley that hugs the well-defined muscles of his biceps, the faded jeans hanging low on his hips.

"Jesus, he's still sexy as fuck," Miranda says, twirling her fuchsia cocktail umbrella.

"Mm-hmm," Jenny agrees, plucking a Maraschino cherry out of Lenny's fruit tray and popping it into her mouth.

I want to roll my eyes at their antics or laugh off their words. Or chime in with something witty. Instead, I look down at my hands, my nails digging into the underside of the bar, my fingers stinging. I try to distract my mind from the sudden, albeit expected, burn of tears that smart behind my nose.

Jaxon Kane is back.

"Don't look now, " Miranda says, alerting me that Jax must be making his way over.

"Evie." His voice is low and husky, smooth and unhurried. It's exactly as I remember and completely different. More mature, worldly... harder.

My body involuntarily reacts to his nearness, to him. My hands grow clammy, my heart races in my chest; I feel my pulse quicken in my throat, throb in my temples. It's thrilling and terrifying and overwhelming. I bite my lower lip, still looking at my hands, urging myself to pull it together.

Taking a deep breath to steady my nerves, I meet his gaze, forcing my lips to curl upwards in what I hope is a friendly, casual smile. I can be normal. "Jax."

A ghost of a grin shadows his lips but it's gone so quickly, it may have been a trick of the light. He smiles easily at my friends, greeting them as though he just saw them a few days ago at the mini-mart. I'm relieved when Jenny and Miranda chat him up, peppering him with random questions and allowing me a moment to collect myself.

It seems like only seconds pass before his eyes cut back to me. They're the same seafoam green mixed with moss that I remember from high school but a graveness lines them now, a maturity loaded with experience, shadowed by sorrow. Nerves skate up my spine at the heady silence and I shiver.

"You're home." I swallow, desperate to fill the still space between us.

"Yeah," he answers, looking around the old, beaten-down bar. He runs a hand over his head, something he does when he's nervous. "How are you?" he asks, turning back to me, his eyes peering into mine.

He holds my gaze for several seconds, and I feel frozen to the spot. A tick pulses in his jaw, and I know whatever he sees in me concerns him. He didn't expect to find me here, to randomly run into me at Raf's. He must think I'm lame, still hanging out in the town bar while he went off and explored the world, helped others, and changed lives.

"Great. How long are you here for?"

He continues to watch me. His eyes track how my knuckles turn white from my grip on the bar, the way I can't stop chewing the left corner of my mouth, and how I'm so nervous to be standing in front of him, I could worry myself away.

"For good," he says finally, rocking back on his heels. "I'm back, Evie."

"Oh."

"Oh?"

"Hey, Jax, you want a beer or something?" Miranda cuts in.

Jax turns to her and shakes his head, an easy grin on his lips.

That's the thing about him; he's always warm, sincere, genuine. He lets others in as easily as I block them out. "No, thanks." He gestures toward a booth in the back. "I'm here with my brothers. Carter's already grabbing drinks."

"Carter's here?"

Jax's head swings toward me. "Yeah. Why? You want to come say hi?"

I shake my head, my skin tingling from his proximity, my heart short-circuiting as a sense of awareness consumes me. Jaxon Kane is here. Talking to me. "That's all right. You guys enjoy catching up."

He tugs the back of his neck before reaching toward me. His fingers squeeze my elbow gently, and I flinch out of habit. Guilt and embarrassment bloom in my cheeks the second I react, and he pulls away as if I've burned him. Maybe I have.

"You okay?"

"Fine. I, uh, I just need some air." I look past him and focus on the door, finally letting go of the bar and taking a half step back. "Good to see you, Jax. Welcome home."

I ignore Jenny's concerned expression and Miranda's wink as I cut around my friends and hurry out the front door of Raf's into the sticky, sweet night air.

Turning to the left, I walk around to the side of the bar, near the entrance to the kitchen. There's enough light that I can see anyone approaching but enough quiet that I can take a minute to process everything that just happened.

He's back.

Holy hell. I can't believe it. I never thought I would see him again. After he left, it felt like my world was ending. That summer, he kept reaching out, phone calls, emails, text messages. Every time I heard from him, the hole in my heart simultaneously stretched and shrank. I looked forward to the sound of his voice even though hearing it cut me to the core.

But then I asked him to stop. Demanded it. Told him to just let me go.

And he did.

I still remember the day he told me he enlisted. It haunts me almost as much as everything that came after.

He's nervous. I can tell the moment I descend the stairs, faltering momentarily on the landing. Whatever he's about to say, I already know I don't want to hear it. I wonder if I can turn around and stumble back up to my room and ignore whatever it is that has that look crossing Jax's face.

"Evie." His voice is low and husky, his hand reaching up to tug on the back of his neck. He won't meet my eyes, and a sinking sensation settles in my stomach, floods through my limbs, and keeps me rooted halfway down the staircase.

"What's going on?" I hate the shaky note in my tone.

Gripping the banister, I take the last three steps slowly, my eyes never leaving Jax as he struggles to look anywhere but at me.

"Can we, um, talk for a minute?" He turns toward the formal sitting room that my mom only uses for her obligatory military entertaining. It's stuffy and serious, and a room I never thought I'd find myself in with Jax.

Still, I follow him inside and perch on the edge of a stiff chair. Folding my hands in my lap, I clench my fingers together to keep them from shaking.

"Are you okay?" I ask, beseeching him with my eyes to look at me.

Finally, he turns toward me and nods, taking a seat across from me.

"Yeah. I, um, I just need to talk to you."

"Okay."

He blows out a deep breath, his cheeks puffing the air out in a long stream that ends on a near whistle. He leans forward in his chair, his elbows resting on his knees. Rocking forward, he moves as if to grab my hand but thinks better of it at the last second, letting his hand fall to his side. "Evie." A wry grin twists the corners of his mouth in a cross between a smile and a grimace. "I can't tell you how much this year, getting to know you, hell, falling in love with you, has changed my life. I want you to know how much you mean to me, how much your believing in me has given me a future I never could have imagined. I'll always be grateful to you, my Maywood, and I'll never forget what you and your family taught me, showed me." He chuckles but it sounds forced. "All of this," he says, gesturing around the great room with his hand, "was inconceivable to me before I knew you."

"You've changed my life too." My voice is quiet but steady, and I'm grateful that the shaking of my hands hasn't yet taken hold of my tongue.

An awkward silence I've never experienced with Jax stretches between us.

"I don't understand what you're trying to say." I admit.

Jax sighs, rubbing his hands together. "You've made me dream, Evie. You've made me realize my future could be full of so many opportunities and chances and, and things I never thought about since my mom passed," he swallows, offering me a sad smile.

"I'm glad." I smile back. "You're so smart and talented, Jax. You could do anything you want. I'm happy we're going to New York together. West Point has been my dream for forever and you're going to love John Jay College. I know you haven't heard back from their financial aid department yet but I'm sure you'll get a scholarship. Even if you have to defer and do a few courses at a community college first; it will all work out."

He nods, his hand tugging the back of his neck again. "I want to do something I could be proud of. Be someone you could be proud of."

"I am proud of you."

He holds my eyes for a beat and in that pause, a flood of emotions flows between us—a torrent of shared moments and unspoken words. And I know whatever comes next is going to level me.

"I've enlisted. I report to Fort Bragg in two weeks." His voice is even and measured, his words belying his calm tone. His eyes are clear and *focused. He watches intently for my reaction, waits for me to give him a piece of my mind like I normally do.*

But I'm too shocked to think clearly. I sit in silence, my heart breaking, my world crumbling. Are we breaking up? I stand shakily, my mind jumping from one thought to the next. My face and neck heat with embarrassment, with rejection. A burn behind my eyelids and nose signals that I'm about to cry.

"Evie," he says gently, reaching for me.

But I escape his grasp, flee past him, and leave the stupid great room.

I bound up the stairs, my steps quickening the closer I get to the top, to the safety of my bedroom. Locking my bedroom door behind me, my back slides down the door until I'm a puddle on the floor, a torrent of tears melting with the sorrow and pain I carry.

Jax is leaving me.

He's enlisted.

He's Army now.

Letting my tears dry on my cheeks, I manage to calm my breathing as my embarrassment morphs into anger.

Today is the last day I will ever think about Jaxon Kane.

No, that's not true.

But today is the last day that I'll see him.

That much I know is certain.

Except it wasn't certain. Because I never left. And now he returned.

"You're going to give yourself a headache." Denver's gravelly voice cuts through the quiet, and I swing around to look at him. "Thinking that hard." He smirks, leaning back against the old brick of Raf's, one foot kicked up behind him, resting against the building. "You want?" He holds out a pack of cigarettes.

I shake my head, briefly alarmed that I didn't hear him approach. He must have exited through the kitchen after heckling the two cooks who work here.

"Haven't seen you around lately," he comments, lighting up a cigarette and taking a long pull.

"I haven't been around."

He exhales a cloud of smoke. "Yeah. You surprised to see him?"

"Yes."

"Eventually, y'all are going to have to talk, y'know? Clear the air."

"Guess so."

Denver chuckles. "I always appreciated this about you, Evie." He gestures toward me with the lit tip of his cigarette.

"What's that?"

"You're a woman of few words." He drops his head back against the brick, looking up at the dark sky. "You tell it like it is but only when you have to. The rest of the time, you give nothing away. Unless you're giving Jax shit but it's been quite some time since I've seen you riled up like that." He tosses the butt and grounds his heel into it.

"I think that's the most you've ever said to me."

He laughs, the sound rich and warm. "Probably. But sometimes, talkin', really talkin', and lettin' go of the past and all the bullshit," he says, shrugging and kicking off the wall, "it can help."

I turn away from him, quiet for a beat, and let his words sink in. I feel him walk closer to me, stopping an arm's length away. He knows better than to touch me, even as a friend, even in a moment of comfort. "Think about it."

Then he's gone, and I'm alone with the black sky and my dark thoughts.

4

JAX

"How'd it go?" Carter asks, sliding a bottle of beer across the grimy table separating us. He nods in the direction of Evie's friends, except Evie is still outside "getting some air."

I shrug, gripping the bottle in my hand. Should I have followed her? What is the protocol when the girl that once made up all the good in your world can't talk to you for two-minutes without bolting?

"She's had it rough," Carter mumbles, watching her friends thoughtfully. "Just give her some time."

"You're kidding me, right? It's been seven years. She's had all the time in the world."

He picks at the label of his beer bottle. "I don't know what to tell you, kid. You took off. A lot changes in seven years, especially when you don't come home to visit." He smiles at me to take the sting out of his words, but still it hurts. Because it's the truth. Isn't that what they say? The truth hurts. Well, it fucking does. "Sure, you say you enlisted for her. Whatever, I get it." He takes a swig from the bottle and shakes his head at me. "But she sure as hell doesn't. And she may never understand that."

"Where's Denver?" I look around for my oldest brother,

wishing he were sitting here just so Carter can shut up with his stupid advice. The guy has banged every female in a fifty-mile radius, and now he's somehow an expert on relationships?

"Having a smoke."

"He should quit that shit. Gonna give himself lung cancer."

"Yeah. Sometimes, we don't know how good we have it 'til we don't."

"Would you stop talking in fucking riddles? Who are you, and what have you done with my brother?" I can't mask the irritation in my tone. Carter and I used to be so close, close enough to tell it like it is. But ever since I got home, he's been circling around me, offering little pieces of advice that land like jabs. Saying stupid shit that makes no damn sense, but I know he's saying it for a reason. A reason I have yet to figure out.

He laughs at me, shaking his head. "You used to be much more level-headed. What'd you become, a hothead in the Army? I thought you had to maintain your wits during war."

"I didn't realize coming home meant stepping into a minefield."

He blows out a breath, tilting his head to the side, studying me. "Well, little brother, I don't think you considered much of anything except yourself these past seven years."

"What's that supposed to mean? I told you, I left because—"

"Because of Evie. Because you didn't want to stand in her way; you wanted her to be free to make her own choices."

"What's your point?"

"That's bullshit, Jax. You left because you had an out." He slams his beer bottle on the table, and it teeters for a moment. "You took your shot and never looked back, and no one is gonna blame you for it but, Jesus, be upfront about it. You left for you, not for Evie or some misguided moral high ground. You did it for yourself." He slides out of the booth. "And it sucks things didn't work out the way you wanted between you and your girl. But you still had family here, you still had us. You could have come home." He turns away. "I gotta piss."

I sit in stunned silence, watching my brother's back as he disappears around the corner.

Anger boils beneath my skin, igniting a fire in my veins. Clenching my hands into fists, I try to calm the inferno raging inside me. I want to punch something. Or Carter. Because as ugly as his words were, they cut me in ways I can't begin to describe.

The truth is fucking painful. It will rip you up and leave you raw and decimated. It will level you with one word, in one moment. The truth doesn't set you free like all those liars spew. It locks you up, cages you in, and turns you inside out until you don't even recognize yourself. And you hate everyone who does.

When I reported to Fort Bragg, I kept myself tied to home through Evie, through my brothers and Daisy. Fine, maybe some of my reasons for enlisting were selfish. I did want to blaze my own path, one that wasn't solely tied to Evie's career aspirations. But I still wanted home to feel like home. When Evie cut our communication, I cut ties with my hometown, opting instead to meet up with my brothers and Daisy in random cities when I had leave. I hurt my family without giving them too much thought because I was too wrapped up in my own hurt. And Carter is right, a lot changes in seven years.

Pushing out of the booth, I leave our empty beer bottles behind and storm out of Raf's, directly colliding with the girl who's had me twisted up in knots since I was seventeen.

"Oof," she wheezes out as her body slams into mine.

"You okay?" I clasp her elbow to steady her, the sharpness of her bone surprising me before I feel the warmth of her skin. Already, I don't want to let go.

She straightens and steps back, my fingers sliding off her elbow and grazing the bare skin of her arm before dropping to my side.

"Fine. Ugh, sorry about that. I didn't see you." She tries to side-step me, and I throw my arm out to stop her.

"It was my fault." I turn her toward me, so I can see her face, try to read her.

Her eyes are like the deep blue of the ocean before a storm, surging. She regards me warily, vulnerability shining around the edges of her irises, causing guilt and remorse to expand in my chest.

Remembering Carter's words, realization slams into me, an awareness I was too angry to accept before. I put that wariness there. I made her uncertain of me. I should have fought harder to be in her life, fought harder for us. Even though I was crushed when Evie cut me off, I hurt her first by leaving.

Awkward, tense silence fills the air around us and I hate it.

I hate looking at the girl who once consumed my whole world; a girl I could see with my eyes closed, and now I can't read her at all. Not even a little.

Evie Maywood was once as unpredictable as the weather: pure sunshine, bolts of thunder, or a calming blue for as far as the eye could see. She was passion and confidence and intensity. She was generous and loyal and honest to a fault. She was quick-witted, quick-tempered, and had a dynamite sense of humor. She was mine.

But this Evie, the one looking up at me now with dull eyes and a paleness that is deeper than skin level, she's not even a shadow of my Maywood.

"For real, Evie. Be straight with me." I tilt my head and smile at her and for a second, just a flicker, everything freezes and it's us again. A cocky as hell, easy-going guy and a beautiful, enthralling girl connected in a way that only the universe could understand.

Then she blinks, and the moment fades into the harsh reality of now.

"I'm fine." Her voice holds a note of finality.

I drop my arm; she walks past me, and the door to Raf's opens and closes.

And it's like losing her all over again.

Fuck. I blow out a deep breath and walk a few steps into the parking lot of Raf's. The overhead lights blaze over the cracked asphalt and errant weeds poking up.

The sound of an engine starting halts my steps as a hunter green F350 begins backing out of a parking space.

Ethan. It's gotta be him.

I turn toward the truck, my hand raised in a half-wave as I remember the Christmas I spent with him and his family in Michigan three years ago. Back then, Den was in lock-up, Carter had a flavor of the month, and Daisy opted to spend the holidays with her roommate's family.

Ethan and I did lights around the house and all the trees. We cut down a huge Christmas tree and laughed our asses off trying to rope it into his truck.

I stride forward to catch him, calling out his name.

The F350 passes me, the guy driving about eighty pounds too heavy and three shades too light to be Ethan. He stares at me strangely before nodding at me.

My hand falls, and I squeeze my eyes shut, opening them in time to see the red tail lights of the F350 trailing down the road.

Ethan's gone.

He's not coming back.

A whistle cuts low to my right and I turn.

"You good?" Denver asks, taking a measured step in my direction, his hands tucked into the front pockets of his jeans.

"Yeah, man."

He pulls a pack from his back pocket and taps out a cigarette, holding the box out to me.

I shake my head.

"I went back inside but couldn't find you or Carter so..."

"Carter went to piss, and I came out to just... I don't know why the fuck I came out."

"To see her."

I shake my head again.

"She's not the same girl she was when you left."

"Yeah, figured that one out real quick."

Denver threads the cigarette between his fingers, twirling it around and around but doesn't light up. "Sometimes coming back is even harder than taking off." His voice is even, but his words are pulled too tight, spoken too sharply. "Could be why you stayed away for so long."

I twist my head to look at him, taking in his ripped jeans, his dark hair pulled back in a sloppy man bun, and the same leather jacket old our man used to rock before he got life in a prison in Alabama. Den looks the same way he did the night before I left. But the seriousness of his expression, the rawness of his gaze, and the honesty of his words are a Denver I've yet to have the pleasure of meeting. It seems like my oldest brother grew up, and I missed that, too.

"Yeah. Sometimes it is," I agree finally.

The right side of Den's mouth lifts, and it seems like he's going to tell me something, reveal an important piece of advice that's going to make my transition back smoother, when the door to Raf's bangs open and Carter steps out.

"There y'all are. I was looking fucking everywhere." He bounds down the steps. "Nothing worthwhile in there to tap."

Den shrugs and I turn away. The most worthwhile reason I can think of to stay is sitting inside on a barstool and wants nothing to do with me. Still, I know Carter wasn't talking about Evie. She was like another sister to him once.

"Wanna take off?" Carter asks Denver.

"Whatever."

"Sure," I throw out, just to be included.

We walk back to Denver's ride in silence, kicking random

rocks and stepping on weeds. Once we're in the SUV and Denver's pulling out of Raf's, I realize that this moment, with the comfortable silence stretching between us and Carter's unsuccessful attempts of trying to score with a girl, is the most familiarity I've experienced with my brothers since coming back.

So I laugh. It's low at first, but gradually it takes over. Soon, I'm hunched forward, scrunching my eyes shut and trying to catch my breath.

I can feel Denver's eyes on me through the rearview mirror. I hear Carter shift his weight in the passenger seat, staring at me over his shoulder.

"I never thought that with me gone, you both would lose your edge," I manage to sputter. "How the hell are the three of us going home alone? Together?"

"What the hell are you laughing about? You always went home alone when we would go out." Carter reminds me.

"I was in high school. And I had a girlfriend my senior year."

Denver snorts in acknowledgement. Carter sits in stunned silence.

We stop at a traffic light, and it's like time stands still. For the second time tonight, my past collides with my present. And my brothers laugh, loudly and uncontrollably, along with me.

5

EVIE

Clicking out of my email, I pull up this week's schedule on my computer screen. Scrolling over the stacked appointments for today, the ringing of the office phone cuts through my concentration.

"Morris Physical Therapy and Rehabilitation," I answer, my hand hovering over the mouse as I listen to the caller.

"Private First Class John Davis."

"Hello Private Davis, what can I do for you today?"

"I'm calling to schedule an appointment with Staff-Sergeant Peters to evaluate my right knee."

I scan the calendar for open slots and note that Peters has a cancellation tomorrow. "We can schedule you for tomorrow at eleven-thirty."

Davis breathes out loudly, as if he was holding his breath, and I can feel his relief through the line. "That would be great. Thank you, Ma'am."

"Sure thing. I'm adding you to his schedule now." I collect his information and add Davis onto the calendar. "We will see you tomorrow."

"Roger that."

Placing the phone back in the receiver, a shadow falls across my desk, forcing me to look up into the familiar but guarded eyes of Jax.

I shudder, placing my hand at the base of my throat.

"Sorry," he says, ducking his head. "I didn't mean to scare you."

"Is there something I can help you with?"

"I'm here to see Staff-Sergeant Peters. He's expecting me."

"You're not on his schedule."

"I know." Jax shifts his weight and stares at me, daring me to contradict him.

I glance at the schedule again to make sure Peters isn't currently conducting an evaluation.

"I'll take you back," I offer, standing from my desk and pushing my chair in neatly.

He follows half a step behind me. I can feel his eyes hovering around my shoulder blades, watching me with a quiet intensity that I don't comment on. We round a corner, and I gesture toward the closed door of Peters' office.

"Staff-Sergeant Peters," I say.

"Thanks. I didn't know you work here."

"I do."

"As the receptionist?" He asks it as a question, but he means it as a statement, surprise coloring his tone.

"Yes." I lift my chin slightly, trying to inject pride into my voice, into my chosen profession. I work as a civilian, but I help support the US Army. I work.

"You've been doing this a long time then?" He widens his stance, his arms crossing over his chest, his biceps bulging in a display of hard muscle and strength. A patch of pocked skin and crisscrossed scars on his left bicep catch my attention as they peek out from below the sleeve of his T-shirt. I squint, studying the damaged skin, desperate to reach out and run my finger over the smooth dips when he clears his throat.

"Four years," I mutter, averting my gaze as embarrassment

floods my cheeks. For four years, I have worked at a job my mom helped secure for me. For four years, I've ridden on the coattails of my family name, a dark stain of embarrassment on their impeccable standards and flourishing careers.

Jax steps forward then, his right hand coming up to rest on the doorframe. "What happened to West Point?"

I look up. His eyes flash with frustration and bewilderment.

"Life. Knock before you enter." I tilt my head toward Peters' door before walking around Jax and retreating to my desk, to scheduling and answering phones and responding to emails. To the predictability of a position where I can never soar too high, grow too much, or be too confident again. To a comfort in knowing I'll always be overlooked.

* * *

Later that evening after the sun has set and the quiet of night pervades my townhouse, I open my laptop and log onto Facebook. Scrolling through posts and pictures of friends and various people whose paths crossed with mine, I admit to myself that I'm stuck. The posts of new job offers and baby showers coupled with the photos of global travel and wedding days forces me to confront that who I am now is so far from the person I aspired to be. That I've been wasting time and potential by merely existing when I could have been moving forward.

Several posts about sexual harassment and assault in the acting industry catch my eye, as does the #MeToo hashtag. I stare at a headline, "Director Abe Collingswood Resigns After Four More Actresses Step Forward," for several moments before reading the article. After clicking on the comments, I'm astounded by all of the brave, bold women who have empathized, shared similar experiences, or simply added #MeToo. A small smile crosses my lips at their courage and honesty.

But then a comment at the bottom of the page captures my

attention. "Stop overreacting. You got what you wanted. Did you not all make a shit-ton of money in his movies?" I slam my laptop shut and wander into the kitchen.

Uncorking a bottle of Merlot and pouring myself a generous glass, I settle back onto the couch and flip to Netflix to watch *Jane the Virgin*. A call from Mom lights up the screen of my phone but I ignore it, sending her to voicemail.

After two episodes, I'm restless. Sleep still hasn't claimed me, the comment on that article weighs heavily on my mind, and each time I close my eyes, I see the disappointment that crossed Jax's face today. I hate that he looked at me like he didn't even recognize me. Like he doesn't even know who I am anymore. But that's fitting, isn't it? I don't recognize myself most of the time.

Resting my head against the cushions of my couch, I let the silence wash over me. It clogs out noises, so I'm left with my even breathing and bitter thoughts.

I could have been someone.

Instead, I allowed the past to consume me. I've watched days turn into weeks, turn into months, then turn into years. I sit and watch and wait.

What am I waiting for?

I finish my glass of wine and set it on the coffee table, not even caring that it will probably leave a ring stain that'll be impossible to remove.

Picking up my laptop again, I open it and navigate to a folder deeply hidden in the hard drive. Inside, I find my applications, letters of recommendations, and transcripts. My old life reminding me of all I gave up.

My eleventh-grade English teacher had written: "Evelyn demonstrates great commitment, discipline, and loyalty to her studies, her classmates, and her community."

"Evie is a true team player, always putting the needs of others before herself. She leads by example." My high school track coach added in his letter.

Seven years ago, I was on a clear path, one that promised exciting opportunities and new experiences. Yet, I'm still sitting here, in my tiny hometown. Tonight, the discrepancy between what is and what could have been is glaring. I can't stop thinking about the past and I know a lot of that has to do with seeing Jax again.

When I told him to let me go, I never believed he really would. I never thought I would be that easy for him to forget about. He reached out once more, a Facebook post, that read "Happy Birthday" when I turned twenty-one. On my twenty-first birthday, clutching a water bottle, his message had felt like a slap in the face.

Seeing him the other night at Raf's, the overwhelming hurt and utter disappointment of his leaving, of his moving forward without me, was a wake-up call I wasn't anticipating.

Although I passed on West Point, these past four years at Morris haven't been awful. In fact, I've learned a lot. On the days that I can clear my mind completely, I even enjoy my work. Helping active duty soldiers return to their squads, sometimes into the midst of combat zones where their absence is felt greatly, where their commitment could change everything is important to me. I feel proud to assist veterans as they rebuild themselves and their lives and come to terms with the people they are now that they've seen things they can't forget. I've suffered with them through moments of anguish and denial. I've witnessed great acts of bravery and acceptance.

In some small way, I've helped, aided, guided, cared for, gave to these soldiers.

I've achieved something I've always valued, albeit not in the way I used to imagine. I've always wanted to help others, that's one of the reasons why I chose to study Psychology.

Why doesn't it feel like enough then?

A sourness in my throat forces me to be honest with myself.

It's because as much as I love being a part of the soldiers' journeys as they heal, as they take tiny shuffles or giant leaps forward, I still want more.

Chewing the corner of my mouth, I mull this over. The physical therapy, my work at Morris, Jax's steady scrutiny and piercing gaze.

I think about my colleague from Morris who recently went to graduate school. I think about Lenny. Things didn't turn out the way they once planned but they still found a way to pursue the futures they desired. That doesn't mean I can't ever achieve my dreams, right?

Pulling my laptop closer, I type "physical therapy degrees" into the search engine.

Scanning the various websites and university admission requirements, I click on several, noting prerequisites and course loads. Suddenly, I'm grateful for my Psychology studies since I've already completed most of the science pre-requisites.

A shiver of excitement runs through me, pushing lightly at my insecurities. A glimmer of hope sparks my heart, reminding me that I am still capable. That just because I've wasted years doesn't mean I must continue to sit and watch and wait.

Instead, it finally dawns on me, I can still become the person I once thought I would grow into. Someone seventeen-year-old me would be proud of. Someone current me can be proud of.

6

JAX

"**W**hy didn't you tell me Evie works at Morris?" I question Carter as I step into the kitchen.

A dribble of milk slides off his chin as he lowers the carton and looks at me over his shoulder. "What?"

"Evie. She works at Morris. As a receptionist." Incredulity colors my tone because I'm shocked as shit. What happened to my Maywood? What happened to the beautiful, vibrant, and insanely motivated girl I kissed good-bye the day before I left for Fort Bragg?

The version of Evie I ran into at Raf's and saw at Morris is distant and detached. She's scarily thin, her eyes are almost empty, and she looks completely worn-out. A sadness I don't understand clings to her.

When we stopped talking seven years ago, I never thought I'd come home and find her here again. I figured I'd walk into Raf's and hear all about a future five-star general. But she's nothing like the Evie I remember. My Maywood may have been reserved and polite in public but in private, she was sassy and spunky and confident as all hell—sometimes, downright argumentative and infuriating. What happened to that girl?

"Yeah," Carter agrees, shutting the refrigerator door and leaning against it, his arms folded over his chest. "So?"

"Why didn't you tell me? She never went to West Point, did she?"

"Not that I know of."

"And you didn't think that was information I should know? I mean, that girl, she was my world and—"

"Was. She was your world. And then you enlisted and—"

"So she could go to West Point without me holding her back. So I could have an actual career." I'm yelling now, indignation coursing through my veins, giving me the edge I need to confront my brother. "I thought," I shake my head, the confession seems stupid now, "I thought we would work it out and end up together."

Carter curses but his tone is softer.

"Why didn't you tell me that she didn't go?"

He pushes off the refrigerator, standing to his full height before dropping into a chair at the kitchen table. "You never asked, kid." His voice holds a note of sympathy. "You got out. You were on your way to do things you never would have done if you stuck around here." He chews his lower lip as if he's carefully choosing his words, "If you knew she didn't go, you would have tried to come back."

I scrub a hand down my face. "So? Would that have been the worst thing?"

He's quiet before he nods, "At the time, yeah, it could have been."

"I don't understand what the hell would make her not go to West Point? It was all she talked about, her family legacy, being an empowered woman like her mom, making a difference. It doesn't make any sense," I say aloud, even though I'm talking to myself.

"You'll have to ask her," Carter responds, standing from the table and walking toward the living room. Before the kitchen door swings closed behind him, he turns to me, "I'm sorry things didn't work out the way you hoped."

I nod at him but can't help wondering that he knows more than he's letting on. That other things stopped him from telling me about Evie.

* * *

"Yo." I smack my open palm against the hood of a Toyota Corolla as I walk up to stand beside Denver's feet.

He slides out from underneath the car, a wrench in his hand, and squints up at me. "What's up?" he asks before sliding back under the car. "Hand me a socket, will ya?"

I poke through his toolbox before finding the socket and passing it to him.

"How're you settling back in?" He asks, his voice muffled.

"All right, I guess. Being back is strange. It's like nothing and everything has changed."

"Yeah. Time away will do that."

I smirk knowing the only time away Denver ever spent was a stint up in Jackson Penitentiary.

"Why didn't you tell me Evie never left?"

The socket clatters to the asphalt, and I hear Denver let loose with a string of colorful profanities. He slides back out from under the Corolla, wiping his fingers on a greasy bandana. "You talk to her?"

I shake my head.

"You should."

"That's what Carter said."

Denver mutters another curse before sitting up, his heels biting into the ground as he slides back and forth on the creeper for a few beats. "He's right."

"I feel like everyone knows something that I don't. Like there's some big secret about Evie that I'm in the dark about."

"Then you'd be right. But you still need to talk to Evie about it. It's for her to tell you... or not. Toss me that bottle." He points to a water bottle to the left of my sneaker.

I tug on the skin at the back of my neck. I know there's nothing I can do to make Denver talk. He does everything on his own time, his own terms, always. Reaching down, I pick up the water bottle and throw it at him a little harder than necessary.

He chuckles as he catches it easily, giving me a glimpse of the new piece inking his inner bicep. Uncapping the top, he takes a long swig. "You ever think we're doing you a favor?" he asks, peering at me over the water bottle.

"What do you mean?"

"The secret... not telling you. Letting all this time pass. You ever think that maybe it's because Carter and I are looking out for you? Trying to protect you?"

"Protect me from what?"

"Regret," he says, a heaviness weighing the one word down, so it takes on new meaning. "Talk to Evie." He lies back and slides under the car, ending our conversation.

I stand still for several seconds, listening to Denver's tinkering and swearing. The heat from the sun blazes down on us. The cracks in the asphalt are larger than I remember, weeds poking up in patches. Our old house looks shittier now, more dilapidated. Old pop cans and gum wrappers decorate the front lawn. All of that is the same, more now, but the same as always. My brothers are the same but not.

It's like nothing has changed at all. Except me.

And because of that one alteration, everything around me seems different.

* * *

The heat of the blaze permeates my gear, stinging my skin like the burn of a jellyfish. Except I feel it everywhere, even in my blood.

"Ethan?" I yell over the rush of blood in my ears. "Ethan!" He was right next to me. I know he was. I reach out blindly, my fingers catching air as I search for him.

Gunshots ring out around me, whizzing past in rapid spurts, their nearness chafing my skin, even through all my gear, even as they miss. Sand kicks up, blinding me. It's everywhere: clogging my ears, filling my nose, lodging in between my teeth.

"Ethan! Answer me," I spit out, crouching low and shuffling two paces to the right where I collide with something. Someone. Him.

A groan.

"Willis." I drop to my knees, my hands quickly searching Ethan's chest and arms, trying to find the source of his pain.

"Jax." It's a wheezy breath like he got kidney punched. Or his lungs are punctured. Or...

"I'm not gonna make it, man."

"Don't say that." I find the hit, my fingers colliding with the hot stream of blood pouring from Ethan's chest. "You're going to be fine. Look at me," I demand, staring at him through the dust of sand and the consistent staccato of rounds piercing the air. Desperate screams of devastating ends and the eerily calm call of commands swirl around us. I add pressure to his wound and stem the bleeding. Ethan's life seeps through my fingers like the sand that chokes me.

"Tell Amy. Tell her... tell her I love her. I've always loved her." His breathing is shallow, his voice faint.

"Tell her yourself. You're gonna see her soon, man. They'll fly you to Germany, and Amy will be there. She'll be all over you, let you eat as many burgers as you want."

"Tell her. Please. Promise me." His eyes bore into mine with the desperation of a man who knows he's about to die.

"I promise."

"Tell her she was it for me. She's it."

"I will."

"Tell her she's going to be an incredible mom. The best."

I swallow thickly, nodding. "Ethan? Ethan!"

The heavy blades of a chopper beating the air sound overhead.

"Ethan, please."

"Grab him." Another voice interrupts my frantic thoughts. A body pushes me aside, hauling Ethan up. Moving him away from me. *"Drop back."*

What? I reach for Ethan. But he's already on the move. He's leaving. He's gone.

And all I have is his blood on my hands.

I jolt awake, the realness of the nightmare consuming me. I taste the hot air, can chew the sand. My hands are outstretched, my fingers reaching for my best friend. My body is hopped up on adrenaline.

Jesus.

I gasp, my chest heaving; I can't suck the oxygen in fast enough. It's like it's about to be cut off.

"Jax? You okay?" Denver's voice calls out as his knuckles rap against my bedroom door before his head pops around.

"Yeah," I wheeze out.

Denver's eyes narrow as he watches me for several seconds before entering my room and walking toward me. "It's almost nine."

"What?" I ask sharply, my hands dropping to my bed. My fingers collide with the sweat spots soaking through my sheets.

"Bad dream?"

I nod.

"Ethan?"

I nod again.

"Fuck." He whistles between his front teeth. "You all right?"

"Yeah."

He sinks to the edge of my bed. "I thought I saw a bunch of fucked up shit in prison, but I doubt it compares to anything you've been through."

"I don't know." I reach up to touch my shoulder, massaging the tender spots around the scarring. Thank God I start PT this week.

He fixes me with a look I don't want to acknowledge. "You gotta talk to someone man. Anyone."

"I'm okay. I'm handling it."

"This is the third time you've woken up screaming in your sleep. This week."

"You keeping count?" I shove the blankets off and swing my legs to the side of my bed. Leaning forward, I rest my elbows on my knees and try to regulate my breathing.

"We're just worried about you."

"I didn't realize you learned how to talk about your feelings and shit in lock up. You could be a professional shrink now."

Denver laughs, a quick bark, as he smacks me upside the head. "Fuck off. I'm just here to give you a heads up."

"'Bout what?"

"Daisy's coming home for spring break."

My head snaps up, and I find Denver watching me closely. I can't stop the smile that breaks out on my face, even as my heart continues to gallop from the fading reminders of Iraq. Daisy's coming home. I missed my little sister almost as much as I missed Evie these past seven years. Sure, I did a hell of lot better at keeping in touch with her, sending emails, FaceTiming when I could, mailing off postcards whenever I was someplace inter-esting that had a functional postal service. But I missed out on so much of her life. She was just fourteen when I left, a kid. And seeing her in random cities whenever I had leave isn't a substitute for all the time I missed while she grew up. "I can't wait to see her."

"I know, man. We all can't wait to see her. Daisy," he says, his lips curling up into a grin, "she's the glue that holds this family together. Always has been."

"When does she fly in?"

"Two weeks from now. Thursday after next. She lands at two pm."

"I'll grab her from the airport."

"I figured." Denver pushes off my bed and tosses me a pair of jeans that are hanging off the chair in the corner of my room. "Get dressed. I'll make you some eggs for breakfast." He closes the door to my bedroom behind him.

I sit still for several seconds, staring at the closed door. It's been forever since Denver made me breakfast; at one time, he did it nearly every morning. My brothers and I were more than just siblings; we were best friends. We've always had each other's backs, looked out for one another, and covered for one another. But deep down, I think we all knew we had to be more because if we weren't, it would mess shit up for Daisy. She didn't deserve that; she already lost too much when she was just a kid. Dad pretty much disappeared after Mom passed and after he got life, we stopped relying on him for anything. Denver, Carter, and I just made it work.

But now Daisy is grown up. I'm back. Denver's moving forward. Carter's... still Carter. But we're all going to be together again, under the same roof, as adults.

And for the strangest reason, I'm really excited about that. It's like all the puzzle pieces are just starting to fit together. And I never realized how much I need the puzzle to be whole.

7

EVIE

C lean soap and mint wrap around me as his shadow hovers over my desk.

I inhale, knowing that when I raise my head, my eyes will fall straight into the moss-green depths of Jax's. He doesn't say anything, just lets me take my time as I come to terms with the fact that he really is back. And will now be a permanent fixture in my life, whether I want him to be or not.

"Good morning, Jax," I finally say, raising my head and letting myself free fall into his eyes for a moment that I wish could stretch an eternity.

"Evie." He smiles at me, laid-back. He rests a hand on my desk, shifting his weight in a casual stance. "How was your weekend?" As he chitchats, he reminds me more of the high school football player from my past than the decorated soldier he's grown into.

"Quiet. Yours?"

"Busy."

"Good."

"Come on, Evie. That's all you're going to give me?" He raises a hand to his chest as if I've wounded him somehow. His smirk is playful; he's always been aware of how irresistible he is.

I raise an eyebrow.

"I think this is fate."

"What is?

"You and me. Both back here. Seeing each other all the time. Meeting on the regular."

I can't stop the smile that plays across my lips. "Jax. You're back here; I never left. And we aren't 'meeting on the regular.' You are a client at my place of employment. That's not fate. That's life in a small town."

"You always were a city girl at heart. This small town could never satisfy dreams as big as yours, Maywood. You could always see past life in our small corner of the country."

"Can I help you with anything?" I shuffle through the folders on my desk, his words piercing a part of me I try to suppress, until I find the one with his name neatly printed across the top in my handwriting. "Do you need a copy of the exercises Peters wants you to start with?"

"Nope, I'm all set." He heaves his gym bag higher on his shoulder, leaning closer to me. "I'm still going with fate," he whispers, before walking toward the locker room without turning around.

I take a deep breath, partly to steady my nerves and partly to inhale his scent one more time.

I'm a masochist like that.

* * *

My palms are sweaty as I stand outside of Peters' office. I've been researching PT programs all week, and I know this is what I want to do. It's perfect for me. The opportunity to work with the military and supporting veterans is what I was born to do, if not actually serving the Army myself. But going the PT route through Baylor's program means I could serve, if I still wanted to.

Just the thought causes my heart to gallop. Of course I want to; it's been my dream since childhood. But can I deal with the scrutiny all over again? If I'm fortunate enough to receive an admissions interview for a PT program, especially the program at Baylor-Army, the interviewer will definitely question why I didn't attend West Point after I accepted and enrolled at the academy. Can I handle having to answer the type of questions I've spent the past seven years avoiding?

I close my eyes. Right now, I should focus on talking to Peters. I can worry about the rest later. Still, my Mom's face the morning I told her I wasn't going to attend West Point flickers through my mind.

She stares at me, her mouth half-open in confusion. Concern tightens the corners of her mouth as she places a hand over mine. "Evie, are you being serious?"

I nod, taking a step closer to her chair at the kitchen table.

She opens and closes her mouth several times, at a loss for what to say.

I stand silently. Pushing my hair behind my ears, I force myself to make eye contact with her. I can do this. I can be honest. I'm not going to West Point. I can't go to West Point. Just the thought of being surrounded by so many guys makes my skin crawl and nausea swell in my chest. It travels upwards until it clogs my throat and catches my tongue, reminding me that I'm better off being silent. Invisible. I wish I were invisible.

"Oh, Evie, it's alright, love. Why don't you take a seat and eat some toast? You look pale. Do you not feel well?"

I nod; I feel like death. Dropping into the chair beside her, I watch as she pops two pieces of toast into the toaster.

"It's normal to feel nervous and anxious before going off to college. It's unsettling knowing that you're moving to a new place, rooming with someone you haven't met before. Maybe your overwhelmed thinking about the course load or academic requirements? It's okay to feel unsure." She chats, buttering my toast and adding a spoonful of

strawberry jam to the center of each piece. She places the plate in front of me and pours me a mug of coffee.

I watch her move around the kitchen, admiring her. At work she's a complete boss; professional, calculated, straightforward. But at home, she's always my mom first, talking and laughing and sitting at the kitchen table drinking coffee from a mug I made in art class. She's the real reason I dreamed of joining the Army. Because she somehow melded both parts of herself, the professional and personal, into the most incredible role model I could ever hope to have in a mother. Especially after my father took off with another woman when I was only eight-years-old.

Mom and I have always been so unbelievably close.

I know now all of that is about to change. Because I can't tell her this. I can't tell anyone.

I envision the disappointment she will be forced to swallow. A general in the US Army, a woman no less, whose own daughter gets accepted at West Point and doesn't attend at the last minute for an unknown reason. She will be gossiped about relentlessly.

The shame of it all bears down on me until my chest rises and falls in rapid succession. Floaters appear in my peripheral vision, and I wonder if I'm going to collapse right here at the kitchen table.

"Evie? What is it?" She stands beside me, leaning closer now and placing the back of her hand against my forehead.

I wrap my hands around the mug of coffee, letting the warmth permeate the frost in my fingers. "I already told you. I'm not going to West Point," I whisper out between my teeth, feeling the sorrow behind my words and watching as her face freezes in confusion.

"Okay. You don't have to. You applied to other colleges and have several options to choose from. You loved the Loyola campus in Maryland." She smiles at me but her eyes are hesitant, the wheels in her head turning as they try to connect the dots.

"I'm not going anywhere." I say, pushing away from the table, my toast untouched, before storming out of the kitchen.

Behind me, I feel the bewilderment and shock rolling off of her, but I don't turn around. I can't.

"Evie?" Peters' voice jolts me from my memory, and I snap my eyes open, turning toward him.

Heat travels up my throat and burns in my cheeks at my embarrassment.

"Can I help you with something?" he prompts after several seconds tick by.

"I'd like to speak with you, sir. If you have a moment."

He glances at his watch and back up at me, nodding briskly. "Of course. I have a few minutes before my next evaluation. Come on in." He holds his office door open for me and I step inside.

The door closes, the latch clicking behind me.

"Evie?" he prods.

"Yes, thank you for agreeing to speak with me."

"What's on your mind?" Peters sits down behind his desk and indicates the chair across from him. I take a seat.

"Well, sir, I've been thinking. I've been working here for four years now and while I love my job and the opportunity to serve the US Army in a civilian capacity, I think I'm ready for a new challenge."

"Okay. What do you have in mind?" He raises his eyebrows, leaning forward until his forearms rest on his desk.

Bubbles pop in my stomach, squeezing up my throat. Once the words are out, it will all be for real. Deep breath. I can do this. Just say it.

"I'm thinking about applying to PT programs. Specifically, Baylor-Army."

"Baylor is incredibly competitive."

"Yes, sir, it is. But I'm up to the challenge."

Peters leans back in his chair, regarding me for several seconds.

My skin begins to itch under his scrutiny. I hold my breath.

"I won't ask you why you didn't attend West Point."

I look away, studying a paperweight that sits in the corner of his desk and contains the US Army Seal.

"I've always thought you had what it takes to serve, Evie."

My eyes meet his again and when I read the sincerity in them, I relax in my chair, relief sweeping through me. "Really?"

Peters nods. "You're a great receptionist, Evie. But you're overqualified for the position." He points this out gently, like a grandfather to a granddaughter. "You have been since your first day."

I literally beam at the man as my heart accelerates. A whole path suddenly opens up before me. It's like I have options now.

"I've looked at the prerequisites and I've completed most of them already. This is my last full semester and if I take two summer classes, I'll complete my B.A. in Psychology." I continue, pulling a folder out of my bag and explaining the course load and admissions process to Peters, even though it dawns on me about three minutes into my explanation that he must be very familiar with the program already.

Still, he sits, and listens to me rattle on, giving me nods of encouragement. Interrupting me briefly to answer a knock on his office door, he holds up one finger to let the person know he needs a minute before returning his attention to me.

Still, I turn in my chair and when I see Jax standing in the doorframe of Peters' office, my nerves build, my hands breaking out into a clammy sweat. He tilts his head at me, offering a reassuring smile.

"Evie?" Peters questions.

I turn back toward him and grasping onto Jax's reassurance, I say, "And that's why I would very much like the opportunity to shadow you as you work with both active duty soldiers and veterans. I would like to assist you in any capacity you see fit."

Silence ensues for several seconds before clapping behind me causes me to jump in my chair and bite back my grin.

Turning toward him again, I take in the sincerity that lights up his face, how his eyes flash with the same excitement coursing through my veins.

We're connected again. Once more on the same page, wanting the same thing, desiring the same outcome. I smile back at his enthusiasm for my future plans, but shut down the electric jolt that crackles through me at the sight of him. Strong, hard muscles bunch under his T-shirt, and his eyes lock on mine, a slight stubble coating his cheeks and chin. I remind myself it will never work. Jax is in my past. I'm here to focus on my future.

My future.

Which, in this moment, resides with Peters, not Jax.

I turn back around.

Peters glances between Jax and I, a spark of amusement passing over his features before he nods at me. "All right, Evie. I'm going to give you a shot."

"Really?"

"Really."

"Whatever you need or want me to do, I'm in. I just want to learn as much as I can and get accepted."

"I understand."

"I'm in too," Jax adds.

I still in my chair, tracking Peters' gaze as he looks over me to Jax. "What do you mean, Sergeant?"

"I volunteer. Let Evie help you on my evals and PT."

My excitement dies as anxiety crawls up my throat. What is he doing? He completely unnerves me and he knows it. I can't work with Peters on him. He's too observant, he'll see too much of me.

"You don't have to do that," I say, turning around again to fix Jax with a stare.

"It's no problem. What do you think, Staff-Sergeant?"

I close my eyes to steady myself before I turn back to Peters. Still, I don't miss the smirk Jax throws my way, or the spark that flares in his eyes.

"What the hell? Why not? Evie, we begin next week. In the meantime, I'm going to get a jump on some paperwork and work up a schedule for you."

"Sounds great. Thank you, sir."

"You start getting the materials ready for your application."

"Will do."

"And you," he says, looking at Jax, "stop wasting time in my office and get to work. I'll meet you by the free weights in five."

"Roger that, sir," Jax says before turning to leave Peters' office. But not before he throws me a wolfish look coupled with a wink.

Not before my heart lodges itself in my throat, and I have to literally remind myself to breathe.

8

EVIE

" S low and steady," Peters murmurs to Jax as he lifts his arm
above his head and moves it in a large circle.

Jax's face is grim, his brow and lips pulled tight as small beads
of sweat break out along his hairline. His breath is labored, as if
he's carrying sandbags up an endless staircase instead of moving
his arm in circles. His shoulder clicks and I grimace.

"One more."

Jax nods, but it's more of a flinch. He chews his lower lip as he
slowly raises his arm again.

I try to maintain a neutral expression, keep my body language
professional and my face blank. But inside, I'm a mess. I hate
seeing him in pain. I keep imagining awful scenarios to explain
how he injured his shoulder. What exactly caused it?

The skin around his shoulder is pockmarked and raw in some
spots, smooth and flat in others. It's damaged and ugly and has
no business marring the perfection that I equate with Jax.

Jax blows out a deep breath through puffed out cheeks, dropping the weight from his hand.

"Well done."

"It's still tight," he comments, taking the towel I hand him and wiping it across his forehead.

"It will be for a while. You've gotta keep at it. Keep running through the exercises. But if something feels different, too much pain, too much noise, speak up, okay?"

"Yes, sir."

Peters claps him on the back with an open palm. "See you Friday," he says in farewell before walking to a leg machine to have a few words with the soldier doing leg presses.

"You okay?" I ask Jax under my breath, completely aware that I don't mean it in the professional sense and not caring.

"Yep."

"You sure?"

Jax leans against a weight rack, eyeing me warily. "Sure."

I swallow, looking down at my feet. I hate the awkwardness that hangs between us. Remembering the way his eyes lit up last week in Peters' office, how for one moment, it seemed like us again, I open my mouth to erase some of the distance between us when Jax beats me to it.

"Evie, I'm sorry." His voice is so low, I look up to make sure he actually spoke the words I didn't realize I've been waiting to hear.

"The way I left," he shakes his head, "I'm sorry I hurt you when I enlisted. And I'm sorry I didn't do more to keep in touch with you, to keep you in my life."

"I told you to stop contacting me." I remind him, confused by his apology but also grateful for it.

Jax drops down to sit on a weight bench so we're almost eye level. He stares at me for several seconds, the green of his eyes darkening, his lips pressing into a thin line. "I don't think you really meant it." He says finally.

I almost sob. I didn't really mean it. I pushed him away because I couldn't bear for him to learn the truth about me. At the time, I didn't want his pity, didn't want him to feel any type of obligation toward me. I wanted him to be there for me because he wanted to not because he had to. And if he wanted to, he never would have left.

But now, looking at him, watching as he massages a splattering of scars around his shoulder, I realize that we were both young, proud, and hurt. We both acted and reacted in ways at eighteen that we wouldn't at twenty-five.

"I pushed you away on purpose." I admit.

"I think so too. Now. Back then, I figured I was being selfish trying to hold on to you when I was the one who left. I bailed on the New York plan. I broke us up. How could you move on if I kept calling? I wasn't being fair to you so I understood when you told me to let you go. But seeing you now, I don't think I should've, Evie."

"What do you mean? Seeing me now?"

The corner of Jax's mouth lifts but it's not quite a smile and it doesn't reach his eyes. "You're different, Maywood. And of course I knew you would grow and change and maybe dye your hair blonde or something in seven years. But it's more than that."

"I'm fine." I snap, my voice harsher than I intend as a chill shoots through me.

He continues to watch me, a flash of sadness, of remorse sparking in his eyes as he stands up from the bench. "Okay. I just wanted to tell you that I'm sorry for the way things ended between us. I'm sorry for hurting you, Evie. That's the last thing I'd ever want to do."

I nod, not trusting my voice. I reach out to grip the weight rack, suddenly feeling unbalanced.

"If you ever need anything, want to talk, whatever, I'm here." He says finally. "Thank you." I whisper, my voice strained.

He steps past me toward the locker room but turns before he clears the free weights. "Want to hear a secret confession?" He asks randomly, a playfulness replacing the seriousness of our conversation.

I glance back up, meeting his eyes. "What?"

"This week, knowing I get to see you, has been the only motivation to get my ass to PT." He smirks for real now, his eyes crinkling in the corners, and a teasing look I recognize flits across his face. "See you Friday, Evie." He snaps his towel at me before tossing it over his shoulder and sauntering to the locker room.

I say saunter, but really it's pure swagger.

I watch him walk away, comparing the outline of his body to the boy I once knew, tracing his hardened back muscles and broad shoulders with the memory of a thinner guy who still managed to walk with all the confidence in the world.

I bite my bottom lip to keep from smiling. Jaxon Kane is really back.

* * *

The sound of running water wakes me the following morning, and I sit up in my bed, completely disoriented. My heart gallops in my chest as my breathing grows erratic. I slide from my bed as quietly as I can, my eyes darting around for anything out of the ordinary.

It has to be Graham. Opening my mouth to call out, I shut it immediately. What if it's not Graham?

But Mom and Graham are the only people with a key to my townhouse.

Did someone break in?

A bolt of adrenaline surges through my veins as fear settles in my chest. Tugging on an old, open-front cardigan, I pull a letter-opener from my desk and hold it in my left hand, my right clutching my phone, 911 already programmed on the screen. My finger hovers above the call button as I walk slowly out of my room, the letter opener held out in front of me.

Peeking into the kitchen, the outline of my brother standing at the sink rinsing out a coffee mug and washing a few utensils, greets me. I almost collapse against the wall in relief. Hiding around the corner, I focus on regulating my breathing and settling my racing heart. Once the panic subsides, I slide the letter opener into the drawer of the hallway console and turn back toward the kitchen.

Walking inside, a smile splits my face and I squeal, startling him as I walk over and throw my arms around his neck. "I didn't know you were coming! Why didn't you call me?"

"Surprise." He kisses my cheek in affection. "I didn't want to wake you and endure your wrath all day. I made coffee."

"I'm not that bad." I turn to the coffee maker and pour myself a cup. Peeking over my shoulder at Graham, I decide he needs another cup, too. Pulling the cream from the refrigerator, I add a splash to both mugs and set them on the table. "Did you bring breakfast?"

He motions to a folded paper bag on the counter, and I can't help the happy moan that falls from my lips. "Cinnamon rolls? From Maddie's? You do love me."

"More than anyone else."

Pulling two rolls from the bag, I press my fingertips into the soft pastry, delighted that they're still warm. I place them on two plates and bring them over to the table, sliding into a chair and motioning for Graham to sit across from me.

"Oh, my God. These are amazing." I bite into the roll, the flaky icing dropping onto my plate like snow flurries.

Graham chuckles, tucking into his own roll. "I know. I told Maddie she should consider franchising, but she won't hear of it."

"That bakery is her baby. She'd never let anyone close enough to even peek at those family recipes. She's completely close-lipped about them."

"Like someone else I know." He raises his eyebrows at me.

"What are you doing here anyway?"

"Can't I just pop in to check on my baby sister? I need a reason to visit you?"

"Of course not. You're always welcome. I just feel like there's another reason you're here."

He glances down at the table, avoiding my eyes, which has warning bells clanging around in my head. I sit up straighter, leaning toward him. "What's wrong?"

His sigh is heavy, his fingertips rustling the page tips of the newspaper on the table. "Hunter was injured. Took some shrapnel to his left eye and his left arm is pretty fucked up."

"What?" I ask in near shock. Hunter is my brother's best friend. His wife and kids still live in our town.

Graham takes another gulp of his coffee as he blinks back the moisture that collects in his eyes. "He's in surgery now. Kelly flew out this morning. I just wanted to be around for Harry and Ella. Their grandparents are staying with them but they'll probably need some help. Kelly's parents are getting up there in years."

"Of course. Is Hunter going to be okay?"

"I fucking hope so."

I reach out, placing my hand on his. "I'm sorry Graham."

"I also got orders."

I close my eyes, hoping that he says anywhere but a war zone. "Where?"

"Germany."

I open my eyes. "Well, that's not bad."

Graham tosses a balled-up napkin at me. "No. It's pretty awesome actually."

"When do you PCS?"

"One month. So, can I crash with you until then?"

"Are you kidding me? Of course!"

"I was planning on it anyway but your excitement is reassuring." He smirks, taking another enormous bite of his cinnamon roll.

I pick at mine, my thoughts still caught on Hunter. I hope he doesn't lose his sight. I hope he's okay. But then the image in my mind transforms from Hunter to Jax and I close my eyes, relieved that he made it home, that he came back, even if he didn't come back to me.

"It will give us some time to hang out. Bond," Graham continues and I open my eyes at the sound of his voice.

"Yeah."

"Not that I want to cramp your style or anything. I won't kill your social life."

"What social life?"

Graham sighs, finishing off his second cup of coffee. Mine's turned cold.

"Evie?"

"Hmm?"

"We have a month to sort you out. I'm not leaving you here to rot away and become a crazy cat lady."

"I don't even like cats."

"Small miracles. This month you're getting back out there. I don't know what's been going on with you these past few years," he says, holding up his hand to silence me before I can fill the air between us with lies, "and you don't have to tell me. But you do need to start moving forward. Find things that fulfill you. Date." He fixes me with a stern, older brother look. "You need to get a life."

"Gee, thanks."

"I'm serious."

"I know." I pick at the pastry icing. "I actually have something new going on."

He raises his eyebrows at me, waiting.

"I haven't told anyone yet."

"What is it?"

"I've started shadowing Staff-Sergeant Peters at Morris. I'm thinking about applying to PT programs."

An ecstatic smile splits Graham's lips, and some of the worry always lurking in the shadows of his face when he looks at me seems to lessen. "Evie, that's incredible. When did this happen?"

"Just recently. I'm not a hundred percent yet. I mean, I am. I just... it's still new."

"Okay. Well... wow. That's really great. I'm proud of you, Noodle." He references a nickname from my childhood that he hasn't called me in years.

I roll my eyes, heat traveling up my neck and fanning out into my cheeks at his praise. "Let's see if I can get in anywhere before we start with all the excitement."

"Are you serious? Any program would be lucky to have you."

"Spoken like a true brother."

"I'm proud of you."

"Stop with all the compliments. You're making me blush."

"Good. I know I haven't been around a lot the past few years, Evie. Between deployment and getting my head straight when I got back, I haven't been here for you the way I want to be. I'm looking forward to hanging out this month. We can catch up on all the stuff I missed the past few years." His voice is gentle but the look he levels at me is serious.

I swallow a sip of my coffee, nodding at his words. It isn't lost on me that he's the second person to look at me with concern and sympathy this week.

9

JAX

"That's full set." Marco, one of the civilian physical therapists at Morris, taps the bar, indicating I should place it back on the rack.

Squeezing my shoulder blades together, a tight soreness pulls against my back. A slow throb already builds in my shoulder.

"Nice work, Kane. I'll see ya around." Marco tosses me a towel, walking over to a woman doing deadlifts in the corner.

I sit up on the bench and mop the sweat from my face. My left arm feels like spaghetti. Apparently, this is progress. Pushing up off the bench, I walk to the locker room, dropping my towel in a bin on the way in.

I'm cranky. Partly because I'm hungry as shit. Partly because my shoulder is throbbing. And partly because I barely saw Evie today. Peters had an emergency so Marco is covering his appointments. Since Evie only shadows Peters, she spent my session answering phones and filing while I spent it thinking about her.

"She looks good, better than usual." A voice from behind a row of lockers says.

A locker clicks shut as another voice asks, "You think it's because Kane's back?"

I stop in my tracks, staring at the space the voices are coming from.

"Nah, he's been gone too long to affect her."

Silence.

"You never know, man. They could get back together."

A nasty laugh. "No way. Trust me, Kane's moved on."

"I guess so."

What the hell? This conversation would be funny if I didn't hear my name dropped into it. Ripping open my locker, I let the door bang against the locker beside it. The voices stop abruptly. Shouldering my gym bag, I'm about to go confront the two assholes and tell them to knock it off. To stop dropping my name and referencing Evie like they know anything about us, when Marco pops his head through the locker room door.

"Kane? Got a minute."

A sharpness infuses the heavy silence as the two dipshits realize I'm in here, too. I can't even hear them breathing. Who the hell are they? And what the fuck did they mean that I couldn't affect her anymore?

"Kane?"

"Yeah. Coming." I close my locker harder than necessary and follow Marco out as he hands me a paper with a new exercise list and explains the tweaks Peters is making to my PT. I cock my head to the side, pretending to listen to him as my eyes latch onto the beautiful girl updating schedules.

"Got it?"

"Yep, thanks." I stuff the paper into my bag. "Catch you later, Marco."

Desperately wanting to turn back into the locker room and knock the two guys gossiping like high school girls out, I stop myself and focus on controlling the anger swirling in my chest. I can't get in a fight at the Morris locker room. If I face disciplinary action, I'll never get to see Evie. Plus, I need to straighten out my shoulder so if I don't re-up when my contract runs out, I'll at least have other career options. A bad arm isn't going to get me anywhere in the private security field.

Walking over to the receptionist desk faster than normal, I lean across it into Evie's space and watch as her eyes widen in alarm before dimming to surprise. Shit. I back up just as quickly, biting down on my tongue to keep from confronting her, straight out asking her why two dicks in the locker room would be running their mouths about her. About us.

"Jax."

"How's it going?"

"Okay. How are you? How's your shoulder today?"

"It's all right. Peters made some adjustments to my PT. I just wish it were coming along faster."

"You're frustrated."

"Exactly."

"I see a lot of soldiers go through this. It's all part of the process. If you're frustrated, it's not necessarily a bad thing. It means you expect more of yourself."

"And that's a good thing? Expecting more of myself?"

"Absolutely. You should always want more for yourself, Jax. You'll get there."

"So go to dinner with me." The words are out of my mouth before I can stop them, and I don't even care. I've wanted to ask her out since the night I saw her again at Raf's, and the two guys in the locker room just gave me the ammo I needed to make my move.

"What?" Her mouth drops open, confusion rippling across her face.

"You just said I should always want more for myself. I do. I want to take you to dinner. I want you back in my life."

"Jax." She rolls back a half step in her chair, even though the desk is separating us.

"Evie. I've always wanted you." The words reverberate in the air between us, ringing with a truthfulness that I could never pretend.

"I, um, Jax." She looks around nervously, her eyes suddenly narrowing as her arms wrap across her middle.

"What's up, Kane?" A guy I graduated with, Gary Reitter, thumps me on the back. "Hey, Evie."

"How's it going, man?" I ask to be polite, but my eyes are still glued to Evie.

"All good. See you around. 'Bye Evie." He tosses her a smile, but her eyes have glazed over, and she's not looking at either one of us anymore.

Gary leaves Morris as I wait for Evie to respond.

"Evie?"

Her eyes jump back to me, startled. "Huh?"

"Go to dinner with me."

Panic and pain burn the blue of her eyes. She shakes her head. "I can't, Jax. I can't do that. I have to get back to work. Have a good weekend." She stands up, swaying as she grabs a stack of folders off her desk and walks away stiffly, dismissing me.

I watch the unsure steps of her departure, confused by her reaction but not ready to give up on her just yet. Evie Maywood, while forever out of my league, is still meant to be in my world. And dinner isn't a marriage proposal. Why the hell can't I still be friends with her, even if I can't fix the mess between us?

* * *

"Remember when we were kids, and we would come back here and pretend to shoot robbers?" Carter's voice startles me as I turn to look at him.

I nod at the memory, a thousand hot summer days and sticky breezes coming back to me. "Yeah. You always got to be the sheriff."

Carter snorts, taking a seat beside me and passing me a beer. "How far is that from the truth?"

"Still better than Denver."

Carter chuckles in his easy-going way, leaning back in his deck chair and taking a long swig of his beer. "Guess so."

I turn to him, bringing the bottle to my lips and letting the bitter taste sweep down my throat. I was never attracted to beer for the taste... rather for the social aspect it's always provided. A link between my brothers and I, a bond between the guys I've served with, a familiarity with anyone sitting around when I step up to the bar at Raf's. It's reliable like that. "What do you mean? You've always been a natural charmer, a bit of wise ass, but legit. With Denver getting sent away and me enlisting, it was always you holding shit down here for us, keeping an eye out for Daisy."

He chews the corner of his mouth, looking out to the edge of our property. It's lifeless, patches of dried grass and dying shrubbery. "Mm-hmm," he comments before chuckling again and punching me in the shoulder with his fist. "I could have killed you fuckers the day Daisy got her period, and I was all alone, left to deal with that shit by myself."

I cringe at the thought, imagining how awful it must have been for Carter. And even more so for Daisy. "What'd you do?"

He shakes his head, running a hand through his hair. "You mean after I assured her she wasn't dying? Jesus, what the hell are they even teaching in Sex Ed these days? I called Lori Filton. Remember her?"

At the sound of her name, an image of Lori Filton, a cheerleader that graduated the year between Carter and me, pops into my head. "She was pretty."

"Yeah. Still is." The corners of Carter's lips turn up. "Anyway, she and I were messing around at the time and so I hit her up, had her come over, explain things to Daisy. She even volunteered to take her to the pharmacy. In that moment, I could have married the girl."

"What happened?"

"Eh, you know. Daisy was all embarrassed and moody for a few days but after that, she was fine."

"No, I mean what happened with Lori?"

"Nothing," he shrugs, "we still kick it sometimes."

I chuckle, raising the bottle to my lips again and mulling that over. Carter has never been serious about a girl. There have always been girls. Always. Ever since he was a little kid and Janie Monroe followed him around on the playground. But there has never been *the* girl. Even Denver has had two serious girlfriends that we all thought could end up a permanent fixture in the Kane family. It didn't work out that way, but it could have. I had Evie. Well, I hope to still have Evie.

But Carter's always been just Carter.

"You see Evie around?" he asks.

"Yup."

"How's she doing?"

"What do you mean?"

"She's quiet these days."

"Do you see her often?" I pick at the label on my beer bottle, a strange heat burning in my stomach. Why does Carter know more about my girl than I do? And why didn't he ever tell me that she passed on West Point?

"Not really."

"Then how do you know she's quiet?"

"Why are you getting pissed at me?"

"I'm not."

He blows out a deep breath. "You left, Jax. You picked up and never looked back."

"I'm sorry."

"What?" Surprise flashes across Carter's features, his mouth dropping open.

"What you said that night at Raf's, about me being selfish, about still having my family," I take a swig of the beer, swallowing back remorse along with the Corona, "you were right. I sucked at keeping in touch with you guys. Random phone calls and meeting up sporadically in New York or DC wasn't enough and I let you down. I get why you're pissed at me and –"

Carter holds up his hand, cutting me off. "I'm not pissed at you."

I raise my eyebrows.

"Fine." He mumbles, drinking some of his beer. "I'm a little pissed."

I grin and he chuckles, reaching over to punch my shoulder again.

"Everyone was gone. And I did the best I could with what I had to work with. Sometimes it seems like that wasn't enough." He admits, draining his beer.

"What do you mean? Stop talking in all these riddles, Carter. What gives?"

My brother watches the edge of our property line but when he turns toward me, his expression deepens into the greatest grief I've ever witnessed from him. He appears sorrowful, even more so than on the morning we buried our mother. He shakes his head, "Forget it. I'm sorry too, Jax. I wish things with Evie turned out the way you wanted them to." He pushes out of the chair then, grabbing his empty beer bottle. I hear the bottle hit the recycling bin and clang loudly against the other glass. The back door slams shut and I stay, listening to the sounds of dusk and staring at the depressing yard.

I finish my beer slowly, thinking over Carter's apology. Carter and I were always close growing up but now that I'm back, things between us have shifted and I'm still trying to sort out my footing. I know I've hurt him; I understand why he's pissed at me. But it's more than that. He wants to lay into me and unload all of the shit he's grappling with but he also wants to protect me from it too. Why would he ever feel like anything he did wasn't enough for us Kane kids?

* * *

My shoulder aches, a deep burn that spreads up the column of my neck and down to the center of my spine. Peters is working me hard and while I'm grateful for his expertise, I hate that Evie sees me in such rough shape, grimacing and grunting and working up a sweat over the simplest exercises. I hate that she's witnessing me in a position where I can't hold it together.

Having her shadow Peters on my PT does bring some benefits, though, like the fact that I get to see her more often. Observe her in her element. She's a natural at the PT, asks intelligent questions, and adds her own opinions into the mix when Peters questions her. Her observations are always carefully crafted, pertinent, and smart.

"How's Graham?" I break the ice during an easy round of bicep curls.

Evie smiles at the mention of her brother. "He's doing well. Back in town actually, at least for the next month before his PCS."

"Yeah? That's nice y'all are getting to spend some time together."

She rolls her eyes, even though she's grinning. "He's killing me. He's got me running with him every morning, and now he wants to throw conditioning into the mix."

I chuckle, recalling how excited Evie would be whenever Graham was coming back to town. They always worked out together. She idolized her big brother and wanted to be exactly like him. Follow in his footsteps.

"Where's he PCSing to?"

"Germany."

I let out a whistle. Germany is cushy. "Sweet."

"He seems pretty excited about it." She hands me a bottle of water as I drop the dumbbell and take a breather before my next set.

"He's crashing with you?"

"Yeah."

"That's good."

"Why?"

"So you're not by yourself," I blurt out before I realize how patronizing the words sound. "You know, so he can keep an eye out for you." I cringe internally, shoving my foot farther down my throat. I know Evie is capable of taking care of herself but seeing how different she is, how thin and fragile she looks, makes me worry about her in new ways.

She surprises me, though. Instead of the shoulder shrug or eye roll I'm expecting, a flash of color spreads across her cheeks and her eyes narrow. For a brief glimpse, she's my Maywood again. "Trust me, I've been taking care of myself just fine for the last seven years. Start your next set." She demands, and I have to swallow back the relief I feel at finally witnessing a reaction from her.

I pick up a heavier set of dumbbells and begin to curl. "I'm sure you've been managing fine on your own. Are you still crazy idealistic and think everyone is inherently good?" I taunt her, not ready to lose sight of the old Evie she's finally showing me.

She stills next to me, and I watch her through the mirror before us as her body stiffens, her gaze turning downwards. Shit. I thought she'd come back at me with a witty comment, not shut down. I finish the set and drop the dumbbells, bending down to snatch up my water bottle.

"Evie, I'm just joking with you, giving you shit. You know I always admired how much you cared about other people, how you saw the world."

She nods her head, the movement jerky. "Sure. I see Gabrielle getting swamped at the front desk." She peers over my shoulder. "Are you okay to work through the rest of the exercises on your own?"

I narrow my eyes at her, fully aware that she's blowing me off, although I have no idea why. "Yeah."

"Great." She passes me the exercise sheet, making a beeline to the front desk and relieving Gabrielle.

I watch her bend over the desk and shuffle through some folders. Her shoulders are tense, her posture rigid. I have no clue what caused her to go from sassy to stoic in an instant but my teasing definitely didn't have the affect I had hoped for.

10

EVIE

"Special delivery," Jax announces, dropping a bag from Maddie's on my desk Monday morning.

"Cinnamon rolls?"

"Still warm."

"Wow, you must have really missed me," I joke.

"You have no idea." He's serious. He did miss me?

"I meant this weekend."

"I meant always."

I roll my eyes, opening the top of the brown paper bag to peek inside and let some of the delicious aroma wash over me. "Thank you."

"Anything for you."

"How was your weekend?"

"Pretty good. Helped Denver work on a few cars he's doing on the side for some extra dough. Transmission changes and shit. Daisy's coming home on Thursday."

"She is? That's awesome. You must be so excited to see her."

"I am. Can't wait actually."

"How does she like Arizona?"

"She likes it too much. Carter says she only visits a few times a year."

"I can't believe she's graduating in May."

"Tell me about it. I haven't seen her in two years. It's like I completely missed her growing up." He tugs on the back of his neck, his mouth flattening into a straight line.

I can't help the sympathetic look I throw his way.

He clears his throat. "How was your weekend?"

"Fine. I caught up on a bunch of assignments and mostly hung out with Graham. We had dinner with Mom. I saw Jenny."

"Don't give too much away."

"It was pretty standard."

"Maybe you need to shake it up next weekend."

Shake it up? I try to smile but it falls flat. Anxiety grips me as I remember him asking me out last week. What was he thinking? The worst part is that for a moment, I desperately wanted to say yes. My heart started racing, and my palms grew clammy and for just that tiny moment, I felt wanted in a way that didn't repulse me. But then I remembered all the things that could go wrong, all the ways he could find out the truth. So I bolted. And that same reaction to flee is building in my body again. I can feel the smile slip from my face, a sourness clenching my stomach as I study my hands so he can't read my eyes. "Nah, I like my weekends the way they are."

"That's not a bad thing. But don't you ever want to, I don't know, do something different? You were the queen of adventure planning. The only girl I knew who planned how to be spontaneous." He chuckles. "But still, you always had a million things you wanted to do or try or see."

"I've changed."

"Look, I get it. Seven years is a long time. I've changed, too."

"I know."

"We could get to know each other again." Is that hopeful hesitation I detect underneath his words?

I force myself to look up and see him grinning, suggestively wagging his eyebrows. I giggle. Literally, giggle before clamping my mouth shut. How the hell does he always get me to respond? How does he always manage to just work past my anxiety and make me comfortable?

"What if you don't like the new me?" I keep my tone playful, teasing. "I could chew with my mouth open or ask too many personal questions. Or snore." Face palm. Why, oh why, did I say that? Snoring would imply sleeping together. Something I shouldn't be thinking about. Something I shouldn't be remembering. I can feel the embarrassment spreading like a million prickly cactuses up my arms and neck.

"Impossible, I'll always like you best," he says seriously, a glint of amusement crossing his face. "Besides," he continues, reaching into the bag and breaking off a bite of pastry, "you've always snored."

"I, what? No." Very articulate, Evie.

"Kane! Stop picking on Evie and get to work." Marco's voice rings out, abruptly ending our conversation. I'm relieved he scolded Jax and not me. So relieved I can't turn around to look at him.

"Yes, sir," Jax answers, his face growing serious.

I can feel him studying me; I'm nervous now that he's going to be upset with me for getting him in trouble. I meet his eyes as he winks.

"Don't sweat it, Maywood. Your snores have always been soft and cute. Like a little puppy." He wrinkles his nose at me, and I shake my head, beaming up at him like the teenage version of myself.

"Go do your exercises."

"Save me a cinnamon roll."

I watch him strut toward the locker room and see how the other women in the gym glance at him from the corners of their eyes, fascinated. I note how the other men look at him openly, enviously. I admire him without him even realizing that I've always admired him. Even though I don't want him to, Jaxon Kane has a claim on me I'll never be able to shake.

Taking a deep breath, I walk through Sanderson High's front doors for my last first day of school. This time next year, if all goes according to plan, I'll be a cadet. I'll have survived the Beast Barracks, better known as Cadet Basic Training. I'll be wearing my uniform. I'll be firmly on the path that my great-grandfather elected when he attended West Point in 1923 before becoming a three-star general. I'll be doing something that matters.

But for now as I step into the humid halls of my high school and dodge a group of freshmen staring at their schedules with wide eyes and panicked expressions, I'll just try to enjoy senior year like Graham suggested. Hurrying down the hallway to my locker, I place several single-subject notebooks along with extra pens and pencils on the top shelf before closing the door. Fixing the strap of my shoulder bag, I walk toward my homeroom and slide into my seat several minutes before the bell rings.

When the bell sounds, I fold my hands on top of my notebook and wait for Mrs. Warren to begin.

"Good morning and welcome to your senior year." Mrs. Warren says, and the class simultaneously quiets and surges with the excited energy of finally being seniors. *"As you know, homeroom is just to take attendance and help you all start your day on the right foot. I recommend using this time to finish up any assignments, catch up on reading, or head to the library to get a jumpstart on projects. Try not to waste this precious time by just hanging out, discussing sports stats, or your weekend plans."* Her eyes cut knowingly to a few guys from the football team and a girl who is polishing her nails.

The door to the classroom opens suddenly, and a guy strolls in, a navy backpack slung over one shoulder. "Hey, sorry I'm late," he announces, not sounding the least bit sorry, before smiling widely at some of his friends and slipping into the open seat next to me.

I roll my eyes. Of course he's late. Jaxon Kane, the good-looking,

*annoyingly likable, and surprisingly smart quarterback. Every guy
wants to be him, and every girl wants to be with him. The most irri-
tating thing about him is that he's actually nice. Not that I've ever
spoken to him. But I've seen him interact with others in the hallways or
cafeteria and while his football friends can be downright jerks, he has
an easy-going vibe that attracts everyone. Even me, I admit, as my
heart rate picks up and my palms dampen.*

*"As I was saying," Mrs. Warren picks back up with her homeroom
rules as pockets of conversation break out around the room.*

*"Hey," Jax says, leaning over the side of his desk toward me. "Got a
pen I could borrow?"*

*"A pen?" I ask. Who comes to the first day of school without a pen?
Before I can grab an extra one from my bag, Silvia Jenkins turns
around in her seat, flicks her strawberry blonde curls over her shoulder,
and fastens her eyes on Jax.*

*"Here you go, Jax." She hands him a pen, a tiny slip of paper rolled
around the end and tucked under the cap. As if she already had her
number prepared and waiting. Was she waiting to give it to him specifically or does she do that for any guy she thinks is hot?*

*"Thanks, Silvia." He smiles that captivating grin again, reaching
out to run his fingertips across her bare shoulder and tugs teasingly on
the strap of her tank top. "You're the best."*

*Her laugh is breathless, and she turns forward in her seat as Mrs.
Warren calls her name out for roll call.*

"Here."

*Jax leans over in my direction again as I sit straight, face-forward,
pretending he doesn't even exist, which is the biggest joke on the planet.
How could someone not realize he exists? I sit quietly, listening to him
breathe beside me, half wishing he would notice me and half wishing I
were invisible.*

"You got a piece of paper I can have?"

My heart sprints.

"Paper?" I repeat, annoyed that I sound like a parrot in his presence.

But really, who doesn't bring a notebook on the first day of school either?

"Yeah, you know, something to write on?" he says it slowly, as if I'm the daft one.

"Jaxon Kane." Mrs. Warren looks up from her attendance binder and zeroes in on him.

"Here."

I huff, pretending to be annoyed when all I am is a nervous wreck that he's talking to me. Me. Flipping open my notebook again, I turn to the second sheet and carefully tug a sheet out along the perforated edge.

Jax chuckles next to me, but I don't give him the time of day.

"Evelyn Maywood," Mrs. Warren calls out.

"Present," I say, my eyes snapping up to the front of the room. "Evie's fine."

She makes a note in her binder before calling out the next name.

I turn in my seat to hand the paper to Jax. "Thank you, Evie," he says my name softly, and a thrill of goose bumps runs up my spine when his warm fingers graze mine as he takes the paper.

I nod, briefly wondering if he knew my name before Mrs. Warren began roll call, then feeling annoyed with myself for caring at all. I mean, why does it matter if Jax Kane knows if I exist? As an Army kid, I've moved loads of times and started over in new schools every few years. But, lucky for me, I've been at Sanderson for my entire high school career. So even though I don't have the childhood memories and long-standing friendships that most of my classmates have cultivated after twelve years of school together, thirteen if you count Kindergarten, I still know everyone in my class. Not that that means everyone knows me. Frustrated with my wayward thoughts, I refuse to make eye contact with Jax for the rest of homeroom.

Still, when he uncurls the slip of paper that Silvia attached to the pen, I can't help but notice the giant smile that stretches across his perfect lips at her phone number.

Or the brief flick of jealousy that ripples through my chest.

11

JAX

Where is she? I'm practically bouncing from one foot to the next as I wait in arrivals, my eyes scanning everyone who leaves baggage claim with their rolling suitcases and duffle bags. It's insane how excited I am to see my sister. I haven't seen her since I flew her to meet me in New York two years ago when I had some leave.

"Daisy! Over here." I hold a hand up to catch her attention as she walks out of baggage claim, pulling her small Samsonite behind her. Holy shit, she's a freaking adult. It's startling how much she's changed in two years. Walking toward me now, a cream blazer over her blouse and her golden-brown hair pulled back in a ponytail, I still picture her as a little girl with freckles and pigtails.

"I knew you would come!" She sails into my arms, almost knocking me over with the force of her enthusiasm. She hugs me tightly, her arms wrapping around my back, her fingers digging into my T-shirt like she's scared I'll disappear if she lets go.

I hug her just as fiercely, tucking her head under my chin and breathing her in. Grasping the ends of her hair, I tug on the soft strands. "No crazy braid running down your back?"

She shakes her head, her hair tickling my chin as she pulls away. "You know I'm not twelve anymore, right?"

"Shut up."

"I'm happy you're home."

"Me too." I take the handle of her suitcase and throw my arm across her shoulders, wanting to keep her close. "You ready?"

She nods, and I press another kiss to the crown of her head as we make our way out of the airport, sidestepping joyous reunions and tearful farewells.

The stuffy air greets us the second the sliding doors open, and Daisy shrugs out of her blazer, folding it neatly over her arm. I tug her toward the parking lot.

"I was stoked when Denver said you were coming home for spring break," I admit.

"Yeah?" She twists her head to peer up at me. "I was pretty stoked to see you myself. I can't believe how long it's been."

"I know. I figured you'd be heading somewhere like Cancun or Puerto Rico to party. It is your last spring break, you know."

Daisy giggles, and the sound pierces my mind. All the times I would make her laugh growing up come back to me in full force.

"I'm fully aware. I was planning to go to St. Barth's with my roommate, Sierra; her family has a house there."

I let out a low whistle, impressed that Daisy at least has friends with access to things that us Kane kids never dreamed of growing up. "What happened? She uninvited you for stealing all her socks?"

Daisy throws her head back and laughs. The sound is wild and carefree, uninhibited, and a smile splits my face. God, I've missed her.

"You remember what a weirdo Carter used to be about his socks? One time, one time," she says, holding up a finger to emphasize her point, "I borrowed a pair of socks and jeez, you'd have thought I stole his piggy bank or something."

"Remember how he used to iron his jeans?"

Another stream of laughter bursts forth, tears shimmering in the corners of her eyes. "Oh, my God! How did he ever get girls? He's such a nerd!"

"I know. It's insane. He somehow managed to fool all the girls coming in and out of his bedroom."

Daisy shakes her head. "I doubt that. They never struck me as the brightest crayons in the box to begin with."

"Good point."

"I miss the big nerd, though. I can't wait to see him. And Den."

"They're excited to see you, too. We're meeting them at Raf's in about thirty minutes. You hungry?"

Daisy looks up at me, beaming. Seriously, her face brightens like the sun. "Yeah, that's perfect. I can't wait for us all to be sitting around a table again. This time, I can even legally drink with y'all."

I give her a sharp look before I realize she's serious. And correct. Daisy can legally drink with us all. Man, sometimes I can't believe I really let seven years go by without ever coming home. So much has changed.

"Don't go crazy."

"Who me?" Daisy pouts innocently, and it strikes me that I have no clue if she's serious or not.

I need to spend a lot of time catching up with my little sister.

* * *

"Here she is. The girl of the hour!" Lenny announces our arrival into Raf's.

Daisy calls out in greeting, walking over to the bar and standing on her tippy toes to lean over the ledge and press a kiss to his cheek. What the fuck?

"Hey, Len. Where're they?" she asks.

"Back corner." He juts his thumb over his shoulder. "Something about not wanting any guy in here to get a good look at you."

"Ah." Daisy rolls her eyes. "Makes sense now."

She continues walking to the back of the bar before looking over her shoulder at me. Her eyebrows lift in question. "You coming?"

"Yeah." I take a step to follow her, my eyes checking every single motherfucker sitting in Raf's and warning them that their eyes best be glued to their burgers and not on my sister.

"Hi ya, fellas!" Daisy calls out as Carter and Denver come into view.

They both look up, their expressions softening when they see her. Sliding out of either side of the booth, my brothers stand to take turns enveloping Daisy in massive hugs.

"I'm happy you're home," Carter murmurs into her hair, genuine affection crossing his face as he pulls back to peer at her. "You're attracting too much attention, though, so try and make yourself ugly when we get home, so I don't have to beat anyone up this visit." He raises his eyebrows, and she laughs, shaking her head. Still, something passes between them, and I narrow my gaze at their exchange. Did Carter really have to beat someone up the last time Daisy was home?

"You hungry?" Denver asks, gesturing for Daisy to sit down before he slides in beside her, effectively hiding her from every patron here. Nice move, Den.

"Starved."

"Me too." I drop into the booth.

"Burgers and beers?" Carter asks, throwing his hand up to catch the server's attention.

"Duh." Daisy says.

Carter orders four burgers and four pints of Heineken.

And then silence descends on our table as we each take a minute to stare at each other. For the first time in seven long years, all four Kane kids are reunited at the place they used to consider their second home. After Mom passed and Dad went to jail, we spent a lot of dinners around this same table. Now, everything is different.

Then Carter farts, and Daisy reaches over the table to punch him in the shoulder, and Den lets loose with crude swearing and I laugh. Really laugh.

And then, it's like nothing has changed at all.

Absolutely nothing.

* * *

I settle into a routine, as being home becomes my new norm. Running in the mornings with Carter, catching glimpses of Denver in the kitchen scrambling eggs for breakfast or boiling water for pasta for dinner. Now, with Daisy's flip-flops stacked in a pile by the front door, it all sort of clicks together, and the house feels like home again. I even mow the lawn.

Therapy at Morris becomes consistent. I see Peters three times a week for rehabilitation. My shoulder burns and crunches and makes a shit ton of sounds a shoulder shouldn't make. It's sore and achy but my range of motion is improving. I never thought getting shot in the shoulder would be a tough injury to come back from; I never expected it to take so long to heal. But slowly, I'm making progress. The skin around my scars pulls and crinkles and looks ugly as shit. But I stick with it, knowing that seeing Peters also means seeing Evie.

She's there every morning when I walk in. Quiet, polite, professional. She greets everyone the same way, except little by little I can tell I'm getting to her. She doesn't look nearly as guarded when she sees me and she talks more openly now. Some days, she even throws me some sass and spunk, which I cling to like a lifeline. Still, I'm hesitant to joke with her too much, not wanting her to push me away like she has in the past.

Every now and then, I see her talking with a guy I know or

don't know, and I feel my stomach clench but it's misguided. She never flirts with anyone, always keeps it strictly professional. She uses a polite detachedness. Besides, she's not mine to claim. Not anymore. So I smile through the frustration I feel and wish her a good morning.

This week I started bringing her coffee. I still remember her order: skinny vanilla latte. Surprise flickered across her face the first morning, but she accepted it gratefully enough, which was just the encouragement I needed to keep it up. Today, I even threw in a chocolate chip cookie, and the look she bestowed on me made my heartbeat quicken like I was still a high school kid.

She's good at her job. Everyone seems to like her. But she's different. She keeps more to herself now, even more so than in high school. She's closed off, a wall erected between her and everyone else. The Evie I used to know was quiet but friendly. This Evie is never friendly, only polite. I watch her from time to time as I work through the sheet Peters worked up for me. She only attends my sessions when I'm working directly with him. The rest of the time, she answers the phone, responds to emails, and files papers. She does the same type of work she did for her mother in high school. She's so damn overqualified it isn't funny.

What is she still doing here?

Why didn't she leave?

The questions plague me daily but with the exception of my brothers, no one seems to know why Evie passed on West Point. The fact that my own brothers know and won't tell me is its own type of torture. On one hand, I'm proud that they're loyal to Evie. It's like she's still a part of my family and Carter and Denver have her back. On the other hand, I want to deck them because I'm their blood, and I feel like they should owe me at least some of their loyalty.

"Working hard," I comment, leaning over her desk after my workout.

"Some of us have to," she quips back, her old sass returning for a brief moment.

I chuckle, remembering all the times she used to give me shit for being a slacker. *You're not going to be able to rely on your good looks to get through life, Jax. One day, you'll be old.*

"What're you doing this weekend? It's Friday night, you know."

"I know. Why are you asking?"

"Can't I just make general conversation?"

"No. You always have ulterior motives."

"So distrustful, Maywood."

"Still so arrogant, Kane. What are *you* doing this weekend?" Her eyes twinkle at me, and I wish I could freeze the moment because she looks so much like herself again.

"Trying to ask me out, Evie?"

She snorts, cute and playful.

"Because if you are, I'd say yes."

She rolls her eyes.

"So ask me."

"I'm not asking you out."

"You girls like the guys to do all the tough parts."

"What's that supposed to mean?"

"We have to deal with all the nerves and self-doubt, work up the courage to approach a beautiful girl, and then convince her to go out with us."

"I don't think you've ever suffered from nerves, self-doubt, or a lack of courage."

"Correct. So, since you already shot me down for dinner, how about a movie?"

"A movie?"

"You know, those things you watch on a big screen while you eat popcorn and try not to blush too hard when I hold your hand."

She laughs for real now, a musical sound like wind chimes in the breeze. "That's all you'll try? Just hand holding."

I hold up the middle three fingers of my right hand. "Boy Scout Oath."

"You were never in the Boy Scouts."

"But I wanted to be."

"I'll go to a movie with you."

I can't stop the grin that splits my face. "I knew I'd wear you down."

"It's embarrassing that that's your strategy."

"Not if it works. I'll pick you up tonight at seven."

"What are we seeing?"

"Whatever's playing at seven-thirty."

She snickers, and I congratulate myself on finally getting her to agree to a date with me.

"I'll meet you there."

"Evie, come on, let me pick you up and—"

"Pretend you're a Boy Scout."

"Fine," I grumble. "But I'm buying the tickets and the popcorn, and if you're lucky and I feel like there's a spark between us, the ice cream sundae afterwards."

She stares at me, a tenderness softening her eyes as she chews her lower lip. "Okay."

"Okay. I'll see you later then."

"See you later."

I walk out of Morris into the bright morning of what promises to be a beautiful day.

12

EVIE

The knock on the door makes me drop my purse on the floor, items scattering everywhere. Naturally. I leave the bag where it is and glance at myself in the mirror over the console in the hallway. Thank God Graham isn't here to witness me freaking out. It's like junior prom all over again, except I'm an adult this time. Lame, lame, lame.

I fumble the lock on the door, pulling it open, about to tell the solicitor on the other side that now isn't a good time. Instead of a stranger, the hot body, sheepish grin, and deep green eyes of Jax slam into me.

"Jax."

He stares at me for several seconds, his eyebrows pulling inward as his bottom lip catches between his teeth. "You look beautiful."

I fight the urge to roll my eyes. "What are you doing here? I thought I was meeting you at the theater?"

He rocks back on his heels, his hands tucked into the front pockets of dark jeans with strategically placed tears. Ducking his head, he says, "I'd make a shitty Boy Scout."

"No kidding."

"I really wanted to pick you up."

"Oh." I glance over my shoulder at my purse splayed on the floor, a tube of lip gloss peeking out from underneath the ottoman. My heartbeat ticks up at his proximity, but secretly I'm pleased. Even though I don't want him to get too comfortable in my space, I want him to want to. Does that even make sense? "Okay, well give me a second." I hold the door open wider. "Do you want to come in?"

"Yes."

I turn back inside, feeling him step into my home behind me. Squatting down, I gather up as many items as I can, tampons included, and toss them back into my purse before he can offer any assistance.

Breathe, Evie. It's just Jax. It's fine.

Inhale. Exhale. Jeez, I didn't expect to see him on the other side of the door looking charming and devilish and stupidly perfect.

"I like your place."

Plopping my purse onto the console, I turn to see Jax taking in my living room, bending slightly at the knees to peer at a framed photo of Jenny, Miranda, and I taken at Raf's last summer.

"I don't remember you being so close with Jenny and Miranda."

"Most of my friends from high school took off after graduation."

He turns to look at me, his mouth opening as if he's about to speak.

"But the three of us have gotten close over the last few years," I blurt out before he has the chance to ask me why I wasn't one of the people taking off after tossing my cap in the air.

He picks up the framed photo, his face thoughtful.

Shouldering the cumbersome purse, I'm grateful for its awkward weight since it gives me something to do with my hands. "Ready to go?"

"Absolutely." Jax places the frame back in place and walks back to my front door. Pulling it open, he gestures for me to exit first.

I wait for him to close the door so I can lock up, listening intently for the three clicks before dropping my keys inside my purse.

He watches me closely, an expression I can't read flickering over his face. "Do you have a sweater or something?" He glances down at my bare shoulders. "Sometimes it's cold inside the theater."

"I grabbed a shawl." I pat the outside of my purse. "I'm a modern day Mary-freaking-Poppins," I titter, nervous.

"You always were prepared for the worst," Jax agrees, gently pressing his fingertips into the small of my back as we walk down the three steps to the parking lot and Denver's waiting SUV. The heat of his fingers seeps into my skin, simultaneously warming and warning me.

A thrill shoots through me at his touch. Nervous anticipation builds in my bloodstream, mixing anxiety and excitement together. Part of me is giddy to be going out on a date with Jax and the other part questions if all of this is too much, too soon. Am I ready to go on a date with anyone? The disastrous ending of my last date flickers through my mind and I shut it down as I reach Denver's SUV.

He opens the passenger door like a gentleman, and I slide onto the seat, clicking in my seat belt and watching him as he walks around the front of the car and tucks his long body behind the steering wheel.

His hair is starting to grow in, making him look more like his senior yearbook photo. He's wearing a pale grey button-down, rolled up to just below his elbows. His skin is tanned, the corded muscles of his forearms on display.

As I sit and stare at his hands and the way they tap out a beat, his long fingers curling loosely around the steering wheel, I realize that we're still sitting in the parking space in front of my townhouse, and Jax hasn't started the engine.

I glance at his face and find him watching me, a small smile playing across his mouth. "Breathe, Evie, it's just me."

"I know."

"If this gets awkward or weird, or if at any time you want me to take you home, just tell me. No questions asked, yeah?"

"Okay," I agree, relief overshadowing my anxiety.

The drive to the theater is quiet, which isn't saying much since it's only about three blocks. Jax parks in the lot and jogs around to my side, pulling the door open for me before I even unclick my seatbelt.

"Uh, thanks." I place my hand tentatively in his as I hop down from the passenger seat. "What's playing?"

Peering up at the old-fashioned movie sign that lists all the movies playing today, an unattractive snort shoots out of my nose. "*Shrek*? Are you kidding me?"

Jax exhales loudly behind me, grinning at the movie sign, my outburst, or both. "They're playing it again, on the big screen for a limited time." His voice changes to that of an announcer on a movie trailer and I laugh.

"Why?"

"Because the musical is coming to Savannah next week. There's a bunch of hype about it."

"That's so funny."

"I know. Remember when we watched it together?" he asks, almost shyly.

I nod, not daring to look at him. We watched *Shrek* in my room one of the first times we ever hung out. He came over to work on our British Literature project and after we finished, we ordered pizza, and he hung around so we could watch a movie. Mom was deployed then and my aunt, who was staying with me, was on a business trip. Alone in the house, I did something so out of character for me: I invited over a boy. Scandal!

Not that he stayed the night or anything crazy. But it was the first time he ever kissed me. It was the first night I admitted to myself that the butterflies in my stomach were because of him and not some random stomach bug I was coming down with.

Staring up at him, I realize I'm pressing my fingertips to my lips, remembering that kiss, remembering him. I drop my hand. "I remember."

His face softens. "You want to watch it with me again?"

I bite the inside of my cheek, trying to contain the smile wanting to burst forth as uneasiness settles in my chest. "As long as you promise not to kiss me this time."

Confusion dims the brightness in Jax's eyes but he nods once.

Stupid, stupid, Evie. I bite my lip, furious with myself for ruining the moment. Annoyed that I let other things taint a special memory between us.

He holds up the three middle fingers of his right hand again. "Scouts' Honor. I'll be a perfect gentleman."

"I'm sure." I roll my eyes, trying to play off my awkwardness when all I feel is a bubble of insecurity. Why does he even want to be here with me? He could be with any woman, literally any female over the age of eighteen in our town, and yet, here he is, taking me to see *Shrek*. "You can still buy me popcorn."

A low rumble works its way out of his chest as he chuckles at me. "You're a real giver. Come on." He holds out his hand, and slowly I place my hand in his, our fingers lacing together, as we cross the street to the movies.

* * *

The final credits roll as the lights brighten in the theater. I pick up my Coke and take one more sip before gathering the discarded bags of popcorn Jax and I plopped on the floor next to our seats.

"I always loved *Shrek*." I stand up, looking around to make sure I didn't leave anything behind.

"Yeah. It's a good movie." Jax takes the popcorn bags and soda cup from my hand. "I got this."

"Thanks."

He leads the way out of our row and down the stairs to the exit. I take in his broad shoulders, his tapered waist, and the way his jeans hang low on his hips. He looks too good to be true. Gorgeous and considerate and humorous all rolled into one. He didn't try anything for the entire movie. Not even hand holding. A big fat nothing.

Hyperaware of every move he made as we sat next to each other in the dark, our breaths mingling over the scent of buttery popcorn and the crunch of M&M's, I waited for him to reach out and lace our fingers together or stretch his arm around my shoulders. Not counting when we both went to reach for some candy at the same time and our fingers brushed, he didn't touch me for the whole movie.

Who is this boy scout, and what has he done with the Jaxon Kane I once knew? I have no idea. But as nervous as I was throughout the first quarter of the movie, I eventually relaxed as every time I glanced over at Jax, he was focused on the relationship unfolding between Shrek and Princess Fiona.

By the time the movie neared the conclusion, I was almost, *almost*, wishing he would reach over and place his hand on mine. Now, that was a huge shock to my system. When was the last time I even wanted a man's attention? Wanted to feel the weight of his hand or the pressure of his fingers against my skin? The last time I was with Jax, seven years ago, that's when.

Gah! What is wrong with me?

Following him toward the exit now, a calmness settles over me. I enjoyed seeing the movie with Jax, liked knowing he was next to me. I didn't freak out once during the film, my thoughts focused on the movie. When I did think of Jax, I didn't veer off into nerve-wracking what if's and mounting doubts. Congratulating myself on getting through this part of the date, I actually hope our night isn't finished yet. I hope he asks me to have an ice cream cone.

He tosses our half-eaten snacks into a garbage can before pushing open the doors into the balmy night air. He pauses, waiting for me to step up beside him and when I do, he looks down at me tenderly, reaching out his hand to lace his fingers with mine once more.

Thank God. I practically sigh in relief.

"So, you up for a sundae?"

I bite my lip to contain my excitement. Staring up at him, I blend the man before me with the boy from so long ago. And even though so much between us has changed, so much has stayed constant and feels familiar. Seems like normal.

"I'd love one."

"Mint chocolate chip?"

A ripple of satisfaction runs through my chest; he remembers my favorite ice cream flavor. It seems like he remembers a lot. Much more than I ever gave him credit for. "Mm-hmm."

"With rainbow sprinkles, extra chocolate syrup, and three cherries?"

"That sounds perfect."

He squeezes my hand, tugging me along as we walk three stores down to Sally's Sweet Shoppe for incredible ice cream and another trip down memory lane.

13

JAX

She winces in the seat across from me, and I lean forward, reaching out a hand to place on her forearm. I'm relieved when she doesn't jump as she's done in the past. The first time she did that, I felt like I got stabbed in the chest. Repeatedly. "Brain freeze?"

She nods, dropping her spoon in the bowl between us.

"You always did love ice cream."

"Guilty pleasure."

"I could think of other guilty pleasures you used to enjoy more." It's out of my mouth before I can check it, and I watch as her cheeks redden and her mouth drops open. Shit. After a beat, she picks her spoon back up, ignoring my comment completely, which is much better than being offended by it.

Stupid.

I know I have to tread lightly with Evie. Be careful with her. I don't know what happened or when, but I know it was drastic. It's the little things now. The way she looks around, always alert at her surroundings. I've seen her zero in on emergency exits several times. She turns inward when a man she doesn't know, or doesn't know well, approaches. Each time I notice one of her defense mechanisms, warning bells clang in my head and an anguish I can't explain fills my chest. She's obviously scared and I want to help her get past it. I want to know what happened to my Maywood but I'm afraid that if I push too hard, she'll retreat into herself and cut me out of her life again.

Seeing her before me, tucking into her ice cream like it's been years since she enjoyed one, almost brings me more pleasure than threading my fingers with hers. Almost. Because in these tiny flashes, it's almost like it's her again. And seeing carefree Evie is like Christmas morning as a kid. Before Mom passed. Before Dad fucked up and was incarcerated. When things were still merry and bright and the spirit of Christmas seemed like magic.

I used to think of Evie as being somewhat magical. The way she believed in me, saw me as more than just a football player with an ego. Knowing her helped me—saved me. Before Evie, I never thought I'd leave our little town. I figured I'd sort things out eventually but the reality is, I probably would have sought out the same type of belonging most kids who don't leave get tangled up in: motorcycle clubs, dealing, dead-end jobs.

"Jax?" She's staring at me, her eyes wide. Her fingers twist around her napkin. It's a nervous habit that irritates me because she never used to do it. It serves as a reminder of all the time I let pass between us.

"Sorry. I spaced out." I shake my head. "Sometimes, it's strange being back."

"I bet. What was it like, over there?" She angles her head, curiosity burning in her eyes.

I hesitate. It's a question I've been asked so many times before by so many people. But it's different with Evie. It's not like I'm the only soldier she knows who's been deployed. She's surrounded by them at work. Her brother serves. Her mom is a general for God's sake. She knows what it's like in Afghanistan. And Iraq. And posts across the world in both friendly and hostile environments. She knows. But she's asking about me.

Is it too much to hope that she's asking because she cares?

So instead of feeding her the bullshit I feed everyone else about it being hot and sandy, I tell her the truth. "It's a place I never want to see again."

"You did three tours."

"Yeah."

"Why'd you keep signing up if you didn't want to go back?"

"My guys. My team. I couldn't let them be one short, you know? A lot of us," I say, blowing out a breath, both wanting and not wanting to talk about this, "we were all in together. It seemed like if one of us didn't re-up, we'd mess with what we had going on."

She nods in understanding. Something almost everyone does but when she does it, it's like she really understands. Probably because she gets me. She always did.

"You lost someone you care about." She squints at me, studying my face. It's a statement when it should have been a question, but like I said, she gets me.

Biting my bottom lip to steady the emotion swelling in my chest and threatening to choke me, I sigh. "Yeah. My best friend."

Expecting her to look away—a new habit she's picked up when she's uncomfortable—she surprises me and keeps her eyes locked on mine. Like the old Evie. The one who didn't shy away from messy, complicated emotions. "I'm really sorry, Jax." Her voice is soft, her words soaked in sincerity.

I clear my throat, a tight smile pinching my cheeks. "Me, too."

She wrinkles her nose, looking so adorable I wish I could reach over and pull her into me. "You don't have to talk about it if you don't want to. Obviously." She shakes her head, her cheeks growing pink. "I didn't mean to pry."

"You didn't. Usually, I hate talking about it. But it's different with you."

She does look away this time, a sign that I need to be careful not push her too hard.

"His name was Ethan," I add, as if it's an afterthought. But really, I want her to know. I want to share him with her since he was my best friend, and she was my girl. Once. They should have known each other. "And I couldn't save him."

Her body jerks back slightly. "What happened?"

My fingers meet to form a steeple in front of my nose as I weigh my words. "It was an IED at first. Followed by shooting. So much shooting I could feel every bullet that grazed by me. The air even stung. Dust and sand everywhere, I couldn't see shit. I knew he was next to me. The guys had been razzing him just moments earlier about Amy's due date. That's his wife. She was eight months pregnant." I smile just thinking about Annabelle, his baby girl. Tiny fingers but the hardest grip I've ever felt from someone so little. "I met Annabelle as soon as I got back. Went straight to Amy's, even before coming here," I explain.

"I'm sure she's perfect."

"She is."

"So Ethan..."

"Killed in action. So fucking stupid, the entire thing. It shouldn't have been him. We were standing as close as you and I are right now. It could have been me; it should have been me. I'm single, no baby girl on the way, nothing to come home to."

She winces at the hard edge barbing my words but I don't care. It's the truth. It should have fucking been me.

"One minute he was there, the next, he was lying on the ground. I was with him at the end." I close my eyes, dropping my hands back to the table. "Worst fucking moment of my life." I blow out a breath, my fingers connecting with the scars on my shoulder. "I got shot up when we fell back. I was so focused on Ethan that I wasn't really paying attention. I actually don't remember much of it."

I feel her fingers tuck into my hand in the space between my thumb and index finger. She squeezes twice, just like she used to when she wanted to get my attention at a party or one of Carter's baseball games or somewhere public.

I open my eyes and look at her, surprised to see moisture gathering in the corners of her eyes and coating her long lashes.

"I'm sorry that happened to Ethan. I really am. But there's nothing you could have done differently. That's the reality of war, Jax. You know that. And even if it's a shitty thing to say out loud, I'm really happy you came home. I'm really relieved it wasn't you."

I breathe out a shaky breath from my nose, letting her fingers rest against my hand. Dropping my head, I nod that I've heard her, scared to voice my thoughts because of how fucked up they are. The truth is that sometimes, I'm really relieved it wasn't me either.

Evie squeezes twice more, and I look up again, the corners of my mouth ticking up at her smile. She remembers, too. "I didn't mean to be such a Debbie downer."

I close my hand tighter around hers, squeezing back. "Nah, I think I can claim that title tonight."

She removes her hand from mine to pick her spoon back up. She plunges it into the bowl, even though the scoop is mostly melted. "I like that we can still talk about things. Real things. I don't really have anyone I can do that with."

"Jenny and Miranda?"

She shrugs, chewing her lower lip in thought. "We're close. Good friends. We have fun together, but it's not like we were inseparable from way back when. Jenny and Miranda have always been tight, and they've sort of adopted me into their group, but I wouldn't say I over share with them."

"Graham? Your mom? Your family was always super close."

A spark of sadness touches her eyes before she blinks it away. "It's different between us now."

"Why?"

"Just is. Things change; time passes. Distance makes things harder."

"Yeah," I agree, thinking of how my relationship with my brothers and Daisy has shifted while I've been gone. "That's how it is with my brothers and Daisy and I, too."

"How is Daisy? It's spring break, right?"

"Yeah. She's all grown up."

"Crazy to think that we're somehow adults now, isn't it?"

"Scary as all hell." I agree, taking a spoon full of mint chocolate chip ice cream. "Evie, I couldn't even believe it was her when she walked toward me at the airport. I saw her in New York two years ago and I didn't think that two years could make such a big difference. It's ridiculous. I can't take her anywhere without guys stopping to stare at her, or worse, approaching her. And some of them used to be my friends!"

Evie bites her bottom lip, and I can tell she's trying to hold her laughter in. "Daisy's always been beautiful."

"Stop. She's my sister. She should be in a nunnery."

"A nunnery?"

I nod, wishing I could somehow convince Daisy to join one.

"You do know that nunnery is also slang for brothel, right?"

My spoon clatters to the ice cream sundae, spraying some chocolate syrup on the table.

"Why do you even know these things?"

Evie shrugs, licking the tip of her spoon. I stare, enthralled, suddenly wishing I could be ice cream instead. My jeans seem to tighten as she smacks her lips together, lowering the spoon.

"I like to read. Unlike some people..." she raises her eyebrows at me, a sweet smile that teases as much as it soothes on her lips.

"I read," I say defensively.

"Really? Like how you were always prepared for British Lit in high school?"

I throw a balled-up napkin at her, tapping her square on the nose. "You can't act like the only reading in the world is Dickens and Austen."

"Dickens and Austen? I'm impressed, Kane. The way I remember it, you didn't even have a pen, never mind the book."

I pick my spoon back up and shovel a scoop of ice cream into my mouth.

I know exactly how she remembers it: my asking to borrow a pen and paper from her in homeroom, us getting paired up for a term-long assignment in class, the boring readings, and the lame lectures. But the time I spent with Evie was captivating. Knowing her changed my life. Falling for her changed everything.

It was the absolute best.

Just like watching her cheeks redden now.

Just like tonight.

14

EVIE

I can't help but blush as I reminisce about the past right in front of Jax. But it feels good too, talking about it, laughing together. I remember everything about the first few times I interacted with him. I remember because knowing him altered everything I thought I knew about love. Losing him solidified all my previous beliefs. Him returning just confuses the hell out of me. Partly because I want so badly to be the girl I was when I first fell for him and partly because I'm not sure I can ever trust another man, even him, again.

"Do you make a habit of being early?" Jax asks innocently as he sits down beside me in homeroom.

"Do you struggle to do so?" I quirk an eyebrow at him, taking in his disheveled appearance.

He smirks, lifting a baseball cap off his head and running a hand through his tousled—correction, tangled—bedhead.

"Sometimes," he admits. "But," he pauses dramatically, "I'm prepared today." Jax holds up a purple notebook. It's thin, and there is a crease in the cover, as if he folded the notebook in half and tucked it into his back pocket. It looks like one of the ninety-nine-cent ones you can

get at the checkout aisle in a grocery store or at a gas station. And what guy would buy a purple one?

"Where'd you scrounge that up?"

He laughs, a deep chuckle that has several other students turning around to look in our direction.

I feel my cheeks flame at the attention, but I can't seem to look away from Jax, the carefree blaze of his moss green eyes, the fact that he is laughing at an insult.

"Found it in a kitchen drawer."

"The junk drawer?" I guess.

He considers this, his expression thoughtful. "Appears that way."

"Did you do the reading for Lit?" Suddenly, I'm desperate to keep this conversation going, to keep Jax's eyes trained on me. Especially now that Silvia has arrived, her eyes glued to Jax, and studying the way he leans over the side of his desk toward me.

"I did. You?"

"Yes."

"Hey, Jax," Silvia practically purrs, grazing her fingertips along Jax's forearm and up his shoulder as she sits in the empty desk on his other side, effectively pulling his attention from me to her.

"Hey," he answers before turning back to grin at me. "'A wonderful fact to reflect upon, that every human creature is constituted to be that profound secret and mystery to every other.'" He quotes Dickens from our reading of A Tale of Two Cities *before winking at me.*

Jax Kane winked at me, after quoting Dickens.

My mouth falls open as I stare back at him, confused as to whether he is openly flirting with me or somehow mocking me.

Before I can determine the intent of his wink, he's talking to Silvia, and I'm staring at the back of his hat, my fingers playing with the edge of my notebook.

That same day we were paired together for an assignment. It forced us to spend a lot of time together outside of school, researching, planning, and brainstorming. At first, we focused on the assignment, but slowly our time together lengthened, and we found ourselves joking around, talking about other things. Music, movies, friends. And later we had quiet conversations about life, love, and relationships. By the time we handed in our final project, I was completely head over heels for Jaxon Kane and wearing his football jersey to every Friday night home game.

I felt in sync with him in a way I never experienced before. I felt whole. He made up a huge part of my world, and the thought of going to New York without him the following fall was enough to send me into a full-on panic attack. So we devised a plan to be together. To take the first steps into our futures as adults together.

Before I knew Jax, my entire high school focus was on being accepted at West Point. Everything I participated in – the track team, volunteering at Veteran's Affairs, my course selections – were for the sake of increasing my odds of acceptance. I didn't have time for boys or dating. Despite my Mom and brother's urgings to be more social and make more friends, I was only interested in pursuing my future goals.

Meeting Jax was like being thrown a curveball. I fell for him hard, fast, and completely. Sometimes, it scared me how much my dreams and goals shifted in relation to his. When he bailed and left, he shattered my heart. And everything that came next, shattered the rest.

Sitting across from him now, seeing flashes of the boy I once loved mixed with the man I don't want to want, but can't help being drawn to, leaves me feeling overwhelmed.

"Evie?" Jax's voice breaks into my trip down memory lane and I look up, my blush deepening.

"Sorry."

"You okay?"

"Yeah, just, remembering."

Jax tugs his lower lip in between his teeth as he regards me. "Sometimes that's painful."

My smile is tight; I'm glad he somehow understands. But then again, he's Jax. He always understands.

"Most of the time."

Jax's hand covers mine, and he flips my hand over so his fingers tickle my palm. "I'm glad you came with me tonight."

"Me too." I reply truthfully. I'm having a good time with Jax, enjoying the easy conversation between us. It's been a long time since I've been out with a guy and let my guard down and the fact that I did so easily with Jax is both comforting and alarming.

"Evie, I know I already said this but I really want you to understand how sorry I am." He looks me straight in the eyes. His gaze is full of sincerity and a mixture of pain and regret; I know he's being honest with me. "The way I handled things between us," he blows out a deep breath between puffed out cheeks. "Fuck. I'm really fucking sorry for hurting you. I never meant to do that. I just didn't want to hold you back. And, if I'm being completely honest with myself, I didn't want to be in your shadow, either."

My eyebrows nock up at this. "My shadow? What are you talking about?"

He hesitates, uncertain how to continue. Raking his teeth across his lower lip, he considers me, the corners of his mouth lifting but never forming into a full smile. "Evie Maywood, you were larger than life. I couldn't believe I was even in your orbit, never mind on your planet. You were bigger than the sun and brighter than every single star combined. Back then, I was scared of being an anchor to your dreams; I was intimidated by your confidence. You knew exactly who you were and what you wanted. Don't get me wrong, I was proud as all hell of you. Amazed by you. But I also needed to go off and do something that could make you be proud of me. Make me bigger than the sun for you."

"You already were."

"No, I wasn't. I may have been that to you, but I wanted to be that for you. There's a difference." His fingertips graze mine as he slowly pulls his hand back to his side of the table.

"You broke my heart. Your leaving destroyed me."

"I know. And for that, I am so unbelievably sorry. It was naïve of me to think things would just work out between us but I really thought they would. That's why I kept emailing and trying to keep in touch. I thought we would work things out and end up together. After you told me to let you go, I knew I was being selfish with your feelings so I stopped calling. I wanted to respect your wishes. But fuck," he pinches the bridge of his nose, "it was really fucking hard. I wrote you so many emails that I never sent. Waited for my brothers to drop crumbs of information that would let me know how you were doing. But they never did and I figured they lost touch with you too once you headed to West Point. I never thought our paths would cross again when I came home. I think that's part of the reason I stayed away so long. I knew it would be disappointing as hell to come back and find you gone."

I close my eyes, a sting of tears pricking behind my eyelids. I want to be so angry with him for enlisting, for leaving. But what he's saying, on some level, makes sense. We were only seventeen when we started dating. Eighteen when we graduated. My future was so clearly planned out, and yet it did sort of seem like Jax was just following me because I wanted him to. Because I needed him to. Because at some point, I began defining myself in relation to him and could no longer fathom a future that didn't include him.

"I get what you're saying," I admit. "And it's not all your fault. I pushed you away too. After you left, the sound of your voice reminded me of all I lost, of losing you. By the end of that summer," I bite my bottom lip hard to keep my tears from falling, "I just wanted simplicity. Uncomplicated. And you were way too complicated for my heart to handle at that point. Still," I level him with my fiercest look, "I did want to punch you in the face or kick you in the balls for leaving the way you did."

Jax laughs, an unexpected burst of energy wrapping us back up in our own world. "There she is." He smiles at me warmly.

I raise my eyebrows.

"My Maywood. She definitely would have punched me in the face or kicked me in the balls if I pissed her off. Glad to see she's still lurking in their somewhere." His eyes soften as if to take the sting out of his words.

I smile back. Because as infuriating as he is, he speaks the truth.

I'm glad that I've still got some of my old sass and attitude too.

We pass the rest of the evening in easy conversation, a comfortable familiarity unfolding between us as we reminisce about high school and trade bits of information about mutual friends and what they're up to now. I confide in Jax about the PT programs I'm applying to, with Baylor-Army at the top of my list. He shares Army stories with me, most of them about the stupid pranks he and the guys in his squad would pull. The banter is simple and uncomplicated and I find myself wanting the night to continue just so we can keep talking.

It's late when Jax walks me to my front door. The light outside flickered on hours ago, and I feel the same giddy butterflies from my teenage years take flight into my ribs. I'm standing on my porch with Jax.

And he's going to kiss me.

The thought fills me with anxiety, excitement, dread and hope. It's such a confusing combination that I don't want to focus on any one feeling and instead count in my head to regulate my breathing. If Jax tries to kiss me, I'm scared I'll freak out. If he doesn't, I might cry from his rejection. There are too many thoughts clattering for attention in my brain and –

"Evie?" Jax asks, interrupting the volcano swirling in my head. He leans the side of his right hand against the doorframe, pressing his weight into it as his face angles to the left. He studies me, his eyes trailing over my face, as if memorizing my features, my expression, me. The left corner of his mouth ticks up as his eyes grow tender. For a beat, he looks just like he did seven years ago. More boy than man. More sweet than spice. "It's just me."

"I know."

"I had fun tonight," he says, his voice low like he's confessing a secret.

"Me too." I take a deep breath as my whirling thoughts quiet down and hope spikes in my chest.

"Maybe we could do it again sometime?" He grins now, his eyes brightening in amusement, and he pushes off the door-frame, standing to his full height before me.

"I'd like that."

"Sometime soon?"

I nod.

"Good." He takes a small step forward, his left thumb brushing against my cheekbone as his right hand cups the back of my neck. "Would you forgive me if I reneged on my Boy Scout Oath?"

"Hmm?" I'm lost in the depth of his eyes. The color darkening with each passing second.

"I'm going to kiss you now." His voice is unhurried as his eyes bore into mine for...permission?

A sigh falls from my lips and Jax blinks slowly, the left side of his mouth tugging up slightly before his lips descend toward mine.

The butterflies beat their wings rapidly in my stomach, and my heart gallops in my chest. I close my eyes, feeling Jax's breath fan across my lips. I breathe him in, partly from memory and partly from the moment, a familiar scent blending with a new, spicy, all-male aroma. I shiver, goosebumps breaking out on my arms. I forgot what this feeling is like, the giddy nervous-ness of a first kiss. Transported back to high school, my eyes flutter closed as I clench my hands, unsure of how to proceed. I haven't done this in so long and Jax must have been with so many –

His mouth captures mine, a sweet pressure that fuses our lips together the same way it did when we were seventeen.

I stand still, rigid even, as my mind links my first kiss with Jax to the present.

His hands grip my shoulders and I relax into him. He kisses me again, increasing the pressure, and I start to melt. It's been so long since I've been kissed. So long since I wanted to be kissed.

Jax's hand slides from my shoulder to the base of my neck to my cheek as my hands come up to rest against his chest. I step into him, and he angles my jaw, deepening our kiss, and dipping his tongue into my mouth.

I try to swallow back my moan but fail miserably, and Jax pulls back, a full-on smile crossing his lips as his eyes gleam.

I blink slowly, as if coming out of a haze. Breathing deeply, my eyes latch onto Jax and I feel cherished in a way I thought I'd never experience again.

"Thank you for tonight, my Maywood." He lets his hand drop from my face, his fingertips trailing down my arm softly.

I nod, my brain foggy, my skin heated.

"Goodnight." He rocks back on his heels, stuffing his hands into his front pockets. "I'll call you soon about that next date."

"Okay." I stare at him, relieved that I didn't freak out, giddy that he kissed me. My heart swells as feelings from the past, emotions I've buried, slowly come back.

Moments tick by as the smile on Jax's face grows, and I continue to stare at him, processing my thoughts and sorting out my emotions.

Jax... kissed me.

After a moment, I realize that I'm an idiot and need to unlock my front door, disappear inside of it, and then crawl under the hardwood floors, never to be heard from again. I can't believe I'm standing here and staring at him like an absolute moron over one, PG-13 rated kiss. But God, it was so good. It felt right. His hands on my shoulders, my neck, my face, were comforting, and not at all invasive like I feared. His kiss was sweet not brutal. He made me feel...safe.

Jeez. My face flames as I feel around in my purse for my keys. Shoving the key into the lock, I turn it quickly before pushing inside. Looking at Jax over my shoulder, I suddenly feel shy. "Thank you again for tonight."

"Sleep well, Evie."

I lift my hand in a small wave, closing the door behind me and turning the locks until the three bolts are in place. Leaning against the door, I slide down until I'm sitting on the floor, my back pressed against it, and my purse next to me. I place my fingertips against my lips, still feeling Jax's kiss linger there.

I kissed Jaxon Kane.

Hours later, when I close my eyes, I wait for the flashbacks to flood my mind. I expect to wake from nightmares. I anticipate the cold dread to pool at the base of my neck and drip down my back. But none of that happens. Whereas the last date I went on ended with me almost slapping the guy after a goodnight peck and filled me with an overwhelming dread that left me reeling for weeks, tonight, I sleep soundly.

* * *

"How was your date?" Jenny slides onto the barstool next to me.

I look at her from the corner of my eye, my fingers shredding a paper straw wrapper into tiny pieces. "How'd you know about that?"

"Carter." She huffs. "You could have told me, you know?"

I turn to face her, taking in the flash of annoyance crossing her features. "I know. Look, I'm sorry. I didn't want to make a big deal about it, and I didn't even know how I felt about it, so..."

Jenny raises her eyebrows expectantly. "So?"

"So?"

She narrows her eyes at me. "How'd it go? What do you think now? Apology accepted, by the way. I'm way too interested to know what happened to be hung up on the fact that you're a liar by omission."

"It went well."

"That sounds like a job interview. What is wrong with you? Were there fireworks? Tension? Something worth mentioning? Like, oh I don't know, I went out with my ex-boyfriend and it was incredible and we had hot, passionate sex all night long."

I take a sip of the water Lenny poured for me when I sat down at the bar. "It was nice. Comfortable. I had a good time."

"Well, Hallelujah for small miracles. Hey, Len, can I get a Jack and Coke?"

"Jack and Coke? It's three in the afternoon."

"Don't be judgey. It's Saturday. And I've had a crappy week."

"Why? What's wrong?"

"I lost a patient last night."

I reach out my hand, dropping it to her forearm. "I'm sorry, Jenny."

"He was so, so young. Still had his whole life ahead of him, you know?"

"What happened?"

"Overdose."

I shudder. I don't know how Jenny does it. Nursing is such a noble profession, but working in the ER, seeing how accidents affect people day after day, night after night, it's heartbreaking.

She thanks Lenny as he drops the drink in front of her. "You're a peach."

"You're still sober," Lenny reminds her, reaching over to pinch her cheek. "You know compliments from sober girls are just creepy."

Jenny and I laugh as Lenny is called away to refill a pint of Bud.

"Are you going to see him again?"

"Jax?"

"No, the other hot guy you've recently started dating."

"Shut up."

"Well, are you?"

I bite back my smile, nodding.

Jenny giggles and bumps her shoulder with mine. "Good."

"It is, isn't it?"

She rolls her eyes. "No need to go on and on about it, Evie. Whew, with all these details, I can hardly contain my excitement."

I throw my paper shreds at her.

She swats them away. "Yes, it's good. It's really, really great."

"Aw, look at y'all sittin' over here, gossipin' and... drinkin'." Carter amps up his southern drawl as he drops his elbow onto the bar next to Jenny, leaning over to sniff her glass. "Jack Daniels. Rough week?" He tilts his head to study her.

Jenny's expression sobers. "I lost a patient last night. It was an overdose."

Carter blanches. "Shit. I'm sorry, Jenny. That fucking blows."

"Orders up," Lenny announces, placing a basket of fries in front of me.

"Really, who are you today?" Jenny asks, shaking off her sorrow and nabbing a fry. "I haven't seen you eat anything remotely delicious in... actually, I can't remember the last time I saw you eat anything at all."

"I eat," I say, biting into a fry to prove my point.

"Must have been that date," Carter teases, grabbing a fry and popping it into his mouth. His eyes twinkle. Yes, they literally twinkle.

I watch him warily, knowing that he knows I've gone out of my way to avoid him for years now. That doesn't mean he's ever stopped being friendly toward me. Nope. Only Carter would continue to act like nothing between us has changed when the truth is, he's seen me at my absolute worst. I cringe just thinking about it.

"How've you been, Evie?" He carries on like I'm not avoiding him.

"Fine."

"That's good. Have fun out with Jax?"

Take a deep breath. Stop being so rude. I force my eyes to meet his. "Yes."

His seafoam green eyes lighten and the warmth in his expression causes a pang of guilt in my stomach. "He did, too."

A lightness sweeps through me hearing Carter's confirmation. Jax had fun, too. Jax and I went on a date. And then we kissed.

Gah! I'm seriously in high school all over again.

"Anyway, I gotta go. I'll let y'all continue talking about how the Kane brothers are the best looking guys in this town."

Jenny snorts but doesn't say anything. Probably because it's true.

"Don't drink too much," he warns, giving her a stern look.

She picks up her glass and takes a sip in response.

"And you, keep eating French fries. And mint chocolate chip ice cream sundaes." He winks at me.

"'Bye Carter," I manage to mumble out.

"'Bye Evie."

I turn my gaze back to Jenny, who is looking at me incredulously. Her eyes are nearly popping out of her face.

"What?"

"You ate ice cream?"

I throw a fry at her. "Shut up."

"A whole scoop?" She teases before pulling me into a side hug.

I pinch her side and she jumps back, flipping me the middle finger. We both crack up, our laughter causing other customers to look at us and smile.

Down the bar, Lenny's head swivels toward us, and he rolls his eyes. "Here we go," he mutters, causing Jenny and I to laugh even harder.

15

JAX

"You wanna go on a hike?" I call out as I cut across the parking lot of Morris and see Evie leaning against the building, her cell phone in hand.

Her eyebrows shoot up when she notices me. "A hike?"

"Yeah."

"Since when do you hike?" Her back straightens as she pushes off the building and stares at me, trying to figure out if I'm for real or not.

"Since I spent countless hours hauling around a shit ton of equipment patrolling sand."

"This from the same man who once told me, a member of the high school track team, that running isn't a sport; it's merely exercise."

"I used to be competitive. And I still don't get how most of the time, y'all just ran against a clock, hoping to win against yourselves."

Her eyebrows dip over her beautiful eyes as she fights curling her lips into a smile.

"Fine. I am competitive. I'll race you to the top of the hill on our hike," I offer.

Her laughter spills out and I grin in response. I'd say anything to get her to laugh like that. It punctures my chest with good times and sweet memories. She needs to do it more.

"You're really pulling out all the stops, you know?"

"How's that?"

"All these little excursions: movies, hiking, stopping by my house." She scratches her nose, and I can tell she's walking a thin line between friendly and flirty and isn't sure which way it's going to go.

I'd pick flirty. Any day of the week. Every single time.

Dropping my voice, I lean closer to her. "I want to spend time with you. I'll do that any way you're willing to. So go hiking with me. And if you're a good sport, I'll let you win the race."

Her eyes flash, a darkening of azure reminding me she once was just as competitive. If not more so. "You'll let me?"

I shrug, keeping my face blank. God, I love teasing her. "Only if you can keep up."

Insulted and indignant, her temper begins to flare, and I want to wrap my arms around her.

"Oh, I can more than keep up. I may not have been traipsing around the desert in a billion degrees, but I've got other tricks up my sleeve."

"Like what?"

"Like... yoga!"

I crack up, bending over as laughter grips my ribs. "Yoga? You do yoga?"

"Yes, its calming and relaxing. It's peaceful." Her back stiffens, her posture defensive. "Besides, it keeps my ass tight." She blinks at me, her signature sass dancing in her eyes as she keeps her face blank.

My mouth literally drops open. She's definitely flirting with me now.

"You've always had a great ass." I chuckle, amused by her

candidness. She blushes, her eyes still shining playfully. "I just never pictured you as someone being so... zen."

"Yeah, well," she sticks her tongue out at me, "we'll see how much you're laughing when you realize how flexible I am." Her eyebrows rise, challenging me.

I stop laughing, clamping my mouth shut as a torrent of images of her in tight yoga pants, contorting her body into impossible positions appear in my mind. They have me battling a surge of jealousy over every fucker in her yoga class and a hard-on all at once.

I blow her a kiss. "There's my rattlesnake."

And what does she do?

She freaking hisses at me.

I sling my arm over her shoulders pulling her against my chest and messing up her hair as we both dissolve in laughter that's as instinctive as it is refreshing. I've missed her feistiness.

She pushes back against my chest, shaking her head at me and wiping the back of her fingers against her eyes as moisture collects there. "God, I've missed you." She bites her lip as soon as the words are out, regarding me with wary eyes as if she's not sure how I'll react.

"Trust me, I've missed you more," I tell her truthfully.

Her cheeks redden again, and her eyes dart away. I can tell she's growing anxious now. Gone are the playful moments of teasing and poking. She's on guard again.

"How about tomorrow?" I ask, trying to put her at ease.

"For the hike?"

"Yeah."

"Okay. Tomorrow."

"Pick you up at eleven."

"I'll make sandwiches. For lunch," she offers sweetly.

"That sounds great. Don't forget to add potato chips to mine."

She snorts, covering her eyes with a hand and peeking at me

through her fingers, playful once more. "Don't remind me. Get out of here, you big ogre."

I drop a kiss to her cheek before she can react, and I'm surprised, and relieved, when she doesn't flinch or step away. "See you tomorrow," I remind her, leaving before she can add anything.

Walking into Morris, I let the memory popping into my head unfold.

Adrenaline is still racing in my veins, causing me to walk as fast as possible when I leave the locker room. I can't believe we fucking won. Actually, I can. I just didn't think we would. Not with the first half going so shitty. But man, that pass to Diego! It was like freaking magic. The door thuds closed behind me, and my eyes scan the parking lot, looking for...

"Good game." She approaches me from the side, wrapping her arms around my middle and squeezing me tightly.

I drop a kiss to the crown of her head, breathing her in.

Jesus. I am a lucky guy. A win like that and a girl like her. Who the hell ever thought it would be like this for me?

"Are you tired? Hungry? Sore?" she continues, peppering my collarbone with small kisses as she snuggles closer, and I wrap my arm around her shoulder, hugging her into me.

"Excited and relieved."

"You should be."

"There's a party at Hudson's. You wanna go?" I look down at her, so I can read her expression.

She wrinkles her nose in the most adorable way possible. "Not really. But please, don't let me hold you back from celebrating with your team. We can do pancakes tomorrow morning or something else over the weekend."

"No way. I'd much rather spend the night with my girl than at a sausage party anyway."

She blushes the lightest shade of pink, compelling me to kiss the corner of her mouth until she turns her face, letting me slant my mouth over hers and dip my tongue in between her lips.

She pulls away, breathless. "What do you want to do?"

"Want to get a bite to eat?"

"Okay."

"I know a place."

"Whatever you want."

Tucking her hand into the crook of my arm like an old couple, we walk to Denver's SUV and climb inside. I chatter on and on about the game and the plays, coming down from the natural high that is Friday night football in a small town in the South. As the starting quarterback, everyone says I can go anywhere I want next year and play football at the D-1 level. But so far, all my scholarship offers have been for partial tuition and I definitely can't swing the prices of a private university. Not even partial payment. Not even for fucking books. Not that it matters, I'm going to New York with Evie anyway.

"We're at your house," she states as we pull up in front.

"We are."

"Why?"

"I'm going to make you dinner."

She turns back to me, surprised. "What? You don't have to do that. You just played an insane game; if anyone is going to cook, it should be me."

I slide the gearstick into park and kill the engine. "Come on. Carter and Denver aren't home, and Daisy's sleeping at a friend's house."

She watches me quietly, a shy smile playing around the edges of her mouth as she mulls this over. Coming to a decision, her face suddenly transforms with resolve, and she squares her shoulders and opens the SUV door.

I bite back a laugh. Evie is the cutest. As tough as a rattlesnake, she always calls me on my shit and lets me know exactly what she's thinking. Unless it's about sex. Then she is all shy and sweet.

I walk next to her up the walkway to my house. It's embarrassing really, the growth of the lawn, the disheveled mulch hugging dying shrubbery. My brothers and I should do a better job at maintaining the place, especially for Daisy. I'm going to talk to them about that.

I unlock the door and push it open as Evie stills next to me.

"Jax." She suddenly sounds uncertain, and I know her mind has jumped to sex. We've only done it a few times and while it's been the most amazing experience I've ever had with a girl, Evie is still shy about it.

"Turn your mind off, Maywood. I'm going to make you the best sandwich in the history of life."

"The history of life?"

"I swear it. You've never had a sandwich like this." I wait for her to cross the threshold before entering behind her and closing the door.

Leading her to the kitchen, she takes a seat at the island while I pull random items out of the refrigerator. "Give me fifteen, yeah?"

"Sure." She flips through a random magazine that one of my brothers must have left lying around. Glancing over, I'm relieved its Motorcycle World and not Playboy. Although, some of the girls could double in both.

I move quickly, efficiently, concocting one of my all-time favorite things to eat.

Sliding a dish before Evie, she glances up, her eyes glowing and her cheeks flushed. "I can't believe you made me dinner."

"Well, I guess we shouldn't really label it as dinner. It's more of the best late-night snack."

"In the history of life."

"Take a bite." I watch her face as she picks up the grilled sandwich and bites into it. She chews thoughtfully, her brows shooting up in surprise before dipping in confusion.

"Are there potato chips on this?" she asks.

I nod. "It's awesome, isn't it?"

"What, exactly, is on this sandwich?"

"I can't tell you all my secrets off the bat, Maywood. You'd never stick around."

"True," she agrees, taking another bite. "It's pretty good. Thank you."

"I don't just share this with anyone, you know?"

"I'm honored," she says, sincerely.

I bite into my own sandwich, closing my eyes and groaning. Dropping my head back, I remember all the times my mom made this exact sandwich for Denver, Carter, and me when we were kids. Back when Daisy was a baby. She always added chips for "an extra special crunch." Sometimes, on random holidays like Valentine's or the first day of Spring, she'd use heart or flower-shaped cookie cutters to make our sandwiches into shapes.

Even though I don't tell Evie any of this, her eyes watch me carefully when I finally open mine and meet her gaze. Her smile is soft, her face almost tender. That's the thing with her; I don't have to say anything at all, and yet she always knows.

16

EVIE

Blue skies and warm sunshine greets me as I roll up my blinds on Saturday morning. The day is beautiful. Picture perfect in a way that casts a happy glow on everything that's about to come. Smiling to myself, I feel a charge, a change in my own energy.

I scoot to the edge of my bed and stuff my feet into slippers as I tug on a robe and head to the kitchen. I'm sure Graham already brewed a fresh pot of coffee. That's hands-down one of the best things about him living with me. The little things, like there being mint chocolate chip ice cream in the freezer and another set of keys in the dish on the hallway console, are comforting in a way I never expected.

"I was about to check that you're still breathing," my brother greets me as I enter the kitchen, making a beeline straight for the coffee pot and filling the mug he left out for me.

"Still here."

"I forgot how cranky you can be in the morning."

"Not cranky." I close my eyes, inhaling the incredible aroma that is coffee, and take a long sip.

"Thank God you didn't end up at West Point. Early mornings really aren't for you."

Swallowing past the lump in my throat that always manages to lodge there at the mention of the military academy, I take a seat at the kitchen table.

"What're you up to today?" Graham asks, peering at me over the top of his newspaper, his left leg crossed casually over his right knee. He looks like such an adult.

"Hiking."

"Hiking?"

"With Jax," I add, just to watch his eyebrows jump into his hairline in surprise.

"You're kidding?" He lowers the newspaper until it rests against the table's edge.

"Nope. He asked me to go hiking." I lean forward, resting my forearms against the edge of the table and wrapping my hands around my mug. "Crazy, right? First the movies and now... a hike." I wrinkle my nose.

"He's trying to win you back." Graham states matter-of-factly, holding up a hand to stop the protests that are about to shoot out of my mouth. "And he's being smart about it. Got to give him credit for that. He's making sure you're comfortable, pulling you back into his orbit." Graham's eyebrows dip down now, furrowing over his nose in thought. "I should really take tips from him."

"Having trouble in paradise?"

"Of course not. Just, well, Jax is really good at what he does."

"What's that supposed to mean?"

"Nothing. He's going about this for your benefit, not his own. He's doing what puts you at ease, biding his time, making sure you're on the same page as him before he moves forward. It's smart. And it means he's serious." He nods to himself as if this settles it, and resumes reading about the current events unfolding in Yemen.

"You're my brother. You're supposed to be on my side. He broke my heart once, you know."

"I'm always on your side, Noodle. And I remember. At the time, I wanted to slug him. But now," he regards me sympathetically, "it's like your becoming more of yourself again. More confident, less guarded. And I know it's got something to do with him so as long as I'm here, I'm on Team Jax." He looks back at his newspaper and I let the issue drop.

I move to stand up when Graham's voice stops me. "Another woman stepped forward."

"Huh?"

He turns the newspaper toward me, pointing at a headline halfway down the page. "Another woman stepped forward against that famous actor. The one in all those action movies. These fucking men and their exploitation of women." He shakes his head, disgusted as the words "sexual assault" jump out at me from the page.

"I thought it was a director."

"That's another case."

"Oh."

Graham watches me closely. "Nothing else to say on the issue? I thought this would have you fuming."

I swallow thickly, shrugging, as I push away from the table. Digging around the pantry for a bag of potato chips, I busy myself with sandwich prep. Throughout the process, my mind mulls over the headline, Graham's words, and the empathetic look he gave me.

* * *

At eleven on the dot, a knock sounds on the front door. Graham looks up eagerly from his perch on the couch, his laptop open on the coffee table.

"I'll get it." He stands.

Rolling my eyes at him, I disappear back into my bedroom to grab my sunscreen and sunglasses. Jesus, you'd think my brother was the one going on the date, er, hike.

I hear Jax and Graham speaking in the hallway, their voices a cadence of familiarity and the past. Shaking my head, I drop the items I need into a small backpack and grab our lunch from the kitchen before meeting them near the front door.

"Morning sunshine." Jax calls out as I walk closer.

"I've been up for hours."

"She just woke up about fifty minutes ago," my sweet brother clarifies.

I scowl at him, and they both laugh at my expense. The joys of having an older brother.

"You ready?" I ask, switching my glare to Jax. Gah! My hard-ass attitude disintegrates the second I look at him. Dressed in a pair of basketball shorts and a tight grey T-shirt, his muscles are on full display, the hardness of his abs evident. I could fall into his arms and swoon. He's wearing a baseball hat, the stubble on his cheeks and chin several days old, and a pair of sunglasses are clutched in his left hand. I swallow hard, dropping my eyes to the floor instead.

"All set. Good seeing you, man. Let's grab a beer while you're home. Catch up, shoot the shit." Jax claps a hand on Graham's shoulder as my brother nods. Enthusiastically, I might add.

"See you later, Graham." I press a quick kiss to his cheek as I pass.

He pats me on the head, tugging on one of the pigtail braids I'm sporting. "Make sure you wear sunblock so you don't burn."

My God. He really is an adult.

The door closes behind me, and I breathe in the day.

Jax and I are going hiking.

* * *

We head toward Sensor's Peak, the twists and curves of the road sharpening the higher we drive. I flip the radio to a country station I like and watch as Jax shoots me some side eye.

"Country?"

"We do live in the south."

"You used to like Pop."

"I used to like a lot of things."

He taps a beat out on the steering wheel, the heel of his hand hitting the top of the wheel every few seconds. Angling his head toward me, he asks, "Do you still like reality TV?"

Of course he brings up the one thing the Kane brothers used to tease me about relentlessly.

"I'm going to take your silence as an affirmative." He decides after a stretch of silence.

"Reality TV is reality."

Jax groans, "You still have the same argument? It's all scripted!"

I place my hands over my ears to tune him out and he laughs, trying to tug my hand away so I'll listen to him blabber on about how reality TV is warping the minds of today's youth.

"Don't knock it 'til you've tried it. I bet you've never watched one episode of *Keeping Up with the Kardashians* or any of *The Real Housewives* shows." I talk over him, my voice growing louder.

"You'd be correct."

"Yeah, well, you're missing out."

He shakes his head, reaching over to thread his fingers through mine. Our clasped hands rest against my bare thigh, my shorts having ridden up when I sat in the SUV. His skin is warm against my own and I find the gesture intimate and sweet. Still, the sight of his hand, a large, male hand against the creaminess of my bare skin sends a shiver down my spine, my heart rate ticking up. He squeezes my hand lightly and I turn toward the window so he won't know how something so small affects me.

"If you tell him I told you, I'll deny it, but I'm pretty sure Denver has seen a few reality TV shows while in lock up."

My head whips toward his. "No way."

Jax nods, biting his lower lip. "Ah fuck it, just ask him about it. His reaction will be worth his being pissed at me."

"Done."

A comfortable silence stretches between us as I hum along to the song on the radio, Jax's hand still clenched in mine. The longer we sit like this, the more I adjust to his hand in my lap and stop worrying about it and start to enjoy the pressure of his fingers against my leg.

He doesn't let go until we're parking, staring at the expanse of greenery and hiking trails before us.

17

JAX

It's hot as a motherfucker, and I'm briefly reminded of a stint I had in the Sahara Desert, across the plains of Sudan, which is a gross exaggeration, but it floods my mind nonetheless. The heat, the itchy swarm of mosquitos, the smell of sulfur, the sound of Ethan's wiseass laugh barking out as he cracks jokes only he finds amusing. It wraps around me like a tornado, sweeping my mind up in its powerful rotation before dropping me just as quickly at the sound of Evie's voice.

"You all right?" The feel of her fingers on my arm, pressing lightly, reminds me that I'm back home. Thousands of miles away from Sudan. Away from Ethan.

"Yeah, sorry." I shrug off her touch, my skin suddenly clammy in a way that has nothing to do with the heat.

She steps back, her lips tightening, her eyes trained over my shoulder.

Damn it. I close my eyes and huff out a breath, clearing my mind and reminding myself that I need to go easy on Evie. She's too affected by discord. Whereas years ago she would have just called me out and told me to cut the shit and spill the beans, this time she looks like she's trying not to cry at my brush off. Her chin quivers as her fingers curl into her hands.

"I get flashbacks," I blurt it out. "Sometimes. I mean, sometimes they're like nightmares and other times just memories. Not necessarily good or bad, they just are. And it throws me for a second."

Her eyes find mine again, deep blue swelling with compassion and understanding that I grasp onto, relief filling me that she's at least looking at me again.

"Do you have them a lot?" She peers at me curiously.

"It depends."

"On?"

"The environment, associations to past memories, that kind of thing."

"What sparked this one?"

"The heat." I admit, tugging on the back of my neck, my hand slipping with the sweat that's gathered there and seeping into the collar of my crewneck. "I don't remember it being this hot in April. It's hot as balls."

She snorts at my expression, and I grin at her.

"I was remembering being stuck in the freaking Sahara of all places."

"Whereabouts?" She begins walking again, and I fall in stride beside her.

"Sudan."

"Darfur?"

"Yeah."

"What happened?"

"Not much. I was just remembering how hot it was, the mosquitos were a bitch, and my friend." I swallow, my throat tight, remembering Ethan, remembering how I told Evie about Ethan, "Ethan just wouldn't stop cracking all these lame ass jokes. They were so bad, they were borderline funny, except none of us understood them."

Evie remains silent, her pace matching mine. Her breathing deepens as the hill grows steeper, but she doesn't say anything, which encourages me to continue.

"He was always joking around. Trying to be funny. Trying to diffuse whatever tension we were all dealing with through humor. Most of the time, he was pretty good at it, too. A real prankster."

"He sounds special," Evie says, sweat pouring down her neck. Soft tendrils of her hair curl around her ears.

"He was the best. Stupidly loyal. Would do anything for any of the guys."

"How're Amy and Annabelle getting on?"

A swell of pride chokes me as I think of Amy and her sweet baby girl. I realize Evie remembers everything I told her about them. "Amy's having a tough time, obviously. And a newborn with colic is probably compounding it."

"What do you know about colic?"

"Daisy had it."

Evie grins but her amusement quickly morphs into sadness. "What will she do now?"

"Amy?"

"Yeah."

"She's planning on moving to Minnesota to be closer to her parents and sister. She wants to raise Annabelle with a sense of family, and having her family around her will be a good support system for them."

"That makes sense."

"Yep. I've gotta call her actually. I've got a buddy relocating to Florida from Michigan. Instead of him renting a U-Haul, I'm going to see if he'll drive down Ethan's truck. Denver and I want to sort out some things on it and then sell it for Amy so she knows she's getting a decent price for it."

"That's nice of you."

"Least I can do."

"Do you honestly think you could have saved him?"

"No." Fuck if that's not hard to admit, but the truth is I wouldn't have been able to save him. No one would. The damage was too devastating. Shot through the chest four times. Blood everywhere. Hot and sticky and pulsing with life until he was gone.

"But you feel guilty," she says it as a statement. She says it as if she knows.

"Every goddamn day."

We walk in silence for nearly a mile. The beauty of the trail surrounds us. The forested canopy provides stretches of shade from filtered sunlight. A light trickle of water rushes over rocks and pools in a bank, filling our ears. Quiet settles between us, and it's comfortable, a constant I once had but lost. The scenery is soothing. The moment is calming.

And Evie's presence is like a salve to my open wounds. It's healing.

* * *

"You remembered the chips." My voice holds a hint of wonder as I bite into my sandwich, the extra crunch like a punch in the chest, reminding me of high school, Evie, Mom, and my brothers.

"Yeah." She tugs her fingers through her hair, dividing it into three parts and quickly re-braiding it.

"You look younger like that."

"Gee, thanks."

I kick lightly against her sneaker. "You know what I mean. Thank you. For lunch." I hold up my sandwich before taking another gigantic bite. I'm hungry and for some reason, food, even something as simple as a sandwich, always tastes better when someone else makes it for you.

"You're welcome. I know it's not the best in the history of life or anything, but I'm glad you like it. I made you two." She tosses me another one.

I shoot her a knowing glance at the reference as I catch the sandwich. Unwrapping the aluminum foil, I'm pleased when more potato chips fall from the roll. "You better watch out, or I'll ask you to marry me."

She rolls her eyes but she's grinning. "If a sandwich is all it takes, you've lowered your standards."

"Hardly." I point to the sandwich she made. "This isn't just a sandwich."

"True," she shifts her weight next to me, her cheeks pink from the hike. Sweat pools at the base of her throat and she swipes at it with the material from her tank top. "What made you decide to come back?" she asks, taking a bite of her own sandwich.

"The night Ethan died, my shoulder took a hit." I clamp my right hand down on my left shoulder, massaging the scars absently.

"Yeah, you told me that."

"That was the night I decided I was done. My tour was pretty much over anyway."

"But why'd you come back here? I mean, you could have gone anywhere."

I take a swig from a water bottle, considering her words. It's true. I could have gone pretty much anywhere. Could always find work in security or even the government sector. I have a few friends in DC now, some in California. There were definitely other options.

"I wanted to be back with my brothers." It isn't until the words spill from my mouth that I realize it's true. I've missed Denver and Carter more than I ever realized.

She nods, her expression thoughtful. She wipes the back of her hand across her mouth before shading her eyes to peer at me.

"And, if I'm being really honest with myself, I was hoping like hell that I'd get to see you, Maywood. I really didn't think you'd be here, but, man, I'm happy you are."

Her eyes widen and she drops her hand, her gaze glued to me.

"I thought everyone would tell me all about you the moment they found out I was back in town. I figured you'd be on your way to a first star by now, maybe married with a kid." I pause, watching her watching me. "And I knew that would hurt like a bitch. But it didn't stop me from hoping."

She lets out a low, unsteady breath.

"Now, you're here. With me." I shake my head over the absurdity of it all. "It makes everything else almost worthwhile. For the first time in a really, really long time, the reality is better than the expectation. More than what I hoped for." I pop the last bite of sandwich into my mouth.

Her eyes track the movement, zeroed in on me, almost like she's in a trance. I reach forward slowly, shifting my weight so I'm hovering inches away from her. I sweep my fingers across her cheekbone, down behind her ear, and grip the side of her neck before dropping my hand to the center of her back.

"I missed you, Maywood. And I'm really fucking happy to be home."

Her eyes flutter closed as she leans into me.

I press a kiss against the crown of her head, breathing her in. She freezes in my arms for just a moment before shifting her weight; her head tilts up until her eyes meet mine.

I inhale sharply, bowled over by the depth of emotion swimming in her eyes, and the flicker of panic that ripples across her features before she settles her expression. Her tongue darts out, touching the center of her bottom lip.

I want to drop my head, press my mouth against hers, and kiss her senseless. But more than that, I want to see what she's going to do.

She turns, straightening until she's sitting on her knees nearly in front of me. Her hands trail up my arms, coming to lock down on my biceps to balance herself. "Jax." Her voice is low, a current of uncertainty licking at the edges.

"I got you, Evie." I raise my left hand until I can hook my palm behind her neck, brushing my thumb against the shell of her ear.

She shudders, her eyes closing, her breath unsteady.

"Jax," she whispers, a plea.

"Tell me what you want, baby." I pull her closer, until she's almost sitting in my lap.

Her eyes open, wide and wild, looking around until they settle on me and bounce between my gaze and my lips.

Her mouth parts, her breathing erratic. Her fingertips play with the edge of my shirtsleeve, her expression a mixture of longing and agony.

Jesus.

I sit up straighter, my hand squeezing lightly on the back of her neck.

"I want you to kiss me," she whispers so softly, so hesitantly, I'm not sure that's what she wants at all.

I hesitate, dipping my eyes to make sure there's certainty in hers.

"For real this time. Please," she adds, a blush blooming in her cheeks.

And that's all the encouragement I need before I bring my lips to hers and touch our mouths gently and kiss her sweetly.

She melts into me then, her body folding into my arms and chest, her lips parting.

Wrapping her in my arms, I deepen the kiss, dipping my tongue into her mouth. She moans and my brain short-circuits. Her chest heaves against mine, her fingertips curling into my skin. I keep one hand pressed against her cheek, my other arm wrapping around her waist, holding her against me, as our kisses start to morph from sweet to bold. At the tipping point from reverence to reckless, Evie pulls back, her eyes clouded with lust, the pulse in her throat beating rapidly, and her expression almost confused.

I run my hand over her braids, clasping onto the ends of her hair to make sure she's looking at me when I tell her, "You make me feel like I'm in high school all over again."

Her cheeks redden, a flush that works its way down her neck as she shakes her head, almost in awe, and lets out a little giggle. Falling forward again, she lets me wrap her up in a hug and hold her to me, our breaths mingling, our thoughts racing.

I hang on to this moment, another example of reality outshining an expectation.

18

EVIE

My muscles are sore and tight when I wake on Monday morning. The hike with Jax was almost like a dream, clinging to the edges of my sleep. Pressing my fingertips against my lips, I remember the kiss we shared, the way his lips felt moving against mine, and the scratch of his stubble brushing against my cheeks, keeping me rooted in the moment. More than that, I remember the exhilaration that filled me afterward, as I buried my face into his sweaty chest and breathed him in. Everything about kissing Jax felt right. He felt like home. I'm practically giddy as the moment we shared comes flooding back.

It was different this time. Not like the sweet kisses he peppered against my lips on my doorstep. That kiss was cautious, feeling me out. This kiss, I could have gotten lost in it if I wasn't careful.

And I didn't even want to be careful.

But what if that's all this amounts to? Just a wonderful moment between two people who once loved each other? What if that kiss was more for closure and less of starting something new? Because let's face it, I can't exactly date Jax. He knows me too well and would see through all the crap I would spew the moment he tried to take our relationship to the next physical level. Kissing is one thing; apparently, it's even a thing I can handle. But I don't know if I could ever be ready for more than that. Jax would never buy it, especially when he knows I was ready for more than kissing so many years ago.

Ugh.

I flip the blinds up and peek into the sunshine outside, letting the warmth of the day encourage me to get moving.

I have the day off, mainly because Gabrielle really needed the extra shift and since I'm not supporting a toddler as a single parent, I handed over the hours without another thought.

Graham knocks twice at my bedroom door. "You up yet?"

"Barely."

He pushes the door open and stands in the frame, a mug of coffee in his hand. "I come baring gifts."

"That could only mean one thing."

"What's that?"

"You want something." I move to the edge of my bed and wipe the sleepiness from my eyes.

Graham chuckles, handing me the mug and waiting while I take several sips of the strong brew, letting the caffeine shock my system.

"So, tell me. What can I do for you?" I meet his eyes over the rim of the mug.

He pulls my desk chair away from the desk, spinning it so it faces me. Sitting down, he leans forward in the chair, letting his forearms rest on his thighs.

"Evie."

"Graham."

"Move to Germany with me."

"What?" I pretty much stutter, little drops of coffee splashing over the rim.

"Just kidding, I was making sure you're awake."

"You're a doofus."

The corners of his eyes crinkle, amused. "No one has called me that in ages."

"I find that hard to believe."

"Mom called twice, said she left you a few messages. She wants to know if we're free to go over for dinner tomorrow night."

"Oh, shit. I completely forgot to call her back! Yeah, sure."

"Good. She's expecting us at eighteen hundred hours."

"Cool."

"What're you doing today?"

"Running some errands. Maybe some yoga. You?"

"Heading over to Hunter's. He'll be back from Germany soon, and Kelly needs some help getting things set up for him before he arrives."

"I'm glad he'll be back soon. Say hi to Kelly and the kids for me."

"Will do." He stands, leaning over to press a kiss to the top of my head. "Don't go back to sleep."

Hmm, tempting. I sit on the side of my bed until I hear the front door close. Then I flop back against the pillows and flip on the TV. Watching an episode of *Jane the Virgin* on Netflix won't mean I won't get my errands done, right?

Three hours later, I force myself to stand up and change into my yoga pants and a tank top. Unrolling my mat, I stretch quickly before going through a series of sun salutations. Within minutes my breathing is controlled, my mind begins to blank, and a peace I only experience during yoga washes through my limbs.

I never thought I'd ever pick up yoga, but I've found it comforting in the past several years. The focus on breath, of being present in the moment, of connecting your mind and body and soul, it has all taken root within me. I now perform my practice daily, feeling a sense of serenity once I open my eyes after savasana.

Rolling my mat back up, I take a quick shower and change into a pair of shorts and a long-sleeve tee. Checking my phone, my stomach flip-flops with a message from Jax. Yes, I am getting butterflies from my ex-boyfriend seven years after we broke up. Gah!

Jax: Hey Evie

Me: Hi

Even though he sent the message nearly two hours earlier, the three dots appear at the bottom of my phone screen immediately, keeping me standing, holding the phone two inches from my face, desperate to see what he texts back.

Jax: What are you up to today?

Hmm, nothing, as per usual. But should I encourage Jax? I don't want to date him. But I do want to see him. Jeez.

Me: Not much. You?

Jax: Want to come grab a bite at Raf's?

Yes. No. Yes.

Deep breath.

Relax.

Me: Sure

Jax: Sweet. Pick you up in 30?

Me: :)

Dropping the phone on my nightstand, my stomach clenches in anticipation. Excitement.

Hope.

I close my eyes and practice ujjayi breathing to steady my nerves. On my final exhale, I open my eyes, square my shoulders, and stalk to my closet. Sliding the mirrored door open, I flip through the hangars, trying to combine an outfit that is casual enough for Raf's but flirty enough for a kind-of, sort-of date.

Pulling shirts and blouses and jeans and shorts from my closet, I toss them onto my bed. It takes me nearly fifteen minutes to settle on a pair of tight jeans with tears and rips through the thighs and knees with a flowing, sage green tank with little copper beads sewed along the neckline. Slipping into light gold, strappy sandals, I dash into the bathroom to pull my hair out of a braid, the long waves hanging around my shoulders. Brushing some blush across my cheekbones and swiping on a coat of mascara, I'm dabbing lip gloss into the center of my bottom lip when a knock on the door has me jumping up in another fit of nerves.

Ujjayi breathing, ujjayi breathing.

My stomach clenches at the thought of seeing Jax again so soon after our hike. It's like we're falling back into a comfortable routine, as if seeing him regularly is a given pattern for our lives. And it's confusing because as much as I want to spend time with him, I don't think he and I will ever be on the same page moving forward. How can we be? I'll never be capable of the type of intimacy expected in a monogamous, serious relationship.

The knock sounds again, this time in a combination. A fast one-two, followed by a languid three.

I hurry to open the door, remembering all the times Jax knocked in the same exact way on my bedroom door to announce his arrival. Just that little reminder of our past has my flaring nerves settling again, and I toss my tube of lip gloss on the hallway console before pulling the front door wide open.

Jax stands on the other side, a navy pair of cargo shorts riding low on his hips, his hands stuffed in his front pockets. He's wearing a heather-grey henley that molds to the toned muscles of his arms and pools around his lean abdomen as his shoulders roll forward, and a sincere smile crosses his lips.

"Wow." His seafoam and moss green eyes take in my appearance, a hint of surprise lightening the color of his irises. "You look beautiful, Evie."

My heart soars at his words, tugging my hope up with it. "Thanks Jax. You clean up well, too."

He cocks his head to the left, his smile still hugging his lips. "You ready to go or...?"

"Just give me a minute. Come on in." I wait for him to enter my home before closing the door and hurrying back into my room to grab my purse and phone.

Meeting him in the hallway, I nearly crash right into him and his hands come out, settling on my upper arms to steady me.

I freeze, the pressure of his fingers searing through my skin, warming me up from the inside out. I look up into his face, biting my bottom lip as my eyes meet his. The air seems to charge between us, infusing a tension that intensifies with each passing second. The green of his eyes darkens, a storm on the horizon. My breath quickens and then gets stuck in my throat, ujjayi breathing completely forgotten. Jax's fingers dig into my shoulders, once, twice, and then he blinks, his eyes closing for a beat too long.

When he opens them again, the storm has subsided, and his easy smirk plays around the edges of his full lips. "You okay?"

I nod. My voice is gone, my breath still stuck somewhere in my windpipe.

"Ready to go?"

I nod again.

He shifts his weight, keeping an arm casually wrapped around my shoulders as we leave my home and step out into the humid air, as casual and comfortable as a real couple.

19

JAX

It's different this time. The moment she opens the door I know it. Can feel it. It's not like when we went hiking or to see *Shrek*. She's more comfortable around me, things between us are more natural, organic. It's like we've taken a step, moved in the direction I've been waiting for her to be ready to move in. And now it's happening. And I have no idea how to not mess it up.

She looks beautiful—her dark hair loose and wavy, sliding over her shoulders, falling to the center of her back. Her blue eyes are sparkling, some of the old mirth and sass laughing along the edges of her irises. She looks... radiant in a way I haven't seen her look since before, a long time ago now.

Her laugh is lighter; I hear it more frequently. There's an almost musical quality to her voice, a cadence of sounds that soars and dips with the emotion behind her words. She's coming back to me. I can feel it. And suddenly, I'm terrified to lose it.

"You okay?" Her eyebrows dip over her cerulean eyes.

I nod, moving my hand over the center console to cup her knee, squeezing gently. She doesn't flinch, and I'm both relieved and panicked.

"Jax?"

I turn to her, careful to check back on the road every few seconds, but her gaze is penetrating. I'm mesmerized by the expression on her face; open and honest and trusting and so, so Evie.

I work to swallow, demanding that I pull myself together. I've run into fires and up narrow stairwells that could collapse at any moment. I've been shot at, shot people, and held my best friend's hand as he inhaled his final breath. I've done things reckless and stupid, necessary and not. But what I've never done is be there for Evie, not the way I should have been. Not the way she deserves.

Turning back to the road, I resolve to be the man she's worthy of, to stop with the second guessing and doubt. To just be here for her, however she needs me to be, for however long she wants me to be. My determination clicks into place and clears the insecurity clouding my thoughts just moments before.

"I'm fine. Sometimes, you make me nervous."

"Me?" She rests her head back against the seat and gently turns it from side to side. "That's ridiculous. How could I ever make you nervous?"

"Because I like you too much. Always have, as I'm sure you know. And I don't want to do anything to mess it up. Not again." I smirk at her, attempting for playful, but my words are too serious, too truthful. We both know it.

She turns to me, her hand covering mine on top of her knee, our fingers lacing together. "You won't. This time I won't let you."

A bark of laughter bubbles from my chest as I pull her closer. This time I won't let her go. Not even for a moment.

Raf's isn't busy when we walk through the front entrance.

The familiar smells kick up to greet us, the regulars are at the bar like always, and it's like nothing has changed. Except it has. Evie's by my side again, her fingers tucked into the crook of my elbow, and more puzzle pieces fall into place.

"Hey, Jax. Ms. Evie," Lenny calls out from behind the bar,

waving a bar towel at us and gesturing around to the wide open tables. "Take a seat wherever. Mindy will be right over."

"Thanks, Lenny." Evie tugs on my hand, pulling me into a corner booth out of the direct traffic of Raf's.

We slide on either side of the table, and I hand her a menu that rests in the corner, even as she rolls her eyes in my direction. We both know it's pointless. We only ever order burgers, fries, and a pint at Raf's. And, occasionally, a piece of pie.

"Mindy's here. That means we can get the cherry pie." Evie leans forward, whispering across the table at me.

"Mindy's that good, huh? Better than Gladys?"

"She's Gladys's granddaughter."

"No kidding."

Evie shakes her head, leaning back abruptly as Mindy approaches our table.

"Hey Evie."

"How's it going, Mindy? How's your grandmother doing?"

Mindy shifts her weight from foot-to-foot, watching me curiously out of the corner of her eye. No doubt she's heard about me, stories both fiction and truth. Small towns are notorious for festering gossip, and ours is no different. "Holding up okay. Good days and bad. Today's a good one. I'll tell her you stopped by." She turns her eyes on me, and I'm struck by how similar they are to Gladys's. "You too. She'll be happy to hear that you're back. And together." Her eyes dart between Evie and me.

"Please tell her hello, and that I would really like to stop by to see her if she doesn't mind," I find myself saying. But after the words are out and I can't take them back, I realize it's the truth. For how much I couldn't wait to leave this town, there are some people and things that are so embedded in my past that coming home without them is almost like not coming home at all. And Gladys is one of those people.

Mindy's face brightens, a dimple in her left cheek flashing. Just like Gladys. "I'm sure she'd like that. What can I get for y'all?"

"Burger, fries, and a water," Evie says, shoving her untouched menu back in the corner of the table.

"Same for me. But add a Heineken and a piece of cherry pie. I hear yours is just as good as Gladys's."

Mindy blushes at the compliment and mumbles a thank you. "I'll get your drinks right over."

She turns and walks toward that bar, calling out one Heineken to Lenny.

Evie turns back to me. "You're really going to visit Gladys?"

"Yeah. I'd like to see her again. You know, for a long time, she was..." I swallow past the unexpected lump that forms in my throat. For a long time, Gladys was the closest thing I had to a maternal figure and when I cut town, I didn't look back. Not long enough to ever check in on her, only knowing tidbits of information Carter would randomly supply. "I'd like to see her."

"She'll be over the moon to see you, too."

"She's not well?"

"Alzheimer's."

The lump in my throat grows, and I have to work to swallow past it. Carter never mentioned that. Hoping to redirect the conversation, I ask, "So, what'd you do today?"

"Honest?"

"Uh, yeah. I don't expect you to lie."

Her nose wrinkles in the most adorable way, "I watched about three hours of *Jane the Virgin*."

"What's that?"

"Stop it! You haven't seen it? It's such a funny show. I think you'd... actually, you wouldn't like it at all. But it's on Netflix, so that's a plus. Do you have any TV shows that you watch?"

"Not really. Usually whatever Carter's got playing in the background. You know us Kane brothers, we're more into—"

"Video games."

"Exactly."

"*War Cry*?"

"How'd you know?"

"As if it would be anything else."

I grin, and she smiles back and it happens again. The air seems to simultaneously expand and squeeze tighter, and it's like it's just us again.

Then Mindy plunks down our drinks, and the stillness explodes, causing Evie and I to look at each other and laugh, and Mindy to look at us like we're crazy. But in a way we are. Always have been.

The remainder of our meal follows like old times. We joke and laugh. Eat our burgers. I pick French fries off of Evie's plate after I finish my own portion. She sips her water, and I order a second beer. We share a piece of cherry pie.

There's smiling and laughing. Trips down memory lane and hints of future plans together.

She tells me about how nervous she is to submit her application for Army-Baylor. I tell her about how relieved I am that my shoulder finally seems to be improving. We share and confide and have a really great time.

When we're leaving Raf's and the door closes behind us, I ask her if she wants to come hang at my house.

When she agrees, I know we're taking another step forward.

Together.

20

EVIE

S tepping inside Jax's house is like stepping back in time. So much of it is exactly as I remember: the photos of his mother on the mantle above the fireplace, the tick marks in the kitchen door way measuring the heights of the Kane siblings stopping abruptly when Daisy turned five, and a dark smudge on the wall leading up the stairs where Denver shot a hockey puck and missed the net.

My fingers toy with my necklace, too many memories swelling in my throat. Too many moments I'd forgotten rushing back in.

Other things, like the couch and the quiet, are foreign to me. The Kane home was always a rough and rumbly concoction of noise, laughter, and swear words. Of forgotten Barbie dolls and *The Babysitter's Club* books dispersed throughout. Things that didn't fit together yet somehow did.

"Hey." Jax nudges me with his shoulder as I stand, frozen, in the center of the living room, taking it all in. His home even smells the same. The usual scent of laundry detergent, a faint reminder of eggs that Denver probably scrambled for breakfast, and something that is purely male. A spiciness that I imagine only lifts when Daisy is home.

"Hmm?"

"Want something to drink?"

"A water would be great." I follow Jax into the kitchen, my eyes catching on the familiar gingham curtains that hang over the window. They're worse for wear now, but I know the boys would never take them down. The kitchen is decorated exactly as their mom left it. Frills and cookie jars and delicate dishtowels.

I take a seat at the old butcher-block island and accept the glass Jax hands me with a smile. Taking a sip, the cool water relieves some of the pressure building in my throat and behind my eyes. I have a sudden urge to cry, although I'm not sure why. It's like I've been bombarded with so much of my old life I'd completely forgotten about. I'm not sure if I'm sad I'd forgotten or because it's not mine anymore, but regardless the remembering aches.

Jax's home, the complete ease and familiarity between us at Raf's, the normalcy of grabbing a bite and then hanging at his place is suddenly too much.

"You okay?"

"Yeah. It's just strange being back here."

"Tell me about it." Jax stands across from me on the island, hunching forward, his forearms resting on the butcher block, so we're eye level.

"It's still so much the same."

"I know. I didn't know what to expect when I came back, but in a way, I'm happy Carter and Daisy didn't change things up."

"Yeah. It's comforting."

"Sometimes." Something I can't place flares in his eyes.

"What?"

"I like seeing you here. Back in my home. In my space."

"Your space?" I snort, my fingertips tracing the rim of my glass, nervous bubbles popping in my stomach. Does that mean this is going to be a regular thing again? Are we moving into dating mode? Could I move into dating mode?

"Yeah. Even stranger than coming back here was not having you in my life anymore."

My inhale stutters. Literally, I gasp for air as if the supply has suddenly been cut off.

"You okay?" Jax comes around the island, his hand wrapping around my shoulder.

I nod, pointing to the glass of water and smiling weakly.

"I caught you by surprise?"

I nod again, working a swallow and steadying my breathing.

He presses a kiss against my cheek so quickly, I'm stunned into thinking I imagined it.

"Well, it's the truth," Jax continues, retreating to his side of the island now that I'm breathing like a normal person again.

"For me, too," I admit. "I've just had a lot more time to accept you being gone."

His brow furrows as he leans closer to me again. "What do you mean?"

"It's easier being the person to leave. You're doing something new, something exciting, starting a new adventure with none of the usual reminders of the past. You got to go. But for me, staying, it really sucked."

Jax drops his gaze to the counter before meeting my eyes again. Pain and frustration and maybe even a little regret churn wildly.

"The first few days after you left, everywhere I went, everything I saw, every single thing in my house, somehow had a memory associated with you. We knew all the same people, hung out at all the usual spots in town. There wasn't anywhere to go or anyone to hang out with that didn't know us as a couple and wanted to talk about what happened."

Sorrow breaks through the storm, coloring his eyes a green so deep I want to fall into them.

"I'm sorry, Evie. I never thought about that. I figured you'd be busy training over the summer and then leave in August for a whole new life at West Point."

"I know."

"I never thought you'd stay. I mean, why would you?" He pins me with a look so intense, I brace myself for the question that's hanging on the tip of his tongue, ready to burst forth and change everything between us. "I know you're not ready to tell me yet. But one day, Evie, one day I'm going to know why you let West Point go."

The relief seeping from my lips is obvious, blatant. He glances away as a flash of pain twists his expression. He thinks I don't trust him.

I hang onto the water glass again, letting the sounds of our mingled breaths wash over me.

I do trust him. The issue is me. I don't trust myself. Because if I tell him the truth and he looks at me differently, I'll break all over again. I'll never heal. And I'll never be able to forgive myself for that.

I'm finally moving forward. I'm going out more, I'm kind of dating, I've been kissed without having a panic attack, and new career opportunities are opening up for me. I can't do anything to mess up all my progress. I won't.

The sound of the front door swinging open causes me to jump in my seat. Jax's eyes slide to the living room as he cranes his neck to hear who is home.

"It's Denver," he explains, although I have no clue how he ascertained that information from the sound of a door closing and heavy footsteps growing closer to the kitchen.

Moments later Denver's frame pushes through the swinging door. His dark hair is pulled into a man bun on the back of his head, and a light beard shadows his jaw. He's wearing a white T-shirt, the vivid ink scrawling down his arms popping in contrast.

"Yo," he greets us, flipping his chin at his brother and offering me a slight smile.

"What's going on?" Jax asks, ducking into the refrigerator and pulling out the Brita to pour Denver a glass of water.

"Not much." Denver accepts the glass and downs the contents in three large gulps. "Fuckin' exhausted."

"You look tired," I comment, taking in the purple smudges underneath his eyes. "You okay?"

Fine lines crinkle around the corners of his eyes as he smiles at me, for real smiles at me. "Shouldn't I be asking you that, Evie?"

Huh? Is he alluding to...? Panic seizes my bones, locking my body down as I stiffen. My shoulders practically touch my earlobes as I tense. My eyes fly everywhere, searching for something to latch on to.

Denver steps forward, cutting Jax off from my line of vision, from seeing my face. "I mean, you've spent, what, the last few hours hanging with Jax and haven't kneed him in the balls yet? I don't know how you stand him," he jokes, clarifying his intent.

I manage the dread that races through my veins.

His eyes are kind as they meet mine, holding my gaze steady.

I focus on my breathing. Inhale. Exhale.

"You're a lucky motherfucker," he addresses his brother, spinning so his back is to me but still blocking me from Jax. "Managing to talk Evie into having a bite with you. Heard y'all were at Raf's?"

"This town is too damn small," Jax says, but his voice is tight and I know he didn't miss the exchange between Denver and me. But I also know he won't call me out on it. Not right at this moment. As long as Denver is here, I'm safe from Jax's burning questions.

Denver must assume the same thing because he starts talking to Jax about a few cars he's looking at and wants to pick up and work on. Jax asks a string of questions, and I use the time to recover. My breathing still erratic, I go through a series of exercises I learned years ago but don't use much anymore. Still, I'm grateful as my heartbeat slows, my skin cools, and my mind clears.

I'm thankful that when Denver rounds the island to grab a plate from a cupboard and Jax turns to face me, I look normal again.

21

JAX

Something happened. Something strange. So fucking weird that I almost feel like I imagined the entire thing, but none of it makes any goddamn sense. I know what I saw. I know what I heard. Denver made a joke and Evie froze, a look of pure terror crossing her face and causing her to nearly hyperventilate. And then, the thing that really sticks out is Denver shielded her from my view so naturally, as if he wasn't even covering for her. As if he wasn't handing her a way out from having to be honest with me.

It's obvious that Carter and Denver know things about Evie that she's keeping from me. That they're keeping from me. As time passes, I'm starting to put pieces together but some of those pieces are so dark and twisted, I can't even stomach the trail they lead me down. And I don't want to jump to conclusions. Not about this.

I definitely think Evie has been hurt. My guess is a past relationship and she got burned by the guy. Not just a usual breakup, but something more sinister. The thought of someone hurting her causes red hot rage to boil in my veins, and makes me want to track the guy down and beat him senseless. The thought of her with someone else is its own type of torture. Maybe I don't have the right to feel that way, but I do. I don't want Evie with any man but me.

It sucks because I know if I flat-out ask her, she'll pull back. I know I need to tread lightly with her, take things slowly, but the not knowing is killing me. What's bothering me even more is I can't connect the dots between Evie, Carter, and Denver. The entire situation is starting to get to me. In fact the more I think about it, the more my concern for Evie blisters into anger toward my brothers.

"Jax?" Evie's voice breaks me from the path my thoughts have turned down.

"Hmm?" I look at her, taking in her appearance. The terror from earlier is gone, her skin smooth, and her eyes are clear once more. Her posture is casual, and she looks completely unaffected. In fact, she almost looks... bored. But I know Evie. And I know that something spooked the hell out of her.

"Is Denver thinking of starting a business or something?"

"Oh, yeah." I clear my throat, "Denver wants to open an auto body shop. Do repairs, rebuilds, that sort of thing."

"That'd be cool. Denver would be great at that. I can totally see him doing it."

"Hey. Don't forget about your boy here." I hate that I sound affronted but... I am. I can fix cars and trucks and pretty much anything almost as well as Den.

"You're going to do it with him?" Her eyes widen, almost in disbelief.

"Mm-hmm. Why? You think I can't keep up?" I joke.

"What about the Army?"

"What about it?"

"You're active."

"Yeah, but only for another few months. Then what?"

"You're not re-upping?"

"Re-upping?" I shake my head, looking at her through narrowed eyes. "No, I'm not re-upping."

She stares at me with incredulity coloring her cheeks. Her eyes widen and her mouth gapes. "Why not?"

"Why not?" I repeat, trying to figure out her line of thinking. My back stiffens, and I know whatever words I say will sound defensive. Because I am defensive as hell. I served three tours and got shot up during the last one. And Ethan died. Ethan died, and I couldn't save him.

The silence stretches between us as she waits for me to answer. Her back is rigid again, her arms crossed over her chest defensively.

"Evie, I served. I did three tours. Missed two weeks of my last tour after my shoulder shit, but I served my country, the military, and the Army."

"I know that."

"Okay."

"But now, what? You're just done?"

"My contract's almost up," I say slowly, as if I'm explaining this to someone whose mother is not a freaking general.

"But your squad, your guys, everything you told me. You said you kept re-upping because you didn't want to leave your guys behind. Because you were all in this together."

"That was before. Things are different now. Most of them would make the same choice as me. Hell, most of them will probably be done when their contracts run out this time too." I tug the back of my neck.

"But you said—"

"I know what I said," I snap at her, my words sharp as bullets. "I said I kept going back because we had a good thing going, and none of us wanted to mess with it."

She sits completely still, as if scared to breathe too loudly. Finally, she nods.

"Ethan is dead, Evie."

She winces, avoiding my eyes.

"So we clearly don't have a good fucking thing going anymore, now do we?" I throw my arms wide, tension and anger reverberating off me in waves.

"Jax."

I step toward her, placing my hand on top of hers on the island. She flinches, and I hold her fingers tighter. I work to lower my voice, to fight against the fury pulsing in my veins at the thought of Ethan gone, of Amy losing her husband, of Annabelle never meeting her father. "Evie, not everyone is on the career track. It's time for me to come home, to stay here, to, I don't know, start something for myself."

"A car shop?" she questions, her tone cold and her voice empty.

I take a step back, pulling my hand away from hers. "Is that not good enough for you?" The words are out of my mouth before I can stop them and I don't care. Where the hell does she get off judging me on this?

"What?" Her eyes flash, a spark of the old Evie resurfacing. I'm so relieved to see her that I don't even care it's me pissing her off. "Of course not! I just, I get that you're hurting, Jax. I know Ethan's death has devastated you, but I still don't understand how you can leave the rest of your guys, your squad, behind like that. Like they don't need you. You're just giving up!"

Ethan's face flashes through my mind, his prankster grin, his easy-going manner. The gurgle in his breathing as he tried to suck in more oxygen assaults my ears. The heat and the sounds and the smells. The uncertainty and the loneliness and the fear. The adrenaline. Shadows of moments and glimpses of memories I tried to bury come bubbling forward. Giving up? I gave nearly all of my self. For seven fucking years.

"At least I tried!" I yell back, slapping an open palm against my chest. Evie's head snaps up, her eyes slamming into me, mixing with memories I hate that I can't forget. "You didn't even show up. What the hell happened to West Point, Evie?"

Her mouth falls open, and her eyes cloud over.

Instantly, I feel like a huge dick. I swore I wouldn't put her on the spot like this. I promised her I'd be here for when she was ready to confide in me. Instead, I pushed too hard, and now she's retreating, building up the walls I've been slowly knocking down.

"Fuck." I scrub my hand over my face and turn around, escaping into the living room, so I don't have to see the hurt overwhelm her. Hurt that I put there after swearing to myself I'd never do that to her again. "Goddamn it."

The kitchen door swings closed behind me.

"Give her some space." Carter's voice is controlled from where he sits on the couch, the remote control clutched in his hand. Yet, I detect a warning wrapped around his words. This is bullshit.

"What do you know that I don't?"

Denver appears on the stairs, his gaze darting between Carter and I. "When'd you get home?" he asks Carter as if it's not completely obvious that I'm trying to get into it with him.

"Denver?" Evie's voice is small behind me, and guilt expands in my chest.

"You okay, Evie?" Carter asks, turning his head to peer around my frame.

She must nod because my brother turns his head to give me one hell of a dirty look.

"Want a lift home?" Denver offers.

Jesus. Are my brothers kidding me right now? "I'll take her."

"A ride would be great. Thanks, Denver." Evie's voice breaks.

I spin to face her. "Evie, wait." My hand is outstretched, about to clasp her forearm, when she backs away as if I hurt her.

"I'll talk to you later, Jax." She mumbles quietly, walking to the front door.

Denver waits for her to walk out in front of him before he

turns and gives me a look I can't decipher. "Don't break anything," he warns Carter and I before pulling the door closed behind him.

My breathing is erratic as I turn toward Carter who sits on the couch as if he doesn't have a care in the world, and the most important thing on his mind is deciding between an NBA and college basketball game.

"What the fuck, Carter?"

"You're coming on too strong. You're going to scare her off."

"You think that's what this is about? That I'm pursuing her too hard?" My left hand squeezes the back of my neck as I pace in front of the TV. "Something happened."

Carter quirks an eyebrow at me. "Yeah? What happened?" He's so infuriatingly calm I feel my blood pressure spike in response.

"I don't know. Denver made a joke, and Evie, she, shut down. Her whole face changing like she was scared or something. I know you know. So just tell me because y'all are driving me crazy. What the hell is going on?"

Carter closes his eyes and tosses his back against the couch cushions. "Just give her some space."

"We were finally moving forward. Things seemed to be clicking between us. I could see her opening up to me, to thinking about a future with me. And then, I have no clue what the hell that was about." I point to the empty kitchen. "She wants me to re-up. How much more time am I supposed to waste?"

His eyes fly open at this. "Why the hell would she want you to re-enlist?"

"Hell if I know. It seems I'm in the dark about everything these days," I snap, moving past him to pull on a pair of sneakers by the front door. "I'm going for a run before I run my fist through your face."

He laughs, easy and unaffected. "I'd like to see you try."

"We're not kids anymore, Carter. I'm stronger than you now."

"Yeah, but you're still ticklish."

I snort. "Fuck off."

"Wear something bright so you don't get hit by a car. It's dusk," he reminds me like we're still kids, and I'm pissed about baseball cards or something trivial.

I pull the front door open and head outside, biting back a reply. My brothers may piss me off sometimes, but they're still my brothers. And deep down, I know they'll always have my back. Even with Evie. Even now.

22

EVIE

"You okay?" Denver's low voice cuts through my thoughts as I buckle my seatbelt.

I look over at him, but he doesn't turn toward me. "Yeah."

"Sure?" He twists to look at me this time, as if to make sure I'm telling the truth.

I nod.

Denver blows out a breath as he starts the ignition and backs out of his driveway, pointing the SUV in the direction of my townhouse. "Still on Silversmith Road?"

"Yes."

We sit in silence for several moments and for some reason, it's comfortable. That's the funny thing. Out of all the Kane brothers, Denver was always the one getting into the most trouble. He was the wild card, the one with all the girls that caused scandals, the one with the rap sheet. He was never charming like Carter or sweet like Jax. He never openly went out of his way for anyone. Most people were so intimidated by him that they didn't dare look him in the eyes directly, drawing a wide circle to stay out of his path.

But Denver always made me feel secure. His watchful eyes

catch everything. He's perceptive and picks up on the undercurrents of passing looks and words. Denver never pushes but somehow always guides. He's always managed to be present for me in a way that didn't require his physical presence.

"He's still in love with you," he says, breaking the silence.

I twist in my seat, pulling one leg up and tucking it underneath me.

"Because he doesn't know better. He still thinks of me as Evie from way back when. If he knew the truth, he wouldn't have the same feelings. He couldn't."

Denver's gaze darts toward me before settling back on the road. He stops at a red light. "That really what you think?"

"Yes."

"Come on, Evie. You know Jax better than that."

"I don't know Jax at all anymore," I say quietly, the argument we had still fresh in my mind. "He's not re-upping."

"You want him to go back to war, so you don't have to tell him the truth?" A tinge of sarcasm colors his tone, but I don't comment on it.

"The Jax I knew would never start something without finishing it."

"What makes you think he isn't finishing something else he started?"

I glare at Denver as his words sink in. "Am I supposed to be the thing he started?"

Denver chuckles, rolling his lower lip between his teeth. His fingers tap out a quiet beat on the steering wheel. "I forgot how sharp you can be when you let your guard down."

I roll my eyes, turning away and facing forward again.

"He's still in love with you, Evie. He's not going anywhere this time. So you can either be straight with him, let him back in, and see where this thing between y'all goes, or you can shoot him down and keep moving on with your life."

I remain silent.

"But you can't keep doing this. Drawing him in and then pushing him away."

I turn to face Denver, my head swinging, "I didn't pursue him."

"I know. But you wanted him to pursue you. If you didn't, you would have shut it down before it ever got to this point. I've seen you the last seven years. Didn't ever hear of you going out on more than one or two dates."

I clench my fingers into fists, my nails digging into my skin. He's right. I didn't let anyone else pursue me. Not really. I had one date playing mini-golf and another one that ended with me nearly hitting the guy. After that, I never let another man get close enough. Except for Jax. If I didn't want his attention, I would have made sure he knew it.

"Tell him the truth, Evie. He's going to find out eventually, and I promise it'll be better coming from you."

Tears prick the backs of my eyes, and I squeeze them shut, knowing that Denver is right. And hating it anyway.

"Am I causing problems between you guys? You know, with you and Carter lying for me?"

"Nah." Denver turns onto my street. "You could never cause problems, little girl. We all like you too much." He cuts me a small smile as he pulls into the parking lot of my townhouse.

"Thanks for the ride, Den."

"Think about what I said. Let me know if you need anything."

"I will." I unclick the seatbelt. My hand is on the lever to open the door when Denver's voice stops me.

"I mean it. Whatever happens between you and my brother," he pauses, a sigh escaping his lips, "you need anything, ever, you call me. Okay?"

"Okay."

"Take it easy."

I open the door and hop down from his SUV. Closing the door behind me, I offer Denver a little wave before making my way to the front door and unlocking it.

Stepping into my townhouse, I close the door and lock up. It isn't until I'm safely inside that the headlights from Denver's SUV swing away, and he pulls out of my complex.

I drop my keys into the little dish and kick off my sandals. Closing my eyes, I scrub my fingers over my face, most likely smearing my eye make-up. Damn, where the hell did I get off judging Jax like that?

Sighing, I plop down on the couch and turn on the TV. Deep down, I know I did it on purpose. The normalcy of our dinner, the familiarity of being back at his house, the easiness with which we fell back into a relationship without even trying is too much. It's too overwhelming. I can't lose myself again. I need to stay focused on PT programs, on my future, on moving forward.

* * *

I ring the bell at eighteen hundred hours. The sound reverberates throughout the wide foyer and seems to echo through the door, pulling me into a thousand memories at once. They vanish just as quickly as the door swings wide open.

"You're here." My brother greets me.

"We could have come together, you know?"

"I was at Hunter's later than I thought I'd be. He comes home in two days."

"Graham! That's wonderful news."

"It is. I can't wait to see him. And, my PCS date got pushed back so I'll get to spend more time with him than I thought. That means you'll also have a roommate for a while longer."

I bump my shoulder against his arm. "That's good news too. For me, at least."

"For me too."

"Evie, there you are. Why are you both still standing in the foyer?" Mom comes gliding into the room, beaming at Graham and me. "It's so nice when we're all here together, isn't it?"

"Yes, it's great. Thanks for doing dinner tonight. I'm so sorry I forgot to call you back." I step closer to Mom.

She waves away my apology. "You look lovely, Evie. I like your skirt." Her fingers smooth the material of my navy and white polka dot skirt as I lean in to hug her.

Inhaling deeply, I hold in her familiar scent. Honey and vanilla. I miss my mom. I wish I could stop avoiding her. I wish I could tell her everything. Just climb into her bed, snuggle next to her and lay my head on her shoulder, and cry as she plays with my hair. I used to be able to do that; now, it would just be awkward.

"Thanks Mom. I got it at Melanie's in Savannah. There's a sale going on."

Mom claps her hands together, "Oh, I love that shop! How are things at Morris?"

She links her arm with mine, and we walk out of the foyer and into the dining room, completely bypassing the formal sitting room where she normally entertains. I know this is for my benefit, because Jax broke up with me there. The gesture is thoughtful and makes me want to hug my mom all over again.

"It's going really well. I wanted to talk to you about a new plan I'm considering."

"Of course, love. What is it?" She gestures to a chair and I sink into to. The table is already set and a charcuterie and cheese board sits in the center. "I'm applying to PT programs."

Mom's face lights up at my announcement but she doesn't look surprised. "I heard that you've been shadowing Staff-Sergeant Peters on his evaluations," she admits.

"I have. I'm learning so much from him; he's a really great teacher."

"He's very good at his job but also a strong mentor." Mom agrees.

Graham trails into the room, taking the seat across from me.

"Before we dive into the details, would you both like some wine?"

Graham and I nod as Mom disappears into the kitchen and returns with three wine glasses arranged in a triangle, balancing between her fingers.

Graham and I each take a glass from her hands and she sits down in the seat next to Graham. Raising her glass in my direction, she says, "To Evie's new endeavor."

Graham raises his glass as well, "To Evie."

I clink glasses with my family and take a sip of my wine. The pinot grigio coupled with their praise warms me from the inside out. Watching their open expressions causes a pang of guilt to swell in my chest. Even as I added space and distance between us, Mom and Graham never stopped loving me, never stopped reaching out, never stopped trying to connect with me in small ways. That's the worst of it. Looking back now, I should have just told Mom the truth. She wouldn't have cared about who judged her. She wouldn't have thought twice about it. I was the one who put all this pressure on myself to live up to this standard, to excel at West Point, to be a general, and embrace my family's legacy.

Mom just loved me. Still does.

"So, Evie, tell me everything. Have you given any thought to Baylor-Army?"

"I have."

"Not that you have to go the military route." She's quick to supply, her hand reaching out between us. "I just said that because I have several colleagues that studied there if you're interested in speaking with any of them for more information."

"I know. Thanks Mom. I am considering Baylor. In fact, I've nearly completed my application, and Peters is going to submit a letter of recommendation."

"Fantastic." Mom claps her hands together. "I'm so proud of you, Evie."

"Well done." Graham adds.

I want to roll my eyes. How the hell can they be proud of me when it's taken me seven years to decide what I want to do with my life? I've been stuck and stalling and their applauding me for something I should have done years ago.

Mom rattles off the names of other programs she thinks I may like, even though none of them are connected to the military. After a few minutes, she steers the conversation to other topics, shooting me a glance from the corner of her eye. I know she changed the topic so I wouldn't feel overwhelmed by discussing PT programs. She wants me to know that just because I've raised the idea doesn't mean she or Graham are going to run with it until I do.

Mom is nothing if not thoughtful and caring. Once upon a time, we were two peas in a pod. But after what happened, and my not heading off to West Point, I felt like I failed her as a daughter. I kept distancing myself from her, pretending I had plans when she invited me to dinner, bailing on our monthly pedicure dates, cutting our phone calls short.

And still, she never gave up or stopped trying.

"Evie," Mom says, breaking through my thoughts. "I saw Jax the other day at the mini-mart. I was already in the car and he was heading inside so I didn't get to talk to him but I had no idea he was back home. Then, Graham tells me you guys have been spending time together."

I nod, my stomach souring as our argument last night comes flooding back. "Yeah, he's been back for nearly two months now. He's one of the guys I'm shadowing Peters on."

"Oh," her brow furrows, "he was injured?"

"Got shot up in the shoulder." Graham throws out.

Mom winces sympathetically, "I hope he heals quickly."

I nod, unable to say more as the thought of Jax and the way I treated him last night burns through me. Mom seems to sense this because she excuses herself to the kitchen and returns with a casserole dish of roast chicken and potatoes.

I'm grateful that no one brings up Jax's name for the remainder of the meal. By dessert and coffee, I'm immersed in the warmth my mom and brother provide, enjoying their company more than I have in a very long time.

23

JAX

My shoulder pops with a crunching sound as I push open the door to Morris. It's busy today, teeming with vets and a few active duty guys hoping to get cleared in time for their deployments.

I sense Evie's presence the moment I clear the door. Completely in tune to her, I know without a shadow of a doubt that when I look up, my eyes will seek her out, and study every nuance of her body language. I still haven't reached out to apologize to her for the way I behaved the other night. I know that we need to talk, that I need to let her tell me things in her own time, but man, if it isn't hard to stare at the woman I love and watch her suffer in silence. Every time I think we're moving forward, we hit a speed bump.

One step forward, two steps back.

Now, here she is, standing by the free weights just outside the men's locker room, talking to a guy I don't recognize. I track her from the corner of my eye, trying, and failing, not to be distracted by the bounce in her ponytail or the easy way she interacts with the soldier. There's a familiarity between them and I hate it.

She's nodding at whatever he's saying, a genuine grin turning the corners of her mouth upward as she laughs. Man, I've missed her laugh. It reminds me of sunshine, summertime, and car rides with the windows open. I scowl that she's not directing her laugh toward me. The other night was more than two steps back, and I need to make it right again. Today.

Clearing my head of my wayward thoughts, I shift my gym bag higher on my shoulder. Before I enter the locker room, I chance one more look in Evie's direction.

The guy places a hand on her forearm, leaning forward to whisper something in her ear. I notice the left side of his face is red, burned and scarred. He has a patch over his left eye. Still, my fingers clench into a fist, arm straining as my shoulder clicks from the exertion. Who the hell is he? She shakes her head, laughing again, and I turn, openly glaring at them now.

I watch, relieved, as he looks up and I finally place him. It's Hunter, her brother's best friend. I heard he just got back from Germany. He was there for several weeks after his eye surgery. Jesus. I avert my gaze; there is seriously something wrong with me.

Pushing into the locker room, I try to get my head on straight. I'm here to heal. To fix my shoulder shit. To finish out my contract. I stash my gym big, give the combination lock a spin, and head out to the weight room.

Glancing around, I notice that Hunter is gone, and Evie is standing off to the side, looking through a manila folder. Her eyebrows are drawn together, and she's chewing her lower lip, deep in thought. She looks adorable.

Starting my first set, I grimace as my shoulder tightens and a throbbing pain radiates up my neck. Screw this. My head is pounding; I'm not focused on anything but clearing the air with Evie, and at this rate, I'm going to injure myself even more. I'm about to bail on all of the exercises and demand that Evie hear me out when two guys I do recognize saunter into Morris as if they own the place and aren't here for PT.

I place them immediately; two kids I graduated high school with.

I watch as they joke between themselves but as they advance closer toward Evie, something shifts. The atmosphere charges, the order of the gym suddenly seems out of balance. Evie's back stiffens and her shoulders slump toward each other as if she wants to curl into herself and become invisible. She shrinks back as one of the guys, Gary Reitter, hits the other one in the stomach with the back of his hand and tips his chin in Evie's direction. Gary, I ran into him months ago, back when I first started here. The other guy, I'm pretty sure his name is Paul, Paul Hawkins, follows along and smirks, a nasty twisting of his mouth and a dangerous look flashing in his eyes.

They're enjoying her discomfort. Getting off on it.

What the hell?

They walk toward Evie, and she turns abruptly, panic crossing her face. I take a step in her direction.

"Hey, Evie," Gary calls out, coming to stand next to her. He tosses an arm around her shoulder and she flinches, her eyes swinging away from him wildly.

"Haven't seen you around much lately," Hawkins comments, an edge to his tone. "Not since the last time we caught up in the parking lot. Before your friends showed up. Remember?"

Evie's chest starts to rise and fall quickly, her breathing erratic, as if she can't suck oxygen into her lungs fast enough.

And that does it.

Her terror, the way it rolls off her and infuses the air with tension, has me seeing red. Not understanding anything that is unfolding between the three of them but knowing that what-ever it is, it's causing Evie severe anxiety, is enough for me to step in. Grinding my fist into my hand, my knuckles crack loudly, and Gary and Hawkins look up, surprise crossing their faces.

Gary drops his arm from around Evie's shoulders. She stands

straight as a board, her eyes trained on a spot on the wall, unblinking.

"Kane," Hawkins remarks, a slow smile working its way across his face. "Man, I didn't know you were in today."

"Everything okay, Evie?" I ignore Gary and Hawkins completely, my focus trained on her. My concern for her safety skyrockets as she doesn't move a muscle. It's as if she's in a trance.

Gary snorts derisively. "That's right." He snaps his fingers between Evie and me. "You two used to be," he says, shaking his head, "whatever you were. It's nice of you to check up on our girl, Evie, after all this time. Isn't it, Hawk?"

Hawkins nods, a menacing smile still on his face. "Sure is. It's been, what? Seven, eight years?"

"Evie?" I reach out slowly, touching her fingers, and she jumps, her eyes latching onto mine. The emptiness I see there is heartbreaking in its intensity. "Come on." I tug her hand gently, pulling her away from Gary and Hawkins and steering her toward the exit of Morris.

Gary and Hawkins keep their eyes trained on my back like a bull's eye. I can feel it, and it causes pure rage to beat through my bloodstream. Adrenaline pulses throughout my body and I have a difficult time focusing on Evie when all I want to do is turn around and pin them both against the wall until they tell me what the hell is going on. After I have my answers, I'll determine how badly I unleash on them. But neither of them would leave Morris walking.

I'm seething, practically shaking with an anger I've never experienced before. The day I heard two guys talking about me and Evie in the locker room flickers through my mind, further fueling my rage. But right now, I know that more than pummeling the two little shits I once graduated with, I need to get Evie out of here. Make sure she feels safe.

"Evie's not feeling well," I say to Marco on the way out. "I'm taking her home."

He glances at her and whatever he reads on her face convinces him I'm telling the truth, because he doesn't question me.

I guide Evie gently out of Morris and into the bright sunlight. She winces, lowering her eyes to the ground. Placing my fingers at the small of her back, I nudge her forward, toward the parking lot where Denver's SUV waits for us. I'm relieved when I feel my keys bounce against my leg, weighing down the pocket of my shorts. I was so distracted by Evie and clearing the air between us that I forgot to stash them in the locker. I pull them out and unlock the SUV.

Helping her into the seat, I buckle her in like a child. Her skin is frighteningly cold, her eyes blank, and her breathing normalizing but still irregular. I jog around the front of the SUV and slide into the driver's seat, turning on the ignition. We sit in silence for several minutes.

I watch as the shaking of her body slowly stops, as her fingers relax in her lap. She closes her eyes, dropping her head back against the headrest.

"Thank you," she whispers, her voice raw and broken.

"Evie," I breathe out, scared that whatever I say will somehow cause her more pain. Treading lightly, I reach across the center console and leave my hand open, palm up, unthreatening. "Evie, what's going on?"

She shakes her head, a bead of moisture leaking from the corner of her eye. She turns toward the window then, trying to inconspicuously wipe the tear away without my noticing.

I stare out the windshield, giving her a minute to collect herself.

When I turn toward her again, she's staring at me, her eyes swirling with so many emotions I can't pull one out to get a solid read on her.

"Can you take me for a coffee?" she asks.

"Of course. But Evie—"

She shakes her head, cutting me off. "Not now, Jax. Please. I can't right now."

"Okay," I agree uneasily, backing out of the parking spot and pulling away from Morris.

In my rearview mirror, I see the outline of Gary and Hawkins watching us.

I slam my fist down against the steering wheel, hopped up on adrenaline and anger and the overwhelming desire to drop the two of them and demand answers. Answers I'm starting to guess at, answers that repulse me almost as much as they devastate me.

Evie slides closer to the car door until she's practically molded against it.

Shit. I scared her. She's scared and upset and needs me.

This time, I'll be damned if I let her down.

24

EVIE

The warmth of the mug between my hands is soothing. I inhale deeply, calming my racing heart and focusing on my breath. I'm okay. Everything is fine. Gary and Paul do not have control over me.

"Cookie? It's chocolate chip." Jax takes a seat in the armchair across from me, holding out a piece of cookie.

I break off a piece and nibble at it. I'm in shock. That's it. Shock. The sugar will help. With each moment that passes, I feel the terror receding. The clamminess of my palms dries, and the wild thoughts ping-ponging around my head begin to quiet. Inhale. Exhale. Breathe in. Breathe out. I run through a round of breathing exercises.

I'm okay. Everything is fine. Gary and Paul do not have control over me.

"You okay?" Jax asks gently.

I nod.

We sit in silence, listening to the sounds of the coffee house around us. Random snippets of conversation from other customers float past my ears. I hear the clink of coffee mugs as they are placed on the tiny wooden tables, the clacking of keyboards as students type out answers to study questions, and lyrics of a song I recognize as one of Graham's favorites growing up.

"Do you want to talk about it?" Jax leans toward me, concern marring his brow.

"Thank you." I deflect, forcing myself to smile at him, so he'll think I'm fine. But really, who am I kidding? "I'm really glad you were there."

He looks away for a moment, and I don't miss how he runs his hand over the top of his head, tugging on the back of his neck. He's frustrated. Angry even. He doesn't understand.

But how could he?

"Evie, please." His green eyes find mine and beseech me to let him in. "Look, I'm sorry about the other night. I shouldn't have snapped at you the way I did. The things I said were—"

"Truthful."

"Out of line."

"You were right. I didn't even show up."

Jax sighs, dropping his head and pinching the bridge of his nose. He takes a deep breath, breaking off a piece of cookie and popping it into his mouth. He chews thoughtfully, his eyes studying me.

"Evie."

"I'm sorry I pushed you. I had no right to question your decision regarding the Army. You made incredible sacrifices to serve your country. And I'm truly sorry that you lost Ethan, a loyal friend, a brave soldier," I tell him truthfully, even though my words sound like I'm reciting something Mom says when she comforts a grieving soldier or family.

Jax's eyes narrow at me, as if he knows I'm just repeating words.

But I have to keep talking. I need to take control of this conversation and redirect the attention away from myself. I need to end things with Jax. I knew it the other night in his kitchen when I could see myself falling right back into a relationship with him. I became overwhelmed for an obvious reason; things between us can never work. I'll never be what he needs and after he learns the truth, I'll never be who he wants. Denver was right; it's not fair to keep letting Jax get close and then pushing him away.

Plus, there's Baylor. If I'm accepted, then I'm leaving here. I need to think about myself and my future. Protecting myself needs to be my number one priority, and I can't give up my trust to Jax just because I did it once before.

Look how well that turned out.

"I'm so happy you're back," I continue, the honesty in my tone more obvious now. "I'm thankful you're safe. But seven years is a long time. A lot has happened. A lot has changed."

"I get that." He leans forward, resting his elbows on his knees. "Evie, what happened back there? What the hell is going on with Gary and Hawkins?"

"Nothing." I swallow a gulp of my latte.

"Nothing? Seriously? They scared the shit out of you."

"I'm fine."

"Evie, please, help me understand. What is going on? Why didn't you go to West Point? Why did you stay here? I never thought, I never realized that," he pauses, trying to find the right words. Trying not to hurt me with them.

"That I wouldn't amount to anything at all?" I supply.

He glares at me. "That's not what I was going to say."

I shrug.

"Why won't you let me in?" He says it more to himself than to me.

"Because I can't handle any more heartbreak," I answer anyway. "I can't handle any more letdowns."

"I never meant to let you down."

"I know. But that doesn't make it any less true."

He rips into the cookie again, almost angrily this time.

"I've let myself down, too. You were right about what you said the other night at your house... I'm sorry too. It wasn't my place to voice an opinion on whatever you decide to do once your contract finishes."

"What if I wanted you to have an opinion on what I decide to do when my contract finishes?"

I can't look at him when I say, "It's not my place and I don't want it to be."

"There's something between us." Jax's voice rises with emotion. He gestures his finger back and forth in the space separating us. "I feel it. I know you feel it. And I'm not just going to ignore it because seven years has passed, and it's a long time and we've changed. All of that is true. But so is the fact that I still care about you. I still want you. I want to be the person you confide in. And I want to give us another chance."

I close my eyes, the honesty burning in his is hypnotizing.

"I'm applying to Baylor-Army. If I'm accepted, I'm moving."

"I know that."

"It's in Texas." I add.

"I know that, too."

"I don't think now is the best time to explore," I gesture between us in the same manner he did, "whatever this is. I need to focus on my future and if things go the way I hope, I'll be living in San Antonio in a few months."

"You're not moving until August or September."

I stare at him, trying to think of a comeback for that. "Correct."

"Evie, what happened with Gary and Hawkins back at Morris?"

Their names cause a shudder to race through my body, and Jax's eyes zero in.

"Look, I'm really happy you're back, Jax. And I hope this car shop with Denver works out the way you want it to and is wildly successful. But right now, I need to focus on a career path and not so much on sorting out a complicated history."

He stares at me like he doesn't even recognize me, his mouth hanging open. The only thing giving away the fury he's feeling is how his fingers shred the cookie into crumbs.

I place my mug on the little table between us. "Thank you for today. Really." I dip my head to catch his eyes and make sure he sees the sincerity and gratitude I hold for him. "The last few weeks have been... wonderful." I manage a smile. "But I can't give you more right now, not like you deserve. I should get going. I'll see you around."

He narrows his eyes, watching me.

I stand up and start to walk past him. I've almost cleared him when his hand shoots out and clamps down on my wrist. I jump, and he immediately lets go.

"I don't know what happened to you, Evie." His voice is so low I have to strain my ears to hear him. "But I'm starting to guess, and none of the scenarios are okay. Every one I imagine ends with me choking the life out of the person who hurt you. What you need to understand now is that I'm not going anywhere. I'm not just giving up. Not on you and not on us. So you focus on your future career path, but I'll be focusing on you."

Goosebumps skate over my skin at his words. Part of me wants to just sit down on his lap, wind my arms around his neck, and cry out all of the feelings bubbling in my chest until his T-shirt is soaked through. And the other part wants to run from him as fast as I can before he can uncover all the ugly truths I keep locked away.

Inhale. Exhale. Breathe in. Breathe out.

"Let me drive you home," he says, standing up.

"That's okay. I'm only a block away, and I'd like to walk."

Ignoring his protests, I move past him. Keeping my eyes trained on the exit, I walk right out the door and out of Jaxon Kane's life.

I'm okay. Everything is fine. Gary and Paul do not have control over me. They can't hurt me anymore.

No one can.

* * *

That night I sit on my couch, wrapped in one of my favorite blankets. A generous glass of wine stains my coffee table. My laptop balances in my lap as I strain my ears against the silence, hoping for just one sound of comfort. Of Graham unlocking the front door. Of a text coming through from Jax.

Something.

I exhale deeply, starting a round of breathing exercises to diffuse the ball of anxiety expanding in my chest. Something's gotta give.

Something.

I'm trying. I really am. I want to move forward, heal, live. I'm tired of just surviving, existing in this state between what happened, who I was, and now who I want to be. Is that awful? Probably. I feel like I'm stuck in limbo. Just biding my time, waiting. Paying my penance. But what the hell am I paying for? I didn't do anything wrong. Not a goddamn thing. And instead of owning that, that I was the victim, that I was wronged, I'm drowning in it. Losing pieces of myself with each day that passes and regressing farther and farther away from the person I'd like to be.

Sometimes, I wonder if I should have moved years ago. Left this town and the people in it behind, the way Jax did. Would changing the scenery, the environment, the atmosphere have helped? Would going someplace where no one knows me, doesn't care that my last name is Army gold, matter? Would it be better?

Is that what I'm trying to do by pinning my hopes on Baylor? Begin fresh?

But Baylor is still Army; it's a different path than the one I envisioned, but it still leads to the same place: military service.

How will I know what I need to heal if I don't try anything

new? I ask myself this a lot. I get all fired up with this spark of how tomorrow is going to be different. Tomorrow, I'm going to make changes. Tomorrow, will be the first step in a series of steps that will define me.

Then tomorrow comes, and panic seizes my throat. Something always happens to set me off. Waking from a nightmare, the smell of his cologne blocking my nose so I can hardly breathe. Seeing his car around town. Hearing their voices as they walk into Morris like they own the place. Always cocky, arrogant, and downright full of themselves. One of them will smile at me, and my insides will shut down, causing me to freeze. The day is lost, and I lie to myself that tomorrow will be different.

Who the hell wants to live like this?

Not a normal person.

But I'm not normal, am I? I can't go out with my girlfriends and let loose. I can't drink beer or sit by myself in the dark. I hate the smell of spicy men's cologne. I practically run past Sephora in the mall. I don't know how to be because my life is filled with triggers that set me off. Little reminders that take hold of my mind and paralyze my body. Ordinary things a normal person would never react to.

I panic. I blank out. I lose focus. And then, who knows what the hell will come out of my mouth? Who knows what I would say in a moment of desperation that would alert everyone to my shame? The stain would seep over my family, embroiling Graham and Mom in a scandal too large to be contained. It would destroy our family name. And even though I know Mom and Graham could care less about that, it would be one more thing that I ruined.

The part that cuts me to the core is that Gary and Paul are Army.

Something I want to be.

Desperately.

Dropping my head back against the cushions, I count to ten slowly. Breathe in. Breathe out. Inhale. Exhale.

When I open my eyes, I review my application for Baylor one more time and then I press submit.

My heart lodges itself in my throat as my stomach churns uneasily.

The page refreshes as I receive confirmation that my application has been successfully submitted.

Oh my God.

I place my laptop on the coffee table and pick up my glass of wine.

Taking a small sip, I smile.

I did it.

I took the first step in a series of steps to redefine myself.

I took the first step.

25

JAX

Cinnamon and sugar invade my car as I drive over to Evie's place, a large, brown paper bag with Maddie's logo on the front sitting on my passenger seat. It was my second run to Maddie's this morning. My first one happened hours earlier when I was on my way to see another woman I adore. Gladys. And man, if visiting with her wasn't a trip down memory lane, a heartwarming experience, and a harsh scolding all rolled into one. Remembering what she gave me earlier, which I stuffed in a drawer in my kitchen when I stopped home to change, makes me smile to myself and turn up the song on the radio.

Gripping the coffee I ordered, I take a sip, wincing as the hot beverage burns my tongue. Dropping the coffee in the cup holder, I curse and turn into Evie's parking lot. I'm nervous. And out of my league on this one.

Parking the SUV I sit for a few minutes, closing my eyes as I try and think through what I want to say. I wish I could call Ethan. A fire that's part pain and part anger ignites in my chest, and I swallow to push it away.

Focus on Evie. Make things right with her.

But how?

Her telling me she couldn't explore a relationship because she needs to focus on her future isn't what bothers me. That's all fine. I will support her in whatever she wants to do. It's that I know Gary and Hawkins scared her. And she reacted by pushing me away again.

I knew something wasn't right with Evie the first night I saw her at Raf's. Even her appearance – her thin shoulders, the sharpness of the bones in her wrists, the dark smudges under her eyes – speaks to an exhaustion that extends beyond a bad night's sleep. But over the past few weeks, she's been filling out, her vitality and vibrancy returning.

Yesterday, she straight up shut down. I know whatever it is has her spooked and anxious around men. I know it's something big and when my mind starts down possible paths, I'm horrified, sickened, and disgusted that someone would hurt her like that. I shove it away and search for signs in Evie that things are getting better. That she's becoming more open, less jumpy, sassier.

That my Maywood is coming back to me.

And she was; she really was.

Sighing, I climb out of the SUV, reaching over the center console to grab the bag of baked goods. Walking over to Evie's townhouse, I climb the steps to her front door and ring the bell.

The door opens a moment later, and Graham stands on the other side. "Hey, Jax."

"What's up, Graham?"

"Come on in, man." He holds the door open wider. "You brought Maddie's?"

I hold the bag up higher, shaking it at him, as I step inside Evie's townhouse and Graham closes the door behind me.

"Thanks." He takes the bag from me and reaches in to grab a cinnamon roll. Biting into the pastry, bits of glazed sugar and cinnamon sprinkle the floor as he walks toward what I assume is the kitchen. "Want a coffee?"

I open my mouth to tell him I have one before I realize I left it in the car. Besides, getting a few pointers from Graham can't be a bad idea. At least I can feel out Evie's mood in advance. "Sure, coffee'd be great." I follow him into Evie's kitchen.

"Take a seat," he throws out, his back to me as he pours two mugs of coffee. "Cream and sugar?"

"Black's fine."

Graham turns toward me, carrying two steaming mugs of coffee to the table. He places one in front of me before taking a seat. The bag from Maddie's sits off to the side between us, next to a stack of napkins and a few plates.

Reaching into the bag, Graham pulls out the cinnamon roll he's already tucked into and plops it on a plate. "These are my favorite."

"Evie's too."

"A family trait," he chuckles. "She's still sleeping."

"Still hating on that sunshine?"

Graham wipes his mouth with a napkin and picks up his coffee mug. "Yep. She's the worst morning person ever. I always wonder what would have happened if she went the Army route. Would she have adapted to the early roll calls and embraced it, or viewed it as the worst part of the day?"

I shrug, taking a gulp of my coffee to avoid saying anything. To avoid asking the question that burns on the tip of my tongue. Why didn't she go the Army route?

"How long do you have left?" I ask instead.

"My orders got delayed. Got a few weeks left here before I ship out to Stuttgart."

I let out a low whistle. "Fancy much? Don't come back with a Porsche or anything wild," I joke, referencing the Porsche factory that exists there.

"Imagine? I wish, man."

I take another sip of coffee.

"So, how've you been?" Graham bites into the cinnamon roll,

more sugar flakes falling onto his plate. "Heard you wrapped up a third tour?"

"Yeah, two weeks early." I point to my shoulder. "But almost done with my contract."

"You re-upping?"

Damn. This is not the conversation I wanted to have with Graham. I wanted to learn more about how to broach things with Evie, not rehash the shit that's going wrong between us.

"Don't think so." I tug the back of my neck, waiting for Graham to lay into me the same way Evie did.

"Career track's not for everyone. You should be proud of your service," he says instead, no judgment in his eyes or tone.

I take another gulp of coffee, growing antsier by the minute.

"You plan to stick around here then?"

"Yeah, thinking about starting an autobody repair with Den."

Graham pops the last bite of cinnamon roll into his mouth and eyes the Maddie's bag, as if debating whether or not to go for a second one. "That's cool. Y'all would do real well with that."

"That's the plan."

Graham reaches into the bag and pulls out another pastry, gesturing between me and the bag, but I shake my head, drinking my coffee instead.

"Does part of that plan include winning back my sister?" he asks so casually I almost choke on the coffee.

Graham chuckles.

I narrow my eyes at him, trying to figure out his line of questioning, but he just stares back at me, open and unaffected.

I sigh. "She's pissed at me."

Graham snorts, taking a huge bite out of the second cinnamon roll. "What else is new? She always gave you shit, remember?"

"I remember." Better than most, I remember feisty, sassy, ballsy Evie.

"She seems better since you've been back," Graham admits, lowering his voice. "More like herself."

I cut him a look, observing the concern mixed with relief that shadows his face.

"Graham, what the hell happened?"

Graham tosses the cinnamon roll on his plate and leans back in his chair. He sighs, a large whoosh of frustration, concern, and uncertainty. "I don't know, man. I really don't. If I did, trust me, I'd tell you just to help you get her back. She was good with you, Jax, real good. When you cut out of here, I could have killed you for breaking her heart. Nights of crying into her pillow, days of skipping meals. I was back for the first week and after I left, Mom said it was more of the same."

I look away, not wanting to hear how much I played a role in Evie's current situation, in making her unsure of herself. Of her place in the world. Did my leaving spur her down a path that led to her current pain? Did I play a role in causing the hurt my girl now struggles to overcome?

"But it was the usual shit of a first heartbreak, you know? I came home more that summer than I had planned, just to keep an eye on her and things seemed to be getting better. She was still intent on West Point, still sticking to her workouts. Sure, she wasn't as bright-eyed as before, but she was still focused."

"What happened?"

"I don't know. Mom told me she woke up one morning, walked into the kitchen, and announced that she wasn't going to West Point anymore. Mom thought she was just nervous and tried to speak with her. Told her to forget West Point and think about one of the other colleges she was accepted to. Evie wouldn't hear it. She just shut everyone out and receded more and more into herself. After a couple months, Mom was out of her mind with worry. She wanted to take Evie to see a therapist and Evie refused. Mom kept trying and finally, Evie just moved out. I came home several times, tried to talk to Evie, tried to understand what happened but," he shakes his head at me, confusion stark against his features, "she didn't even respond. She nodded at everything I said and then thanked me for my concern. She was so polite. Detached. Nothing like herself. I pleaded with her to tell me what was wrong, to forget about West Point if she wanted, but to tell me what made her change her mind. Was she nervous? Getting cold feet about moving to New York? About the military commitment? But she didn't give me anything to work with."

I don't say anything. What is there to say?

"She started taking classes at the community college, then transferred to Savannah State University. She tried full-time, then part-time. Then switched to online classes which is what she's doing now to wrap up a degree in Psychology. She worked odd jobs, babysitting and shit. Finally, Mom convinced her to think about something more stable and reliable. That's when she started at Morris. She seemed a bit better after that; I guess it was having some consistent human interaction." He snorts, the sarcasm heavy. "The first real spark I've seen since that summer is when you came back. And for that," he says, raising his mug in my direction, "I'm grateful to you, Jax. So forget the bullshit of before, of whatever happened between y'all. If you're planning to stick around and you still love my sister, then help bring her back. And I'll do whatever I can to help you."

I watch him for a few moments, noting how worried he is, how much he cares about Evie, and how much he lost when she pulled away from him. I think about Daisy and how I would feel the same way if she drastically changed overnight. It must be infuriating for him, the same way it is for me.

"Thank you, Graham," I tell him. "I want her back. I never wanted to let her go in the first place. I just thought, fuck, I don't know, I was stupid back then, a kid. I thought I'd hold her back."

"I know."

"You do?"

Graham nods. "And if things didn't play out the way they did, you probably would have," he says, grinning at me to take the bite out of his words. "You and Evie were young, real young. And she was full of dreams and plans and goals."

"Exactly."

"But things are different now, Jax. She's not the same girl she was in high school; you need to go slow with her, move cautiously. She's all kinds of hurt now, and it extends way past having her high school boyfriend enlist."

I place my coffee mug on the table with resolve that I'm in this for the long game. "Can I see her?"

He gestures toward her bedroom, "Wake her up nicely, or she'll be a pain in my ass for the rest of the day."

"Yeah, okay. And thanks."

"Anytime." He waves me out of the kitchen, and I walk toward Evie's room, intent on not letting her push me away any further, intent on winning her back.

26

EVIE

A knock on the door wakes me.

I squint at the sunlight filtering through the blinds in my room and pull my pillow on top of my face to block out the rays.

"Evie?" Jax taps his knuckle against the door, a quick one-two followed by a third tap.

Ugh.

"It's me."

Of course, it is.

I squeeze my eyes shut tight and wonder if I just feign sleep, maybe it will claim me once more, and I won't have to do this.

Another rap against the door.

Still, I don't move.

Lowered voices converse outside my bedroom and then the distinct sound of the door swinging wide open has me sitting straight up in bed, my pillow falling to the floor.

"Morning, sunshine." Jax walks into my room like it's an everyday occurrence. Bending to retrieve my pillow, he tosses it at me, collapsing in a flop at the foot of my bed. "How'd you sleep?"

I throw myself back, my head hitting the mattress as I think about how incredibly unattractive I must look: hair like a bird's nest, leftover makeup still smudged under my eyes, teeth that haven't been brushed.

Why is this my life?

"I brought you Maddie's."

Hmm. Perking up some, I manage to pull myself up once more and face Jax.

"Why are you here?"

"I wanted us to talk."

"At the crack of dawn?"

"It's eleven."

"It's my day off."

A grin glances off the corners of Jax's mouth as he watches me with amusement. "Still hating on the sunshine?"

"Obviously."

"Would a cinnamon roll and coffee make it any easier?"

I look at him, trying not to soften so soon, and nod.

"Come on." He holds a hand out to me and pulls me closer to the edge of my bed. "You better hurry before your brother eats them all."

That gets my attention and has me throwing off the covers and springing into action. "Graham Robert Maywood! You better not be eating all my cinnamon rolls."

"Your cinnamon rolls?" my brother returns, his voice filled with laughter. "Jax is my friend too!"

I storm into the kitchen, Jax on my heels, and I am relieved when I see a full mug of coffee and a warm cinnamon roll on a plate set by my place at the table. "Thank you," I manage to say to my brother.

He presses a quick kiss to my cheek. "Anything for you, Noodle. I gotta head out. I'm meeting up with Hunter. See you later?"

"Okay," I say, dropping into my chair.

"Good seeing you, man." Graham shakes Jax's hand, clasping

him on the shoulder. A silent look of understanding passes between them but I can't discern the look.

"Take it easy, Graham." Jax sits down at the table, picking up a half-filled mug of coffee and taking a gulp.

Graham gives us one last wave without turning around before loping to the front door and leaving, the door closing behind him.

"Thanks for bringing Maddie's."

"You're welcome."

I take a massive bite, stuffing my face to buy me a few moments without having to say anything. Embarrassment for yesterday and for what Jax witnessed weighs heavily in my chest. Do I confront it or just pretend it never happened? Does he think less of me now for freaking out the way I did?

"Evie," Jax says, filling the silence, "I'm sorry about yesterday. About the way things went down. All of it. But I meant what I said; I'm not giving up on us. So you can try and push me away, you can try and walk right past me, but until you look me straight in the eyes and tell me to fall back, I'm not going anywhere."

Some of the uneasiness bouncing around my stomach settles, and I realize I'm relieved that he's here. That he cares enough to seek me out, to keep fighting for a relationship that sometimes seems completely hopeless to me.

"Jax," I sigh, "there are things that I'm not ready to tell you. Things that I'm not sure I'll ever be ready to tell you."

He watches me closely, his green eyes full of compassion.

"I can't... I can't give you what you need."

"What do I need?" he asks almost playfully, a small smile flickering across his full lips.

"Someone who is whole."

"Nah. I just need my Maywood." He reaches out gently, his thumb stroking my cheekbone. "I'll take you even with all your holes."

I snort at his lame attempt at a joke. "About yesterday, I—"

"I want to show you something. Will you come to my house for a few?" He cuts me off, a seriousness filling his face.

I look down at my pajamas and back up at him. "Can I have a few minutes?"

"Take all the time you need, love. I'm not going anywhere."

I bite my lower lip, knowing deep down that his words are two-fold. Now that he's back, he's not going to give up on me. Or on us.

Hope flickers lightly in my chest but I'm scared to grasp at it, scared if I try too hard it will flicker out before it has a chance to really shine. I know Jax is telling me the truth; I know he won't let me slip away. Thinking of all the progress I've made since he's come home, it's obvious that my healing is related to him too. He was the one who got me questioning things in my life, thinking about options, wanting more for myself.

And deep down, in my heart of hearts, I know that I want him for myself too. I'm just scared of him not wanting me back once he knows everything.

* * *

I insist on driving myself to Jax's house, partly because it doesn't make sense for him to shuttle me back and forth, and partly because I need some space from him to make sure I keep my head clear. Jaxon Kane has the unique ability to reduce me to a pile of mush with just one look. And even though I'm relieved and giddy he's not going to let me go, I also know that I can't dive into this with him. I'm not capable of exhibiting the feelings and emotions that I want to. I can't even bear the thought of having to be intimate with him, of his hands touching me, sliding over my skin, underneath my clothes. I just... can't. Kissing is one thing, but the thought of all the things that come after kissing shadow my thoughts and make my heart race.

And what about Baylor? I'm determined that if I get in, I will go. It's time. It's been time for years, and I can't waste any more of it blinking. Would Jax still want me if I move to another state? Would he come with me? How could he if he's opening an auto-body repair shop with Denver?

Could we ever have any type of future together?

Parking in front of his house, I turn off the ignition and climb out of my car, ambling to his front door where he waits for me, sitting casually on the porch.

Tucking my hands into the pockets of my jean shorts, I stand a few feet away from him, taking in his light brown hair falling slightly over his forehead, the deep green of his eyes, the slash of his cheekbones, and the cut of his jaw. He's too beautiful to be real most of the time. The scar around his eyebrow glints in the sunlight as he turns toward the door. The sight of it settles me, a comfort, as I remember the Jaxon Kane from years ago.

"Come on." He stands, holding out a hand.

I take it tentatively and follow him inside, waiting until the door closes behind us.

Following him into the kitchen, I mentally cringe at the way things unfolded between us the last time we were here. I shouldn't have reacted the way I did; I shouldn't have questioned his future with the Army.

"Stop overthinking everything." His smooth voice cuts through my mental berating, and I offer a shaky smile, sliding onto a bar stool at the island.

"What do you want to show me?"

His face reddens, almost as if he's blushing. Ducking his head, he walks over to a drawer and pulls out an old purple notebook. A heavy crease cuts the notebook nearly in half, and spirally paper worms dart out of the binding. He holds the notebook up and I laugh.

"Scrounge that up in the junk drawer?" I joke.

He shakes his head. "Gladys gave it to me."

"Gladys?"

"Yeah. I went to see her this morning. Mindy was there, said she was having a really good day. She was happy to see me. Really happy." His eyebrows furrow together as if this confuses him.

"Of course, she was. She adores you. Adores all you Kane boys, even when you're raising hell and causing all kinds of trouble."

"It's crazy, isn't it?"

"No, she knows y'all are good boys at heart."

"Don't let Den hear you say that."

"Den's changed, too."

"He has, hasn't he?"

"Yeah."

Jax nods, his eyes suddenly faraway, as if he's lost in thought, fixated on things that happened long ago. "I guess so. Anyway," he says, meeting my gaze again, his eyes amused now, "we started talking, and then she told me she had to return something to me. Mindy was just as confused as I was and tried to have Gladys sit back down, but she was so insistent." He chuckles. "You remember how she could be?"

I nod; Gladys could be a hell raiser herself if the situation called for it.

"She went into her room for a few, Mindy trailing her, probably scared what she was going to bring out, and then she returned with this." He passes me the old notebook from the year we had British Literature together in high school.

"Gladys reminded me that sometimes just showing up isn't enough. That you have to be honest and sincere and remorseful. She demanded that I offer you the apology you deserve because she said I'd never win you back otherwise."

My eyebrows shoot up to my hairline, and I can't stop the nervous giggle falling from my lips. "Win me back?"

Jax's eyes darken and his features settle into sharp angles of determination. His next words are whispered earnestly, "I'm sorry, Evie. I'm sorry for the way I left town. I'm sorry for the way I left you. But most of all, I'm sorry for making you feel like I didn't want you anymore. For making you question yourself. You are the bravest, most badass woman I know, and it breaks my heart that my actions made you feel insecure or less than who you are."

I stare at him, my breath lodged in my throat, and my hands pressed between my thighs to keep them from shaking.

"I missed you so much those first few months, that's why I kept reaching out. I thought we'd get back together. Once you asked me to stop, I cut off my communication with everyone from here. Deleted Facebook and the rest of my social media accounts for about a year. Avoided all calls from my brothers and blew off emails from Daisy. I was scared that if I spoke to them, I'd ask about you, and I'd regret ending things between us in the first place. Hell, after you asked me to back off, I did regret ending things between us at all. I was furious with myself for not going with you to New York."

Tears prick behind my eyes at his honesty and at the hurt he also endured. The realization of what we should have been and what we are couldn't be farther apart.

"And I hated myself for it. Hated myself for hurting you. I knew I was in love with you; I knew there would never be another girl who came close. But I wanted to make my own way, I wanted to carve my own path. I wanted us to both have successful, exciting careers. And I didn't figure out early enough how to make that happen for both of us while staying together."

I shake my head at his words, tears spilling over my eyelids and tracking my cheeks.

"As time passed, it got easier. I became close with my squad, traveled the world, got lost in the distance I put between us. After Ethan..." He tugs the back of his neck, his fingers pinching the skin at the base. "I wanted to come home. I wanted to be done with distance and space; I wanted roots." He looks at me, his eyes softening. "I never thought you'd be here, Maywood. God, how I hoped, but I didn't believe it until I got back. Until I saw you at

Raf's. So I figure this is some big, cosmic joke, my getting a second chance with you. Having the opportunity to win you back. I know it's been a long time; I know a lot has changed. But I also know that I'm still crazy in love with you, and there will never be anyone else for me. You're it. So," he exhales shakily, flipping the notebook open and ruffling pages until he finds the one he's looking for. He turns the notebook around so I can read it and sighs. "Gladys suggested I begin with this."

27

JAX

DEAR EVIE,

I f you're reading this, it's because I'm gone. I know I told you I was leaving, but the truth is I didn't actually think I'd go through with it. Not even after I signed my name to enlist. Not even after I told my brothers and Daisy and packed my bag. Not even after I kissed you goodbye.

The day I told you I enlisted, you looked at me with so much sadness and disappointment. Much more than anyone else ever has. And it fucking hurt. Partly because I hate disappointing you and making you cry, and partly because I know no one will ever feel for me as much as you do.

I'm sorry for hurting you, Evie. I'm sorry for not being enough for you. I know that you say I am, and that may be true now, but it won't be in the future. You are filled up with goodness and dreams bigger than anything I've ever imagined. You've made me see an entire world beyond the borders of our town; a world I didn't even think to consider.

You've got a beautiful future ahead of you, Evie. You're smart, determined, sassy as all hell, and the most selfless person I know. I have to let you go, so you can go off and be that person. If I don't, I'll hold you back, and I would never want to do that to you. So even though you don't believe me now, I promise one day you will.

Whatever I do next, whomever I grow into, anything good that I accomplish is because of you. Knowing you has given me a future. You rescued me, Evie, and I'll always be grateful. I hope one day you can remember me and smile the way I always do when I think of you.

Jax

Her eyes scan across the last line, and I drop my dog tags next to the letter before she can look up. Her fingers reach out, tracing along the small beads and across the indentation of my name on the plates.

"Jax?" She looks up, her eyes watery and her cheeks stained from where her tears fell.

"I want to thank you, Evie."

"Thank me? For what?"

"For me. For everything. I never would have amounted to anything much if I hadn't met you, if you hadn't pushed me to be better. To want more."

"I didn't do anything, Jax." She looks down, watching her toes as they scrape back and forth against the bottom rung of the barstool.

"You did. You did so much more than you even realize."

She shakes her head and pushes back from the island, sliding off the barstool, as if my words are difficult to hear.

I take a step in her direction.

"Stop it." She whirls toward me, streaks of anger blazing red patches on her cheeks. "I didn't do anything. I haven't accomplished anything. I've been here. This entire time, I've been here, watching the rest of the world pass me by."

"You saved my life." I pull my dog tags from the island and push them toward her.

"Stop."

"This is what I owe you." I force the folded tags into her hands.

She laughs but it's jarring, a bitter undercurrent edging her next words. "Are you kidding me? You owe me your dog tags?"

"Yes!"

A tear escapes from her left eye, tracing her cheek slowly as she shakes her head. "I don't want them."

"Why?"

"I don't want this!" She gestures between us, the chain of the tags wrapping around her fingers as the nameplate swings wildly. My whole life wrapped up in her hands, the way it always should have been.

"I don't want this," she says quieter this time, the tears coming faster. "I wanted you."

"You have me. That's what I'm telling you. The letter, the dog tags, all of it. This is me. I never should have left, but we're getting a second chance, and this is all I have left to give. The truth and the future."

A heavy silence settles between us, adding weight to the words we speak. Evie's breathing and my racing heart are the only sounds beating in my eardrums. I need her to understand. I need her to see me. Really see me, the way she used to. "Evie, please."

She looks at me with such sadness I feel my soul splinter. Shards of the past infiltrate into the now, and it's like I'm staring at seventeen-year-old Evie and the woman she should have become compared to the woman she is. Broken, dejected, a shell.

Sifting the dog tags between her fingers, her lips curl gently. "These ruined everything, you know that? If you hadn't enlisted, if you hadn't left..." She shakes her head. "I'm not whole anymore. Do you understand that? Your letter is beautiful. I wish I read it seven years ago. It doesn't matter now because I didn't go on to accomplish any of my dreams. Not one. I'm not—I can't be every-thing you need."

"I just need you."

"You say that now. Just like I said it years ago. This time our roles are reversed, and I don't know if I can give you more."

"You don't have to."

"Jaxon."

"Evie, listen to me." I step forward, closing my fingers around her hand, letting the mistakes and achievements of my past wrap around our wrists, binding us together. "I said I was leaving because it was the best thing for you, the right thing to do. I told myself that you could never reach your dreams with me always holding you back."

She hiccups, her eyes boring into mine.

"But I was scared and stupid. I was a kid, and I had no idea what to do with all the things I felt for you then. You were so sure of yourself, so confident in your future path. You always knew exactly who you are and I-I didn't. Carter told me I was selfish and he was right. But I was eighteen and however misguided my intentions were, I swear I never meant to hurt you the way I did. I never expected to come home and find you here. And I sure as hell never expected for you to be —"

"Like this?" she whispers.

"What happened? Why won't you let me in?"

She pulls back and steps behind the barstool, so it's between us, giving herself distance from me. The war of emotions playing out on her face is brutal to witness, so I can't imagine how she must feel. Finally, she collapses on the barstool as if her legs can't support her weight anymore.

I step closer, but give her the time she needs to collect her thoughts.

"If I let you in and you leave, I'll be nothing. Don't you see? You can reduce me to nothing. And I don't want to be nothing."

"You could never be nothing. God, Evie, you're everything."

Her fingers play with the chain of my dog tags, her thumb running over each bead of stainless steel. Time seems to slow as she places the tags on the counter and turns toward me. I angle my body until I'm standing straight in front of her, watching every emotion as it flashes across her face. Her hands reach up and she lays them flat against my chest. Slowly, they slide upwards until they glide over my shoulders, her fingers intertwining behind my neck. Her breathing is rapid, her eyes piercing mine with a desperation I can't place. She tugs against my neck gently, pulling my face toward hers.

Confusion clouds my mind as I try to follow her thought process but I don't question her, even as warnings rattle in my head. Instead, I dip my face to hers and capture her lips with mine.

28

EVIE

His lips are warm as they touch mine. For a moment, I'm transported to a million years ago. To a hot summer night, fireflies, and the boy who held my heart. He shuffles forward, deepening the kiss and the memory fades, replaced by the man who stands before me now. His hands reach up to touch my cheeks and his fingers lace through my hair, holding my head steady.

I moan, my fingers digging into his scalp. I melt into him, dissolving into the safety I know he provides—once provided.

Jax's thumb brushes against my cheek, and I part my lips, allowing his tongue to dip in and dance with mine. His hand drops to my back, pulling me closer until I'm perched on the edge of the barstool, and the only thing stopping me from falling is him. I cling to him, my frustration from earlier evaporating into a wild need to lose myself in him once more. Until the past and the hurt and memories dissolve, and we're both holding onto this moment as if it's the only one that's ever existed.

My eyes flutter closed, and I breathe him in, kissing him back, my skin on fire, my heart racing. He breaks the kiss, moving his lips along my jaw, behind my ear, and down my neck.

"Evie." It's a whisper, but it's loaded with so much promise, so much longing, so much.

I guide his lips back to mine and stand on the bottom rung of the barstool, so we're nearly the same height. Bracing my hands against his shoulders for leverage, my lips clash with his fiercely as I pour all the feelings I'm too scared to say into his mouth.

He smells like soap and summer and mint. He tastes like home. His skin is hot where it touches mine, infusing me with a thrill that travels throughout my body, causing my fingers to twist in his T-shirt, as if it were possible to pull him closer.

"Evie," he whispers again. "God, I missed you. You feel so good." The tip of his tongue traces my lower lip before accessing my mouth again.

So good.

I'm going to make this so good for you.

I shudder, remembering the harsh laugh, the ugly words coming from the wrong mouth.

"No." I shake my head, placing my palms on his chest and shoving hard, losing my balance and teetering sideways. "Don't touch me, please."

Jax's hands settle me on the floor as I push him back to ensure there's space between us.

I'm transported back in time. Stuck in a night that ended but lives on in my thoughts and nightmares. So long ago, so much of it I don't remember at all. But the parts I do, it's as if they occurred yesterday or an hour ago.

Jax's eyes snap open, his nostrils flaring. I see him before me, bewilderment crossing his face and uncertainty burning in his eyes. But I also see the shadowy outline of someone else. Of two of them.

"Evie." His voice is steady now, his hand reaching out to me.

I retreat immediately, wrapping my arms around my stomach as if they can somehow hold me together.

"Evie, what's wrong? Whatever I did, I'm sorry. I didn't mean to make you uncomfortable," Jax explains, his voice low and soothing.

"I have to go." I look around frantically, as if searching for an emergency exit from my life. My voice is empty save for the edge of panic, my head caught up in a different moment. Goosebumps break out along my skin and a clammy coldness spreads from the base of my neck to the small of my back.

"Wait." Jax reaches for me again, but I flinch at the possibility of his touch. He backs up slowly, his hands raised in surrender.

I'm gasping for air, the lack of oxygen clawing at my throat. My hands reach up, clasping the base of my neck.

"Evie, you're okay." Jax's voice is even and calm. Unhurried. "You're having a panic attack, baby. Please sit down." He takes a step closer and when I continue to stand and stare, he jumps into action, pressing gently on my shoulder until I collapse in a chair he pulled from the kitchen table. He guides my head down until it's in between my knees. "Breathe, Evie. In and out. You're okay. It's just me and you. Everything is going to be okay." He rubs soothing circles on my back, his touch light.

I focus on his words, my eyes trained on the floor and fixed on a spot of cereal crumbs. Little by little, my breathing regulates, and I come back to the present, the shadows banished once more. I listen to the sounds of my breath, tune in to the inhales and exhales, keeping my mind blank from the thoughts wanting to invade and pull me back into darkness. I ignore the insecurities and doubts bubbling up in my chest.

"I'm right here, baby. I'm not going anywhere."

I grasp onto his voice like a lifeline and let his touch bring me back to the now. Here. With him.

After several moments, I raise my head. Turning to look at him, the devastation I read in his eyes levels me. "Jax."

"Shh," he hushes me, pulling me closer and wrapping my entire body in his.

We sit in silence on two chairs in his kitchen with the familiar gingham curtains hanging over the sink for a long, long time.

* * *

Eventually, dusk falls, and the Kane household fills with the warm voices of men. Carter and Denver come home from wherever they were all day, joking nonstop, and pretending like it's normal that I would be back in their home after I left so dramatically the last time I was here.

Jax watches me closely and I know there is so much we need to talk about. So many things I need to tell him. His eyes burn with curiosity and guilt. And fear. But for the moment, I'm grateful for the reprieve Denver and Carter provide. Delaying the inevitable with Jax for a little while longer, I hang on to the comfortable familiarity of the Kane home.

"You guys wanna get a pizza?" Den asks, popping the tab on a soda can.

"Sure," I say, relieved to be included again. The Kane family was once like my own and in a lot of ways, I missed Denver, Carter, and Daisy just as much as I missed Jax. When he left, I lost so much more than just him.

"Pepperoni and onions," Carter decides, grabbing a bottle from the six-pack in the fridge and sliding onto the chair next to me. "Hi, Evie."

"Hey, Carter."

"How was your day?"

I can't stop the smile forming on my face. Carter's always been too charming for his own good. "Not too bad. How was yours?"

He shrugs, taking a swig of beer. "Coulda been better. I ran into a girl that hates my guts. Kathy Hayes from high school, remember her?"

I nod, absently, trying to focus on what he's saying as the

smell of beer wafts toward me, bringing me back to high school along with his words.

The music is loud, and a thread of static runs through the beat, causing a slight jump in the speaker like a tick. I walk up slowly, intimidated by the crowd of my peers spilling out of the house onto the front lawn and hanging over the railings of the wrap-around porch, beer bottles and red Solo cups in their hands. It's one of the final parties of summer. It's one of the last youthful moments of innocence and wreaking havoc and the now. Next week, I report to BUDS. I begin my future as a West Point cadet. And all of these people, the ones I've co-existed with in the hallways of high school or sat next to in class the past four years, will also take the first step on their own paths. Away, here, it doesn't matter. A bittersweet tang hangs in the air as if everyone knows and feels it: tonight is the end.

So I make myself walk up the steps to the front porch. Force myself to smile at acquaintances and exchange pleasantries with people I know but who've never known me. Not really. Jax's been gone for nine weeks now, and still I feel like a stranger coming to a party like this without him. Before he left, the reassuring weight of his arm resting around my shoulders and the calloused palm of his hand pressed against my hip would have relaxed me. The low rumble of his voice in my ear or the laziness of his laugh would have reassured me. I would have belonged here because I was with him and he belonged here. He belonged everywhere he went, owned the room or the house or the entire town with his easygoing affability and humor.

Stepping over the threshold into the house, I'm swallowed by the swarm of the hive—the buzzing bodies of classmates and people from town. I glance around nervously, hoping to land on a friendly face that can pull me away from the center of the room to one of the shadows; I want someone to exchange a few words and laughs with and maybe even pull me into a goodbye hug that won't matter tomorrow when Carter walks up next to me, playfully bumping my shoulder with his.

"I didn't take this to be your scene." *He presses a quick kiss to my cheek and hands me a bottle of beer.*

I take the bottle from his fingers gratefully, relieved that I have something to do with my hands. Clinging to the neck of the bottle, I return the smile. "It's not."

"Then why come?" He places his hand on the small of my back and gently guides me out of the busy foyer into the kitchen where some juniors are huddled around a keg, and a guy makes out with a girl in the corner. He's pushed between her thighs as she sits on the edge of the countertop, her fingers tangled in his hair.

"To say good-bye, I guess."

He nods, bumping fists with a guy who passes us, someone I recognize from the football team. Someone who knew Jax. A lump forms in my throat at the thought of him, and I struggle to swallow past it, to push it back into the recesses of my chest so it can bubble up at another time.

"You think you'll miss this place?" he asks seriously, pivoting to face me and leaning against the stove, his legs crossed at the ankles.

"No," I answer honestly.

"Yeah, I wouldn't either if I could get out. You hear from Jax at all?"

"A bit. He's called and emailed me a few times."

He blows out a deep breath. "Look, Evie, I know his leaving was tough on you. Tough on all of us really, especially Daisy." His face sobers at the mention of his little sister. "But he had to go. You know that, right? It had nothing to do with you and everything to do with him. He needed to find himself a bit, do something on his own. He couldn't just follow you to New York and wait in the wings while you changed the world." He dips his head to catch my eyes, grinning to take the sting out of his words. "He'd never be fulfilled doing that, you know? It's better this way. Now you can go to West Point with a clear head, be focused on your future, without having to worry about Jax or be distracted by him." He gives me a knowing look. "And he can become a man on his own terms. Feel me?"

"Sure." I take a sip of the beer, the gulp pushing past the lump forming in my throat once more. I know what he says is true. Logically, it makes sense. Eighteen-year-olds falling in love barely have a chance

at happiness these days. Toss in military service, training, and moving around, and it's a near impossibility. Someone will have to sacrifice, give up dreams, plans, and hopes, and Jax didn't want that someone to be him. I get it.

"So, don't worry about him. He made his choice and he picked enlisting. You've made your decision and are heading to West Point. Life is about to change for you. It's your last night in your old life. Let yourself have some fun and enjoy everything this shithole of a town has to offer." He throws his arm wide, encompassing the party filled with drunk graduates. Carter smirks, his dimples deepening as he bends his knees to catch my gaze. "I promise you, you won't be coming back here. Might as well drink up tonight and party with the rest of us losers before you go and blaze your own trail, Evie Maywood. And despite whatever these fuckers say, or don't say, I'm rooting for you."

A real smile crosses my face at his words.

"Ah, there she is." He pulls me into a one-armed hug, pushing off the stove. "You were always too good for my brother anyway. Here's to one last hurrah." He clinks his beer bottle against mine.

"Yeah," I agree, taking another gulp of the beer.

"Have fun tonight but be careful, and let me know if you need anything, yeah?"

"I will."

"Now, I gotta go see about that blonde over there. Catch you later." He nods in the direction of a girl in the grade below me. Kathy Hayes. Her platinum blonde hair screams out from the crowd, her curves clad in a tight shirt and low-riding jeans. She tosses her hair over her shoulder and stands straighter, pushing her chest out, as Carter approaches. He wraps his arms around her waist, dipping his hands into the back pockets of her jeans and tugging her against him as she tips back her head and laughs. Her hands come up to rest on his shoulders. It's easy and carefree, familiar as if they've done this dance before.

It's a sense of certainty, of knowing one's place in the world, and knowing that they belong at this party, in this moment, together.

It's something I've never known except for the brief times I was wrapped up in Jax.

It's something I'm going to try for tonight. Just tonight.

Carefree and fun and present in the moment.

For one last time in this shithole town I hope I never return to.

"Evie. Hey, you all right?" Carter's face swims before me as he waves his fingers in front of my nose.

I note immediately that even though he's peering at me closely, he doesn't make any move to touch me.

Jax is beside me in a moment, kneeling at my side. He places a hand on my knee, and I flinch in reaction. Carter looks away, and Jax's eyes shut, so I won't read the hurt in them.

"I'm going to see if Den needs anything," Carter mutters, pushing away from the table.

Jax slides into his vacant chair and leans forward, his elbows on his knees and his eyes focused on me. "Evie, love, what happened?"

29

JAX

The fear receding from the depths of her eyes causes my chest to seize up. She looks like she literally saw a ghost at the mention of Kathy Hayes. It doesn't make any sense. Once Carter's out of the room and Evie and I have the kitchen to ourselves, I lean forward and ask her the question that's been burning me from the inside out since the first night we ran into each other. And this time, I think she may actually tell me the truth.

Too much has transpired between us today. First, the letter, then the panic attack, now this. She's on the verge of having a breakthrough or breaking; too much has happened in the past few hours to pretend otherwise.

Her eyes take on the glassy shine of faraway thoughts, and her hands clench into fists, her knuckles turning white. "I went to a party. The last party of the summer. I always hated those parties, but I made myself go. I thought one day, I'll look back and wish I said goodbye to senior year, to this life, to all of it properly," she says, her voice low, monotonous. "So I went. Carter was there. He told me to be careful, to let him know if I needed anything. I started drinking, dancing and laughing—a stupid night of being carefree, of trying to fit in with everyone else one last time. And then everything became disconnected. I felt disjointed. Aware but unable to connect my own thoughts." She stares over my shoulder, her mind faraway. "Gary Reitter and Paul Hawkins..." Her breath catches, and her eyes squeeze shut. "We were in a room."

Horror grips me and I feel the exact moment my blood turns to ice. I know the words that are going to spill from Evie's lips before she murmurs them; I think a part of me has known for a while, but I'm still not ready to accept them. I sit in stunned silence, both desperate for her to stop and anxious for her to continue.

"They raped me. After they drugged me. They raped me, Jax." Her eyes latch onto mine as the truth spills from her pretty mouth with words she should never say. "I couldn't, I couldn't move. But I could see them and hear them. They kept laughing and calling me General Maywood. I still feel it over and over and so many little things remind me of that night, creep up on me when I least expect it." She pauses, her eyes regard me warily.

My hands grip the base of the chair she sits on until my fingers feel like they're going to snap. My mind is already playing out the scene. Acid eats at my stomach, bile creeps up my throat, and anger boils my icy blood to lava.

"Carter found me."

I recoil at this, as if she slapped me. What the fuck? My eyes bore into hers as I work my jaw back and forth, knowing that I can't interrupt her to ask any questions. She needs to tell me this on her own terms, at her own pace.

"He pulled them off me, cracked Gary's jaw and broke Paul's nose. I was so cold. I remember that. I was shaking so much I could hear my teeth clicking. Carter took care of everything. Denver came, and they wanted to take me to the hospital. They wanted to file a police report."

"You didn't go?" I whisper, still processing that my brothers tried to save my girl when I didn't. My brothers have known this secret the whole time and haven't said one word in the past seven years.

She closes her eyes. "I was scared and tired, and I just wanted to go home. They took me home, and I crawled into my bed and," she says, biting her bottom lip, "I never really got up again. At least, not the me you knew."

"Evie." I swallow past the guilt that's building in my throat, hating myself more in this moment than I ever did in Iraq. "I'm so sorry. I'm so sorry that happened to you. I'm sorry I wasn't there to protect you. I should have—"

"It's not your fault, Jax." She opens her eyes and squeezes my fingers, and I place my other palm over hers, reluctant to ever let her go again.

"It is." I nod to emphasize my point. "If I was there, that never would have happened."

"Maybe." She shrugs. "But you can't protect me from everything. It could have just as easily happened at some bar in New York City or after a night out at Raf's. I think I blamed your leaving for so long because it was much easier than admitting the truth to myself." She smiles sadly. "I was too confident, flaunted the fact that I thought I was better than everyone. That's what they said that night and that's how they taunt me every time I run into them now." She bites her lip hard and I can tell the words are painful for her to say. "'Not so confident now are you, General Maywood.' They started with me in the Morris parking lot right before you got back. Jenny and Miranda saw them and wanted me to report them but I, I can't." Her eyes plead with me to understand.

A tick in my jaw pulses with the anger raging inside. I want to chase them down and make them hurt for hurting Evie, for all the hell they put her through. I want to—

"As time passed, I became more and more fearful of filing a report. It was stupid really, the best chance I had of them being held accountable for what they did would have been to report the incident immediately. But I was," her eyes fill with tears and she pauses, taking a moment to wipe the back of her fingers across her eyes.

I stay frozen to the spot, my fingers still gripping the seat of her chair. Too scared if I move to grab her a tissue, she'll stop talking, I wait for her to continue.

"I was so ashamed," she cries and my heart shatters in my chest at the anguish in her voice. "I was so scared. I kept thinking about what everyone would think of me. I kept thinking about Mom and Graham and the Army. What if no one believed me? If I had been raped, why didn't I report it that night? That's what people would ask. And the thought of having to answer everyone's questions was too overwhelming. So I just tried to forget the whole thing and then," she sobs harder now and I squeeze her fingers lightly to let her know I'm here for her, "they became Army!" Her eyes blaze with anger, her lips raw from where she raked her teeth over them.

"Evie, you have nothing to feel ashamed about. You're so brave, so courageous to—"

"No," she shakes her head vehemently and I stop talking. "Don't say that. Don't you see how weak I am? If I couldn't get past that, how was I ever going to be a leader? Possibly lead people into war zones and on missions where the risks and stakes are so much higher?"

"No." The harshness of my tone takes her by surprise and she shrinks back. "Evie, you are the strongest person I've ever known. Carrying that around, dealing with it all by yourself for all these years... I'm in awe of you. You never allowed yourself to heal. That doesn't make you weak. Stubborn maybe."

She snorts as tears leak from the corners of her eyes.

"But never weak."

She drops her head forward so it leans against my shoulder. "I'm stuck, Jax. I need to move forward, but I don't know how."

"I understand that."

"I have flashbacks, little triggers that set me off. Like the mention of Kathy Hayes, the smell of beer." She pulls back slightly and points her chin at Carter's beer bottle. I stand quickly, grabbing the bottle and moving to the sink to pour it down the drain. "Nightmares. I hate the quiet. I'm scared of the dark," she continues as I sit back down again.

"It's PTSD."

"No," she says, shaking her head. "I see the guys who come back from war with PTSD. The things they witnessed, the guilt they live with, it's not the same thing."

"Doesn't matter. Baby, you know this, you're a Psychology major. You've experienced a traumatic event. PTSD isn't just for soldiers. It's for anyone who experienced or witnessed something traumatic. And flashbacks, nightmares, triggers, they're all part of it."

"How do you know so much about this?"

"Because I have it," I admit on an exhale. "And it sucks. But you don't, we don't, have to figure it all out alone."

Her eyes bore into mine, wide with hope and vulnerability and... trust.

"We'll figure it all out together, I promise."

"What if we can't?"

"I'm not saying it's going to be easy, love. There's a lot we don't know about each other now. There's a lot that's happened. There's a lot we're both dealing with. But if we don't try, we'd be giving up on ourselves. And I'm tired of doing that."

She snuggles closer to me again, bending at the waist and pressing her ear against my heart. My fingers lace through her hair, stroke her cheek, and keep her against me. She breathes me in for a few moments before pulling back and offering me a gift— the first true smile I've seen cross her face since I've been back.

"You really want to be with me?"

"More than anything."

"Okay. Yes."

Taking her hand in mine, I kiss her open palm. "Evie, will you be my girlfriend?" I grin up at her, the tension subsiding into something lighter.

She regards me shyly, her eyes shimmering with the moisture of her tears. "Yes, Jax. I'll be your girlfriend."

"It's like high school all over again."

"Nope," she says, shaking her head, "no letterman jacket this time."

"I gave you my dog tags."

She tilts her head to the left, as if considering this concession. "That's true. They're even better."

"Really? Why's that?"

"Because they're for forever."

Tugging her hand, I pull her closer until she falls into me. Then I drop a kiss on her forehead before my lips seek hers again. I move slowly and carefully but she meets me halfway. Sealing the deal.

* * *

We leave before the pizza ever arrives, slipping out the back door so Evie doesn't have to see my brothers so soon after confiding in me what happened that night. Although she seems okay, relieved even, she wants to go home, and I don't blame her. Confiding in someone about something that's held you hostage for years, something you've never felt comfortable talking about for the first time is emotionally draining. It's clear to me Evie is exhausted.

The entire ride to her townhouse I keep my palm on her knee, as if by touching her, I can keep her with me.

"You sure you don't mind driving me? You'll just have to take me back tomorrow to get my car?" she asks for the third time.

"Just means I get to see you first thing tomorrow." I look over at her. "Besides, you look like you'd fall asleep at the wheel."

She punches me in the shoulder and relief settles in my chest. We can do this, Evie and me. We can make this work.

Pulling into the complex of her townhouse, I park in front of her place and turn off the ignition.

Evie turns and raises her eyebrows at me.

"What? You think I'm not going to walk my girl inside."

She rolls her eyes and folds her hands together, placing them neatly in her lap. "Then I'll sit here and wait while you also get my door."

"That's a given, baby." I hop out of the SUV and jog around the front until I'm on the passenger side, pulling open her door. "My lady." I extend my hand to her.

She takes it and steps down, grinning at me. "Thank you, kind sir."

I thread my fingers with hers as we walk the short distance and take the three steps to her front door. Standing underneath the porch light, I stare at her, completely in awe of her, of everything she's been through, of how resilient and strong she is.

"You're beautiful, Evie."

She scrunches her nose at me as if she doubts my words.

"I mean it. You're a survivor. There's nothing ugly about that."

She cocks her head to the side, studying me. "So are you."

30

EVIE

"**A**ll right, Noodle, tell me what's going on?" my brother asks, plopping down too close next to me on the couch, so his weight sends me bouncing on my cushion.

"Hmm? Nothing," I deflect, never breaking my attention from the article I'm reading on my laptop. The #MeToo movement is growing as so many strong women around the world come forward with stories of sexual harassment and assault. They range in ages, races, socioeconomic statuses, and career choices. Their bravery is inspiring on so many levels and I aspire to be like them.

Graham closes my laptop on my fingers. "Nice try. But I know something is up."

"Graham! How do you know I wasn't working on something important?"

He kicks his feet up on the coffee table, chuckling at me. "Because I'm your brother and know you. If you were working, and not just reading an article, you would have saved it three seconds ago. Now, you're just avoiding the question. So something is definitely wrong. Tell me."

I stick my tongue out at him and place my laptop on the coffee table. Kicking my feet up and under me, I pull a throw blanket across my knees and settle back, fixing Graham with a look.

"Okay, I'll start," he volunteers like he's doing me a favor. "Jax is back in your life."

I roll my eyes.

"That was a nice move, him walking you to your front door. Very old school. How're things going?"

"What is this, twenty questions?"

"Hardly. That was, I don't know, three questions at most."

"Want a tea?"

Graham studies me for a second, his gaze sweeping over me from head to toe, before nodding. "Sure."

I scuttle into the kitchen and place the kettle on the stove. Busying myself with preparing the tea, I clear my head and settle my nerves. As the kettle begins to whistle, I turn off the stove and pour two cups of tea.

Turning around, Graham is in the entrance of the kitchen, staring at me.

"You okay?"

"Yes, why?"

"You've been crying."

I blow out a deep breath. "Yes."

"Something happen with Jax?"

I shake my head, indicating that we should relocate our conversation to the living room.

Graham follows me closely, sitting next to me on the couch. I flip on the TV for background noise and for a few seconds, we both stare at it even though neither of us is watching it.

"I miss you, Noodle."

"Me too," I murmur, glancing at him from the corner of my eye.

"Why were you crying today?"

"I told Jax some things." I pause, blowing on my tea. "Things that happened the summer he left. Things I haven't told anyone before."

My brother blows out a deep breath, his face trained on my profile as he watches me. "I don't know what went down that summer, but I know it changed you. Since Jax has been back, you seem like yourself again, or closer to it, than you have in a very long time."

"I'm getting there." I take a sip of tea.

"Listen, Evie, I know I haven't been around a lot these past few years. All my updates come from Mom, and how much she worries about you. I know whatever happened that summer changed you. I'm sorry if I wasn't there for you the way I should have been. To be honest, I was caught up in my life, my own shit. And I assumed you were just dealing with a broken heart. The end of a high school relationship. Seeing you now, being here," he pauses, as if saying the words aloud is painful, "it was more than that, wasn't it?"

Nodding, I take another sip, letting the scalding tea burn my throat.

"I'm here now, Evie."

I turn and look at my brother, noting his concerned expression and the tightness around his eyes. I don't think I ever could have told him had I not told Jax. But now that I have, now that I know I have the support of at least one person I can count on, could I maybe make it two?

Inhaling sharply, I place my tea on the coffee table and plunge forward. "I was raped."

Graham's face falls, a sheen of shock washing over his features, followed by confusion. And then he's pulling me into a hug so warm, so caring, so supportive that I find myself crying all over again.

Graham lets me cry, keeps me wrapped up in his embrace, until my sobs turn into hiccups, and my tears dry on my skin. He doesn't say anything, just murmurs comforting sounds and rubs my back, letting me know that he's here for me.

When the last hiccup subsides, I pull back, rubbing the backs of my hands across my eyes and offer a shaky smile.

"Evie." Graham's voice breaks and when I witness the loss in his eyes, I almost feel guilty for not confiding in him sooner.

When did I pull so far away from him that I felt I couldn't tell him things? At one time, I told him everything, even the things he didn't want to know or didn't ask about. Why did I let that change?

"I'm sorry," we say in unison before laughing, the sound nervous.

"You first," he says, leaning against the couch and picking up his mug.

"I'm sorry for not telling you sooner."

"I'm sorry you felt like you couldn't."

"It's not you. I didn't, I couldn't tell anyone. I was so embarrassed, ashamed really."

"Why? Evie, no one who loves you would ever think any less of you for that."

"I know but I felt, God, I felt so stupid. So weak. They kept saying how I was too confident for my own good, flaunted that I thought I was better than everyone, that I was going places. And in some ways, I felt that they were right. I was confident, so sure of myself, so sure of West Point and my future." I swallow nervously. "I guess in some twisted way, I felt like I deserved it."

"They?"

"There were two of them."

Graham's eyes close as all color drains from his face. He tips his head back so it rests against the couch cushions and I watch as two tears leak from the corners of his eyes. When he opens them, they bleed with pain and sorrow. "Does anyone else know?"

"I told Jax earlier."

Graham swallows thickly. "I'm happy you feel like you can confide in him."

"Denver and Carter know too. They were there that night."

Graham pinches the bridge of his nose as his eyes shutter closed again. "Who were the guys? If you don't feel like talking about it, I—"

"No, I want to tell you," I admit, the honesty of my words surprising the both of us. I wrap my hands around my mug and settle back, resting my head against the cushions. Then I tell my brother the entire story. Starting with the day Jax broke my heart and ending with today.

Graham is quiet throughout my entire story, watching me closely, flashes of pain sparking in his eyes at certain moments.

When I finish, he pulls me back in for another hug and kisses the top of my head. "I'm amazed by you, Evie. I'm so incredibly proud of you, and I'm here for anything you need moving forward. I'm here. Got me?"

I nod, burying my face into the familiar smell of his T-shirt.

"You can tell me anything, Evie, absolutely anything. It would never change the way I see you or how much I love you."

"I know that now."

"What about Mom?"

"I'd like to tell her, too. She deserves to know and I, I miss her."

"I'll go with you if you'd like?"

"Okay. Tomorrow."

"Okay."

"Want to watch TV and hang out?" I ask, suddenly needing some normalcy to balance out all the serious conversation.

My brother keeps an arm wrapped around me as he picks up the remote. "After something that heavy, I'll even indulge you and watch one of those awful reality TV shows you like."

I pinch his side. "Comic relief?"

He pulls me closer. "Something like that."

I snuggle into his side as he presses play on an episode of *Keeping Up with the Kardashians*.

* * *

Graham comes with me the next morning to my mom's house. Her features sharpen in surprise as she opens the door. "What's wrong?" she asks, her hand reaching up to clasp the pendant she always wears around her neck—a gift Graham and I bought her for Mother's Day years ago.

"Nothing." Graham says, stepping forward and pressing a kiss to her cheek. "We just wanted to come by for breakfast."

"Of course." She holds the door open, gesturing for us to enter. "I love when we're all home together." Her eyes flick to me and her smile dies on her lips. "Evie, are you all right?"

I take a deep breath and smile weakly. "Have you made coffee yet?"

"Yes, come on into the kitchen." She turns, and Graham and I follow her.

Graham shoots me a reassuring look.

Within minutes, Mom has the table set with fresh fruit, hot coffee, muffins, and toast in the toaster.

"What's going on? Would you like eggs?" Her eyes dart over to Graham as he shakes his head.

"Mom, Evie would like to tell you something."

Mom turns toward me, her face so open, her eyes so kind that I want her to reach out and pull me into a hug.

My throat is suddenly dry and it's difficult to swallow. I don't want to hurt my mom and I know she's going to be devastated when she learns the truth. She's probably going to blame herself for not knowing, for not figuring it out sooner. I'm sure she'll wonder why I felt like I couldn't tell her. She'll blame herself for that too, trying to think of examples where she made me feel like I couldn't trust her.

"Evie?"

I blink. Inhale. Exhale. I can do this.

"Mom," I begin, my voice barely audible. I clear my throat. "I want to explain to you why I didn't go to West Point." My fingertips clench the tablecloth, giving my hands something to do so they don't sit on top of the table and tremble.

"Evie, it's okay. You don't owe me an explanation or—"

"Mom, I need to tell you." I plead and her eyes widen, her words trailing off.

I take a fortifying breath as Graham reaches over to place a palm in the center of my back for moral support.

"Mom, I was raped. By two guys I went to high school with. At a senior party," I rasp out.

My mother stares at me in shock before her eyes fill with tears, and her hand comes up to cover her mouth. "Evie." My name is a strangled whisper as she shakes her head. "Oh, God, Evelyn, I am so sorry." Tears escape over her bottom eyelashes, her fingers clutching the pendant at her throat. "When? How? Oh, my darling girl." She stands, coming around to my side of the table and wrapping me in her arms, pressing my head against her stomach.

I close my eyes, surprised when I feel my own tears track my cheeks. I didn't think it was possible to cry this much. We remain in silence for several minutes, me wrapped in my mother's embrace, and my brother's hand rubbing small circles along my spine. My family enfolds me in a shroud of support.

I'm not sure how much time passes, but eventually my mom pulls her chair around the table and sits next to me, clasping my hands in hers. "What happened?"

I open my mouth, and the entire story spills out. I watch as her eyes narrow in anger, widen in surprise, and practically fall out of her head when she learns that Gary and Paul are both Army now. I tell her everything and when I'm done, she pulls me into a hug and whispers apologies over and over into my hair.

Breakfast rolls into lunch, and my brother steps out to pick up some pizzas. We're sitting in the living room when Mom asks me the question that no one else has since the actual incident.

"How do you want to handle this?"

"What do you mean?"

"Would you like to file a police report? Press charges? I'll support whatever decision you make, Evie. We will do whatever will help you heal."

"Mom, they're Army. They're practically untouchable."

"No, they weren't Army at the time of the attack and even if they were, there are still channels we can access. If you want to."

"I never took a rape kit."

"But there was a witness."

"Yes." I think of Carter.

"Take some time, love. Think about it."

"I want to press charges." The words shoot out of my mouth quickly, surprising us both.

"Okay."

"I don't want them to do what they did to me to anyone else. And even though I should have spoken up sooner..." I shake my head. "I keep reading all of these articles about the #MeToo Movement. There are so many stories of incredible women coming forward, some many years later, and naming their attackers. They are so brave, resilient. I want to be strong like them. And I want to make sure that my silence doesn't allow Gary or Paul to do something similar to someone else. I'm going to do now what I should have done then."

"I'll go with you to file the report," Mom offers. She looks at me, her eyes softening. "If you'd like me to."

"Yes, I would. Thank you."

Graham returns, and Mom and I drop the issue. The three of us sit around the table, eating pizza, and talking. It feels so much like Friday night dinners in high school that for once, I remember the past and feel lighter.

When I arrive home from Mom's later in the day, Jax is sitting on the steps in front of my townhouse. He smiles when he sees me but it's tight and I know he's still worried about me, worried about everything that unfolded the day before.

"Hey Jax." Graham calls out before turning to me. "I'm going to swing by and see Hunter, let you two talk. Call me if you need anything, okay?"

"Okay. Thanks for coming with me today, Graham."

"Of course."

I climb out of Graham's rental car and wave as he drives off.

"Hey." I turn toward Jax.

"Hey yourself. How are you today?" He asks, standing up as I walk closer.

"I'm good."

"Yeah?"

"Yeah." I place my hand in his when I get close enough and tug him up the stairs. He kisses my cheek sweetly as I fumble with the locks. Once we're inside my townhouse, we sit down in my living room.

Jax raises his eyebrows at me questioningly, "Did you talk to Graham?"

"Yep, and Mom."

"Really?"

I blow out a deep breath and watch his face as I say, "I'm going to press charges tomorrow."

Jax rolls his bottom lip in between his teeth as he looks away and I note the moisture that collects in his eyes. After a moment, he looks at me, his eyes brighter. "That's incredible, Evie. I'm proud of you. Whatever you want to do, however you want to handle this, I'm behind you one hundred percent."

"I know."

"We all are."

"Thank you." I lean forward and kiss him lightly.

He holds my face delicately in his hands and kisses me with a sweetness, a reverence, I didn't know existed.

My heart soars in my chest at the understanding and compassion I'm receiving for admitting a shame I let cripple me for way too long.

* * *

Mom and I head down to the police station early the next morning. Several officers slant their eyes in question at my mom as we walk inside and ask to speak with the Chief of Police. Mom doesn't bat an eye under the extra scrutiny; after we are called to enter Chief Allen's office, Mom sits down and looks at me, waiting for me to speak the words I need to say in order to move forward.

Chief Allen offers me an encouraging nod, and Mom leans over and grasps my fingers in hers.

I take a deep breath and tell Chief Allen my story. I'm surprised as he regards me sympathetically, taking time to walk me through the process and explain to me in detail what my options are.

"You do understand that a rape charge is much harder to stick without evidence and years after the incident occurred?" Chief Allen asks gently.

"Yes, sir."

"It's going to be harder to prove the rape than if you had pressed charges immediately and had a rape kit performed."

"I understand."

"Okay. Whenever you're ready, I'll take your statement."

I take a deep breath and officially file a police report.

Chief Allen explains that after turning it over to detectives, someone will be in touch to discuss how to proceed.

I nod, shaking his hand to thank him for his time.

Stepping out of the police station, Mom and I hold hands,

and she squeezes my fingertips. I exhale a massive sigh, letting go of so many feelings, emotions, and thoughts that have been suffocating me for years.

I squeeze Mom's fingers back, feeling lighter than I ever thought possible.

* * *

That night, I find the article from months ago about the four actresses who stepped forward and named a famous director for sexual assault. Re-reading the article, I take my time going through all of the comments. Once I've read them all, I take a fortifying breath and add my own.

#MeToo

31

JAX

Walking into my house several nights later, my mind is on Evie, still reeling from everything she's been through. I've been caught up in a daze since she confided in me, going through the motions each day, barely paying attention to what I'm doing. I'm so proud of her for confiding in her family and accepting their support. I'm in awe of her for pressing charges against Gary and Paul. When I'm with her, I want to be the support she needs, someone she can rely on and trust completely.

But I'm also struggling to accept what happened to her. I can't swallow the fact that two guys we graduated with violated her, hurt her, and continued to torture her about it. Guilt explodes in my chest every time I think about what Evie endured and how I could have prevented it if I had been there. If I had stayed. I know she says it wasn't my fault but I doubt that would have happened to her if I hadn't enlisted, if we never broke up.

I unlock the front door and push it open, tripping over air and practically falling inside, the door bouncing against the wall and alerting my family to my arrival.

Daisy looks up from her seat on the couch, startled. "Jax? Everything okay?"

"Hey, man," Denver says, walking into the living room from the kitchen, a bottle of beer half-raised to his mouth. "Haven't seen much of you lately. You missed dinner again."

I look up, momentarily confused, before I remember that Denver was making chicken parmigiana for dinner tonight and I had said I would be here.

Denver narrows his eyes at me, understanding dawning in his eyes. "You talked to Evie."

"Yeah."

"Damn," he mutters under his breath, placing the beer bottle on an end table.

"What's going on with Evie?" Daisy asks, shifting her weight to see me better.

"What are you doing here?" I turn to stare at her, my voice scratchy.

Denver shakes his head at me as Daisy looks at the floor.

"Is Carter home?" I ask, and both Daisy and Den nod.

"I really need to talk to him. Carter!" I call out, the emotion in my voice obvious as Daisy winces, and Denver takes a step toward me. "Carter!"

Carter bounds down the stairs, his shirt off, his jeans unbuttoned. A petite blonde trails behind him, the first three buttons of her shirt popped open, her hair falling out of her ponytail: Lori Filton.

"Hey," Carter stares at me for a beat too long before escorting Lori to the front door. "I'll call you later, babe."

She presses a kiss to the underside of his jaw and shrugs, closing the door behind her.

Heavy silence descends on our home as the four of us stare at each other. I move to the couch and sit on the end opposite of my sister while Carter takes a seat in an armchair, and Denver hovers nearby, his eyes bouncing from one of us to the next.

"You need a beer?" Denver asks quietly.

I pinch the bridge of my nose, thinking of how the smell of beer is a trigger for Evie. "Got anything stronger?"

"Yeah," he disappears into the kitchen. Through the door, I hear the clink of ice against a glass.

"What's going on?" Daisy turns toward me, her eyes questioning.

"Are you supposed to be home?" I ask her, my eyebrows drawing together. I would have remembered if Denver or Carter mentioned her coming back so soon after spring break.

"No," she sighs, "but can we talk about it later?"

I nod, my head about to burst with everything that happened with Evie. I'm not sure if I can handle much more tonight. Especially not where Daisy's concerned. Absently, my fingertips massage the scars on my shoulder. It doesn't make any sense, but my shoulder throbs and aches with pain I haven't felt in a long time.

Denver returns and passes me a glass with three fingers of scotch and one large, square ice cube. He tosses a beer bottle to Carter and picks up his beer from the end table, raising it to his lips.

I clutch the scotch gratefully, taking a sip and closing my eyes. When I open them, all three of my siblings are staring at me, Denver and Carter with uncertainty and Daisy with concern.

I blow out a large breath, my cheeks puffing to the sides as I grip the back of my neck. "Dais, I'm real happy to see you, but could you give us a minute?"

My sister rolls her eyes at me, "I'm not a kid anymore, Jax, whatever is going on, you can tell me."

Den shakes his head, "It's not like that, Dais. Jax can't tell you because it's not his story to tell."

"Then how come you and Carter can stay."

"Because we knew the story before him. It has nothing to do with any of us or our family, okay?"

She stands up from the couch reluctantly and glances between the three of us. "You guys aren't in trouble, right?"

"No." I assure her.

"Okay. I'll be in my room."

"Thank you." I tell her and from the seriousness of my tone, she offers me a sympathetic smile before walking up the stairs without any more questions.

I wait until I hear her bedroom door close and then I fix my gaze on Carter. "What happened that night?"

Carter's face twists, a sharp anguish shuddering over his features. His expression is pained when he sighs and leans forward, his elbows resting on his knees, his head dropping to the floor.

When Carter looks up, he stares straight at me, his eyes bleeding with a pain that borders on torture. "How much did she tell you?"

"Everything."

Carter rubs the beer bottle between his palms. "Evie came to a party Eric Minz was having. One of those last summer parties that the entire senior class shows up to. A last hurrah. Evie came. I saw her walk in, look around. She was awkward; you know how much she hated the party scene, how much she shied away from attention like that."

Denver and I nod.

"Anyway, she showed up. I grabbed her a beer. We BS'ed for a few minutes, and then I saw Kathy Hayes. Remember her?"

"Cute blonde, a cheerleader?" Den asks.

"Yeah. So I left Evie. Chatted up Kathy. A little while later, Paul Hawkins asks me where he can score some E." Carter stops suddenly, desperation surging from his eyes as he fixes me with a pleading look. "I didn't know, Jax. I swear to God, I didn't know."

My blood ices in my veins as I start to put two and two together.

"They drugged her with E?"

Carter nods.

Denver mutters a string of curses under his breath as Carter hangs his head again.

"No." My voice is strangled. "No. Tell me you didn't supply it, Carter. Tell me you fucking didn't."

"I'm sorry."

"Sorry?" I spring forward from the couch to tackle my brother to the floor. My shoulder screams in pain from the sudden movement, but I block it out, focusing on pummeling him. When I get close enough, I realize that he doesn't even flinch. He just sits there. Ready to accept the hit, guilt and horror stamped on his face.

Denver jumps up, placing a warning hand out in my direction.

Spinning on my foot, I put my first through the nearest wall, the impact jarring my shoulder.

"I thought they were just after a good time." Carter's voice lacks emotion. "I swear to you, I didn't know they were going after Evie. Or any woman! I would never—God. I'm so fucking sorry, Jax."

"Does she know?" I whirl on him, my hands still clenched, hot fury pouring from my mouth, my pores. "She didn't say anything to me about E. Or you dealing."

He shakes his head.

"You need to tell her," Denver says quietly. I expect him to be looking at me but his eyes are boring into Carter's.

"I know."

"Jesus," Denver mutters. "When we took her home that night, you never told me."

"I didn't realize it then," Carter explains truthfully. "I put two and two together later and at that point, I... Fuck. I didn't know what to do. You were gone." He nods in my direction. "You were on probation." He looks at Denver. "Was I supposed to turn myself in? Probably. But what would have happened to Daisy?

Foster system?" He exhales loudly, his fingers digging into his temples on either side of his head. "I didn't know what to do."

I groan, my fingertips massaging the scars on my shoulder. "She filed a police report," I say, looking up at Carter as understanding dawns in his eyes.

"I'll give a statement."

Staring at my brother, I can tell that this devastated him. Ate at him. Consumed parts of him for the last seven years. Regret swells in my chest, an acrid taste working up my throat and sweeping over my taste buds as I watch Carter struggle. Culpability lingers as I realize that while I was off pursuing an out and Denver was keeping his nose clean and Daisy was working towards college, Carter was the one keeping it all together, so the rest of us could do what we wanted. Carter was the one left behind to hold the reins and make sense of the damage and keep the rest of us blinded from the truth, so that we wouldn't have to be burdened.

"Why the hell were you dealing, man? I was on fucking probation. You know how bad that could have been for our family? Child Services was looking for any reason to pull Daisy from this house back then." Den speaks up, his tone barbed with anger.

Carter drops his head back against the top of the chair. "I know. I did it for her."

"What are you talking about? For who?" I ask.

"Daisy. She had her heart set on ASU," he answers honestly.

"You told me she got a scholarship." I say.

Silence.

"Fuck." Denver looks away, and I hang my head.

Everything fell on Carter, and he kept it together for as long as he could. Even dealing with all the fall out on his own.

"I'm sorry," I tell him, looking him straight in the eye, so he can see all the meaning I can't convey with words. "I really am."

"Me too, Jax. For all of us."

* * *

That night I can't sleep. Every time my eyes close, I see her, drunk and drugged at a party, being taken advantage of. I see Gary and Hawkins. I see so many things I don't want to see, can't stand to see, that it's easier to stay awake.

When I'm not thinking about Evie, thoughts of Ethan infiltrate my head, the heat of fire, the feel of coarse sand, the rusty tang of blood.

At three in the morning, I kick off my blankets and exit my room, going downstairs to make myself a sandwich. I hope Carter bought more potato chips on his last grocery run.

Walking into the kitchen, I halt, the sight of Daisy sitting at the island crying as unexpected as it is painful.

"Dais?"

She turns to me, wiping her knuckles across her cheeks and trying to smile. "Hey. Couldn't sleep?"

"Nope." I walk closer to the island. "You hungry?"

She shrugs.

"I'm going to make some sandwiches." I turn toward the cupboards and start pulling out random items, relieved when a new bag of chips falls out of the snack cabinet. Plugging in the sandwich press, I continue to focus on my task to give my sister some time to pull it together.

"Why're you crying?" I finally ask after a few minutes of silence.

She sighs, still trying to get her sobs under control. "It's stupid."

"I'm sure it's not." I chance a glance at her, and she's shaking her head.

"It is," she insists, "I'm being dramatic."

"Dais, come on, you've always been a Drama Queen, but I can count on one hand how many times you've sat around crying. The fact that something is bothering you, enough that you're home from school and crying in the kitchen in the middle of the night, means it's not stupid. Not to you. So what gives?"

She takes a sip from the water glass in front of her and offers me a half smile. "I had a job lined up for after graduation."

"Congratulations! Why didn't you—"

"It fell through."

"Oh. Damn. I'm sorry, Daisy."

She presses her fingertips into her eyelids, "I'm graduating in a few weeks and I don't even have anything to show for it!"

"That's not true. You have lots to show for it."

"Like what?"

"Friends who have places in St. Barth's," I remind her, my heart swelling a little when she laughs.

"I just, I want you guys to be proud of me," she admits, picking up the sandwich I slide in front of her.

"We are proud of you. Incredibly, stupidly proud of you. So much so that we brag about you all the time."

She rolls her eyes, but a small smile flickers across her lips. "What am I supposed to do now?"

"You're supposed to enjoy the rest of your senior year of college. Have fun with your friends. Take your final exams and apply for new positions. Just because one job fell through doesn't mean there won't be another. In fact, maybe your next opportunity will be even better and you'll be grateful that this one didn't work out. Don't sweat it. Come home for the summer, and let your big brothers spoil you rotten. And I bet if you do all those things, you'll have a new job lined up in a few months."

She bites into the sandwich, her eyes flashing to mine with surprise as the potato chips crunch. Chewing thoughtfully, she finally nods. "You really think I'll sort it all out?"

"I know you will."

"And you won't hate it if I'm around for the entire summer, annoying you guys and yelling at you for leaving the toilet seat up?"

"I'd miss it if you weren't."

She takes another bite of her sandwich. "Okay, then. I'll come home."

"I'll help you move back," I tell her, taking a bite of my own sandwich and closing my eyes at the extra crunch that pops in my mouth.

I'm startled when I feel Daisy's arms around me, but as I open my eyes and hug her back, another puzzle piece snaps in, and I remember that this is why I came home in the first place.

32

EVIE

Steaming espresso and hints of cinnamon sprinkles and buttery goodness greets me as I step inside Kindred Spirits Bakery. I love it here. It's easy to get lost, holed up in a big, comfy armchair, watching the world pass by outside the floor-to-ceiling windows, a book in my lap and a latte in my hand.

I breathe in the soothing scent of fresh baked goods and look around at the occupied tables. Craning my neck to the left, I spot him in the back, sitting at a two-top with a cup of coffee near his hand, biting into a doughnut. He fidgets restlessly, his toes tapping out a beat on the rung of his stool. Nerves is not a look I am accustomed to associating with Carter, and I feel my own blood pressure spike as I watch him.

"Can I get you something?" The barista asks and I jump, turning toward her as I realize the line has dwindled, and it's my turn to order.

"Skinny vanilla latte, please. And," I say, peeking in the front display window of treats, "a chocolate croissant."

"Eight eighty-three." She cups her hand out as I fork over a twenty.

Waiting for my order, I dawdle, wasting time before I alert Carter to my presence.

It was strange that he called me this morning, completely out of the blue, and asked me to meet him here. Of course, I've seen him around over the past seven years. It's hard not to run into someone you're actively trying to avoid. Although he's always been friendly and kind when our paths have crossed, he's never directly sought me out. Not since a week after the incident when he came by to check on me, and I made him swear he would never tell anyone what happened, especially Jax.

But here we are, about to sit down and grab a coffee like old friends catching up. He's got to be here because of Jax or something Jax-related, and that makes me nervous. I'm grateful for the caffeine in a cup the barista hands me, and I take a long sip, burning the roof of my mouth but calming myself at the same time.

Walking toward Carter's table, he looks up as I approach, and a hesitant grin ticks the corners of his mouth upward.

"Hey."

"Hi." I smile back, settling myself on the stool across from him. "Want some?" I push the plate with my croissant in his direction.

"Nah, thanks." He gestures toward his empty plate. "I already had two doughnuts." Carter leans back in his seat, his fingers playing with a napkin. "I wish I'd seen you come in, I would have gotten your coffee and croissant."

"It's okay."

"Thanks for coming."

"I'm still not sure why you invited me here."

"I know. I, uh, I wanted to talk to you."

"Is everything okay with Jax?" I fumble my croissant, my nerves making me clumsy.

"Jax?" Carter leans forward again, resting his elbows on the table. "Yeah. Jax is fine. This isn't about Jax."

"It's not?"

"No. I, Jesus, I need to tell you something, Evie."

"Okay."

"Things between us used to be so easy. You were like another sister to me once."

"I know. I, um, I'm sorry, Carter. I know you were just trying to help me that night, and afterwards I completely pushed you away. Pretended like I didn't even know you and that, that was pretty horrible of me," I admit. What is wrong with me? It's like now that I told Jax the truth, I have to just keep on spilling my guts to everyone I encounter. But it's freeing in a way I never expected.

"No, you were right to dismiss me. I fucked up." His eyes darken, and the usual easygoingness and good times I've always associated with Carter turns serious, foreboding. "Evie, there is no easy way for me to say this, so I'm just going to say it. And then, if you want to leave or kick me in the nuts or never see me again, we'll do that. Okay?"

"Carter, you're freaking me out. Just tell me whatever it is."

"That night, with Paul and Gary, at the party," he pauses, eyeing me to make sure I'm following along. As if anything could ever make me forget anything about that night.

"Yes, I remember."

"Right. Well, a little while after I saw you at the party, Paul hit me up for E." He watches me expectantly.

"E?"

"Ecstasy."

"The drug?"

"Yes."

"Oh. Okay." I continue to sit and stare, trying to figure out what he's telling me.

"It's my fault, Evie." He lowers his voice, his eyes pleading with me to understand. "That night. Everything that happened. It's my fault. I sold him the drug that—"

"Ohhh," I breathe out, realization finally slapping me in the face. My hand covers my mouth, my fingertips pressing against my lips; the same lips that drank alcohol laced with... Ecstasy. I knew I was drugged that night but I didn't realize what it was or that it would have been so easy for Gary and Paul to access.

"Evie, I am so sorry. I should have told you sooner. I didn't even realize it that night and then afterward, when I figured it out, I didn't know what to do. I was such a chicken shit coward. That night destroyed your life and ruined everything you worked so hard for. I saw you struggling, watched you shrink away from everyone, and I lied to you for all these years." He scrubs a hand over his face, his eyes pleading, and his face shadowed with guilt. "I understand if you hate me, Evie, but I need you to know that Jax had no idea. Neither did Denver. And I'm so fucking sorry."

Shock locks down my limbs. A bubble of hysteria works up my throat, erupting from my lips in a giggle. I giggle.

Carter places a tentative hand on my wrist, beseeching me to look at him. "Evie, you're okay."

Why do people keep saying that to me? Of course, I'm okay. If that night didn't kill me, there's not much else that will.

I was drugged with Ecstasy. A party drug. I couldn't even party correctly. I failed at my last hurrah attempt as well. What a disaster.

"Evie?"

"Hmm?"

"You all right?"

I blink, Carter Kane coming back into focus before me. His brows are drawn, his green eyes anxious, and concern heavy in the thin line of his lips. "Carter," I say, sounding dazed. Reaching out, I grasp my latte and take a sip, the hot espresso and steamed milk connecting me back to the here and now.

"Evie, can I call someone for you? Do you need anything? Do you feel sick?"

I take a steadying breath. "I'm fine. I, I didn't expect you to say that, and it caught me by surprise."

"I understand if you hate me, but please, please don't take what I did out on Jax. He loves you and—"

"I don't hate you."

"What?" Surprise flickers across Carter's face, and he shakes his head to disagree with me.

"Carter, you didn't do anything. What happened isn't your fault. At all," I say calmly, a strange serenity washing over me now that the truth about that night is being brought to light. I'm talking about it more and instead of driving me to seek consolation inwards and retreating from the world, it's causing me to realize that I do have a support system. And I can latch onto them to move forward.

"Evie, I sold Paul the Ecstasy that he used to—"

"You don't know that," I cut him off, removing my hand from under his and hunching forward. "Maybe Paul took that pill and used something else on me. And even if he did use the pill you sold him, do you really think that if Paul hadn't bought E from you then there was no one else at the party that would have supplied it?"

Carter considers this for a second. "Well, no, but that doesn't mean—"

"And did you know what he was planning to do with it? That Gary was involved? That they used drugs before to roofie unsuspecting girls?"

"Of course not." He sounds appalled.

"Exactly."

"But it still came from me."

"What if the situation had been different?"

"I don't understand."

"What if I hadn't been drugged that night? What if I just drank too much and got sloppy, and Gary and Paul shuffled me into a bedroom and took advantage of me? Would that be Eric Minz's fault for supplying beer at his party?"

Carter exhales loudly, chewing the corner of his mouth. He

looks like Jax when he does that, and I soften toward him. He's completely torn up about this. I wonder what else he's shouldered for the past seven years. How has carrying around this burden affected him?

"What if it had been Daisy?"

He stares at me in horror. "Did something happen to Daisy?"

"No," I reassure him quickly. "I'm saying, what if that scenario happened to Daisy? Would you and your brothers blame the guy who sold the drugs, or the guys who did the act?"

He rakes his fingers over his hair. "I get it. Your point, I mean. I get where you're coming from. But, Jesus, I feel sick over this."

"Thank you."

"Huh?"

"For caring about me enough to worry about me like that."

He chuckles anxiously, a release of tension, and leans back again. "I didn't know what I expected, but it definitely wasn't your forgiveness."

"You're not guilty of anything, Carter."

"I still should have told you sooner."

"I don't know if it would have helped."

His eyebrows dip together over his nose. "Why not?"

I tap my fingertips softly against my coffee, "I haven't really allowed myself to come to terms with that night until recently. Until Jax." Pausing, I try to sort out my thoughts, so I can make sense of them before I confide in Carter. "I hadn't told anyone what had happened."

Carter's eyebrows spike up at this. "No one?"

"Not until the other night. I told Jax, and then I told my brother. Then my mom. I'm going to tell Jenny and Miranda when I see them this weekend. I filed a police report. I was so scared for so long to tell anyone about it because a part of me thought I deserved it."

"Oh, Evie, why would you ever think that?" Carter's voice is pained as he leans toward me again, placing a hand gently on my wrist.

"That night I remember them mocking me. Calling me General." I snort. "I did think I was too good for this town. I was too confident, so sure of what I was going to do next, where I was going in life. Sure, I was polite because I had to be, but I know I ruffled a lot of feathers with my opinions and sass and focus on my future. I think I was scared if I told anyone, they either wouldn't believe me or think I deserved what I got."

"Evie, no one, absolutely no one, ever deserves to be treated like that."

"I know that now. But it wasn't until I said it out loud, until I confided in Jax, talked to Graham, that I began to believe it."

Carter heaves a sigh, his hand going to my chocolate croissant before he takes a bite, swallowing half the pastry.

"Stress eating?"

He snorts, shaking his head at me. "I'm glad you filed the report. I'll give a statement. I witnessed it, and I'll gladly tell the police everything I saw."

"You sure? You'll have to tell them about the Ecstasy."

He pins me with his eyes, his face serious. "I'll tell them everything."

"Thank you, Carter. If you had told me earlier, it might not have mattered. I'm glad you told me now because I'm ready to move forward. And nothing about that night was your fault. In fact, you saved me before it got worse."

"Maybe you could tell that to Jax," he jokes.

"I will."

"I'm kidding."

"I'm not."

He breaks off another piece of my croissant and pops it into his mouth. "Can we be friends again?"

"I'd like that," I say honestly, drinking more of my latte and considering how much better, lighter, cleaner I feel since confiding in others, filing a police report, taking some control over the situation. Now, talking with Carter, I'm starting to realize that by keeping silent, I've been gagging myself in more ways than one. I've never been open to fully accepting what happened to me that night and how it changed me, so how could I expect to move forward?

"Hey, could you do me a favor?"

"Anything."

"I want to move past this, Carter. I really, really want to reclaim my life. I hate feeling like such a failure, like I blew my future, and am resigned to spending the rest of my life going through the motions and being petrified of every guy I'm in close quarters with."

"That's how you feel?"

"It's like I'm underwater. All the time. Everything around me is unfolding, and I can hear it and see it, but it's distorted some-how. I know I can reach the surface if I try, but it seems almost safer to just let myself sink, so I don't have to deal with everything that's above water."

"What if everything above water is what you really want?"

"But what if I fail?"

"You could never fail, Evie. You've already survived so much. Plus, not attaining something doesn't necessarily mean failure. It's a learning experience. It means you were brave and bold enough to try. If you look at it like that, then failure isn't even a possibility."

"Could you help me?"

"Of course. What would you like me to do?"

"Help me be, I don't know, normal again. And don't go easy on me. I know if I ask Jax he'll say yes but he won't push me too hard. He feels guilty about the entire thing and we need time to sort our history out before he'll ever feel comfortable giving me tough love."

"Evie Maywood, you are and have always been a lot of things, but normal was never one of them." He flashes me his signature grin, his seafoam green eyes softening. He looks more like the Carter I know. "You've always been too authentic to just be normal."

His words center me. The Kane boys were the only ones who've ever celebrated my awkwardness. "Help me fit in then?"

"Whatever it takes." He holds out his pinkie.

"What are you doing?"

"Pinkie-swearing, duh."

"We're not five."

"But this is how I give you my word."

I roll my eyes, linking my finger with his.

"I'm glad you're back in my life, Evie. But mostly, I'm happy you're back in Jax's."

"Me too."

33

JAX

"Got a minute?" I stand beside Denver's feet as he works on an old Chevrolet El-Camino.

His hand gropes the ground as he curses. "Yeah, hand me a flashlight, will ya?"

I kick the flashlight that's a few inches from his fingers closer, and he grasps it, his hand disappearing underneath the car again.

Several minutes tick by as I listen to my brother's heavy breathing, colorful swearing, and random mutterings. Eventually, he slides out from underneath the car and shields his eyes, squinting up at me. "What's up?"

"I need to talk to you. Want a Coke or something?"

"Sure. I'm getting hungry anyway." He pushes himself into a sitting position, swiping his water bottle off the ground, before standing up and heading toward the house.

We walk inside and straight into the kitchen. Denver makes a beeline for the refrigerator. "Daisy made pasta before she took off. Leftovers okay?"

"Sounds good."

I slide onto a barstool and wait patiently as Denver heats up a couple of plates. When he's sitting beside me, two Cokes popped open and steaming dishes of pasta in tomato sauce in front of us, he fixes me with a look. "You can't open the autobody shop with me."

I sigh, not surprised that he already figured it out, but wishing I had the chance to explain myself before he jumped to any conclusions.

"Den, it's not that I don't want to. Going into business with you would be great and I—"

He holds up a hand, silencing me as he shovels a forkful of pasta into his mouth. "You don't have to explain, Jax." He swallows loudly, taking a swig of soda. "I'm happy for you, man."

"What are you talking about?"

"You and Evie, it's for real, isn't it?"

"Yeah."

"So, you'd be an idiot to go into business with me and chain yourself to being here when your girl's got plans in motion to be somewhere else."

"You know about Baylor?"

He nods, his expression easy and relaxed. "She's gonna get in. They'd be stupid not to take her."

"I know." I think about Evie and how she'll probably be the first in her class.

"So, San Antonio?"

"Nothing's decided yet."

"It'll be good for y'all," he continues, as if I didn't speak at all. "Getting a fresh start somewhere else. A new place that doesn't hold all these memories and connections. Small towns are great when you need a neighbor's hand, but they blow when you're trying to get out from under past mistakes."

"Yeah." I watch him, wondering if he ever thinks of leaving, starting over someplace new. A place where no one would know he spent time in lock-up. "You ever think about it?"

"Nah." He shakes his head. "I don't mind the looks and the talk because no one ever expected anything else from me." A sad smile ghosts his mouth before he turns to look at me. "My story isn't a scandal; it was a given."

"You've done real good turning things around, Den."

He shrugs. "I've done all right."

"I'm sorry about the autobody repair."

"Don't be."

"What're you going to do now?" I ask, taking my first bite of pasta.

"Don't worry about me, kid. I'll figure something out. Stay focused on your girl and the future y'all are building." He taps his Coke can next to mine. "I'm proud of you."

An unexpected lump swells in my throat at Denver's words. Seven years ago, those words never would have crossed his lips. It's funny though, because now that he said them, I realize how much they mean to me.

"I'm proud of you too, Den."

He smirks, taking another bite of pasta. "What've you got going on this weekend?"

"Not much."

"Wanna take a trip?"

"Where?"

"Arizona."

"Ari—" I pause, my thoughts finally catching up to his. "Daisy's graduation."

"I wanna see her throw her cap in the air," Denver admits.

"Yeah, I'd like that, too."

"All right." He stands up, picking up his plate and walking over to the sink. "I'm sure Carter'll wanna come. I'll check flights. We'll leave on Friday. Surprise her."

"She'll love it."

"Yeah."

"Need help with the El-Camino?"

Denver turns to me, staring for a minute. A flash of something undecipherable flits in his eyes before he reaches up to mess with his hair and nods. "That'd be great. Thanks, Jax."

"No problem." I follow him out of the kitchen and into the bright sunlight and heat.

We drop to the cracked asphalt with the weeds poking through and the shitty, dilapidated state of our front yard. This time, it doesn't bother me as much as it once did. I guess because this time I'm more focused on spending time with my brother and less on our surroundings.

This time it feels like home.

* * *

"I wish I could come with you guys," Evie tells me later that night, a bowl of mint chocolate chip ice cream resting in her lap as we hang out in her living room.

"Me too."

"Daisy's going to be so surprised."

I nod, thinking about my sister and how much I'm looking forward to surprising her. How much I'm looking forward to traveling with my brothers.

"Any news from Chief Allen?"

She scrapes her spoon against the bottom of her bowl. "They're building a case. He told me with Carter's statement they have enough evidence to go forward. Turns out, other girls have pressed charges against Gary, although my report is the first to name Paul. All together, they think they have enough evidence to prosecute Gary. Paul will probably take a plea."

"That's good news, Evie."

"Yeah. And since Carter's selling the Ecstasy is past the statute of limitations, it's not even a thing."

I raise my eyebrows at this. "For real?"

"It's been more than four years, so the state can't take legal action. Plus, Chief Allen is much more focused on nabbing Gary than punishing Carter for slipping his friends Ecstasy. It helps that everyone was eighteen at the time."

I mull this over, relieved to hear my brother isn't facing legal issues. Even though I never pressured him to speak up in defense of Evie, I was grateful he did. He walked straight into the police station without batting an eye and laid everything out for Chief Allen.

"You hear anything else yet?"

"You mean Baylor?"

"Yeah."

"No, it's too soon. But I promise you'll be the first to know."

"You're going to get in."

"You really want to move to Texas?"

"I want to move wherever you are, Maywood. Texas, Japan, outer space, doesn't matter."

She snorts, tossing a throw pillow at me, which I catch easily and prop behind my shoulder.

"What are you going to do there?"

"For work?"

"Yeah," she raises a spoonful of melting ice cream to her mouth.

"I got a few things in the works."

Her eyes grow serious. "Like what? Why didn't you tell me?"

I shrug, running a hand over the top of my head. My hair is longer than I've had it since before I enlisted, and sometimes the feel of it surprises me. I doubt I'll ever sport a man-bun like Den, but for now I like that I don't have to shave it all the time. "Nothing's a done deal, and I didn't want you to get all stressed out about it."

"Jax, I'm not getting stressed, but we have to talk about these things."

"Okay."

"I'm serious."

"Me too." I reach over and pull her feet into my lap. "Communication is the key to successful relationships, you know?"

She rolls her eyes, eating another spoonful of ice cream before placing her bowl on the coffee table. "Where'd you hear that?"

"Carter."

We look at each other and then burst into laughter.

"He's the worst at relationships!"

It's the truth. The fact that my brother dropped that knowledge on me this morning made my day up until now. Because the sound of Evie's laughter will always trump Carter's attempts at sounding smart.

"So, tell me about the things you have in the works."

"Security."

"Security?"

"Yeah. I reached out to a few guys I served with. They started up a security company and think I could be a good fit."

"But I haven't heard back from Baylor yet."

"That's why it's in the works but there's no pressure, so I didn't tell you about it." I squeeze her toes gently.

"Oh."

"Come here." I tug on her feet, pulling her in my direction.

She giggles, and I latch onto the sound. Once Evie is settled in my lap, I kiss her lips softly. "You love me?"

"I love you."

"You want to build a future with me."

She nods, her breath mingling with mine.

"Then don't worry about anything else. Going forward, we'll figure it all out together."

"All of it?" Her voice sounds both nervous and breathless.

I press a kiss to the side of her neck. "All of it."

"Even the nightmares and flashbacks?"

"Especially those."

"Even the nights when I can't finish something with you that I start?"

I pull back, my gaze meeting hers. The fear and vulnerability shining in her baby blues squeezes my heart and makes my chest feel funny.

"I don't care about anything but your happiness, Evie. I want you to feel safe and comfortable. We'll do everything at our own pace. There's no pressure or expectations. Not with us, okay?"

"Okay." She responds, relief evident in her tone.

"We'll talk about everything first. Take it slow. Feel me?"

"Yes. Because communication is key, right?"

I swat at her, catching her off guard by tickling her. She flails around in my lap, but I keep her pinned against me. She throws her head back in laughter, and she looks so beautiful, so carefree, that I vow to get to a point where she can feel like this all the time.

Once her giggles subside, a small smile crosses her full lips, and I can't help myself from leaning forward and nipping at them before kissing her. "I love you, my Maywood."

"I love you more, Jaxon Kane."

TWO MONTHS LATER

34

EVIE

"Is this okay?" he asks gently, his brow furrowed as he watches me closely, searching for signs of panic.

"Yes."

He rolls his lower lip into his mouth, still studying me. "You sure? There's no rush. Or pressure."

"I'm sure."

He leans down and presses a kiss to the underside of my jaw. Hovering over me, I feel him everywhere and squeeze my eyes shut tight. He kisses behind my ear and must feel me stiffen because he pulls back sharply.

"Evie?"

"Yes?"

"Open your eyes."

I force my eyes open, regarding him warily. Guarded. I want nothing more than to turn my head to the wall and get through this. I can do this. I can.

It's been two months since I pressed charges against Gary and Paul. Jax and I have been spending countless hours together, working through our complicated history, and battling our personal demons together. We've been wading around the intimacy elements of a relationship but I know I want this with him.

It's a step forward. One that I really want to take.

"I need to be able to read you. To make sure this is okay. That you're okay."

"I'm fine."

"You're not fine." He pushes back, resting on his heels as his thumb strokes my cheek. "I don't want to rush this with you." Holding up his hand before I can interrupt, he says, "For your sake... and mine." Dropping a kiss to the top of my head, he rolls over me, pulling the comforter up so we're tucked in tight. Like kids in a sleeping bag at summer camp instead of two consenting adults about to have sex.

He picks up the remote and turns on the TV, navigating to Netflix.

I roll my eyes when he stops at *Jane the Virgin*.

"What are we doing?" I ask.

"We're hanging. Netflix and chill, I think is what the cool kids are calling it."

"I think the chill part is code for sex, and it seems like you just squashed that."

"I'm not ready," he says seriously, taking all the embarrass-ment and insecurities that overwhelm me and owning them like it's the most natural thing in the world. Like it's as easy as breathing.

I titter nervously.

"Besides, I'm waiting for you to seduce me."

"What?" My voice sounds too high even to my own ears.

Jax turns his head toward me and winks. "I am. Kind of like how you asked me out."

"I didn't ask you out."

"Whatever you say, Maywood." He presses the volume button up as the show starts. Then he wraps his arm around me and tugs me into him so that my head rests in the crook of his shoulder.

The good one. "I don't care what we do... or watch... as long as I'm with you." The simplicity in his tone warms me. And makes me feel complete, whole.

I snuggle into him, pressing a kiss to the side of his neck and turning my face to the television.

We watch *Jane the Virgin*, lying in his bed, and it feels so right, so normal, that I remind myself not to overthink it and to just enjoy the moment.

To just enjoy the feel of Jax's arms around me.

The smell of mint and soap.

The feel of his stubble when he turns his head, and it rubs against my forehead.

To be fully present in this moment.

Eventually, my eyes close, and I doze off into a peaceful sleep: one with no nightmares, no flashbacks, and no memories that I can't escape.

Except, of course, the ones that I want to run to and not from.

* * *

"Open it!" he demands, more excited than I've seen him since our high school football team won State our senior year.

"I'm too nervous." My hands shake as I hold the envelope in between them. I drove straight over to Jax's the second I saw the envelope in my mailbox. "It's too thin. It's going to be a rejection. Acceptance letters usually come in a big packet."

Jax waves off my reservations, his eyes practically dancing with excitement. "Open the letter, Evie."

I exhale loudly, offering myself a little mental pep talk, reminding myself that not getting in won't be the end of the world. That I'll definitely survive.

"Evie," Jax says, impatience heavy in his tone.

Tucking my index finger under the envelope flap and tugging

it up, I pull out the single sheet of folded paper and open it. My eyes quickly scan the first line.

Holy hell.

My heart jumps into my throat as my body locks down and my eyes widen.

I'm in shock.

"Pinch me."

Jax reaches over and digs his fingers into my arm.

"Ouch! What the hell?"

"You told me to pinch you."

"I didn't mean for you to literally pinch me!" I wave my arm, the letter flailing between us.

"You got in." A giant smile stretches across his face.

"I got in!"

He lifts me in his arms, swinging me around and whooping loudly as I clutch the letter to my chest, scared to let it go. I need to read it about a million more times in order to believe that I, Evelyn Maywood, was really accepted into Baylor-Army's Physical Therapy Program.

Jax settles me on my feet and steps forward, his hands framing my face as he holds my head in between his palms. His eyes bore into mine, moss green overflowing with pride. "I knew you could do it. You've always been a badass, Maywood."

I roll my eyes at his compliment, but my lips tug upward into a smile. A huge one.

"Come on, let's tell them." He points his chin toward his front door where his siblings are hanging out in the living room.

"Give me a second." I pull out my cell phone from the back pocket of my jeans. "I want to call my mom."

"Okay." Jax sits down on the front steps of his house while I walk down into the driveway and hold the phone to my ear.

"Evie?" Mom answers on the first ring.

"Mom, I got in!"

A beat of silence passes before, "Oh Evie! Congratulations! I never had any doubt. When did you find out?"

"I just opened the letter."

"I'm so proud of you, sweetheart. You're going to be an incredible physical therapist."

"Thank you, Mom," I say, her words warming me more than she'll ever know. Over the past few months, Mom and I have been spending more time together, falling back into the old comforts of past routines. Now that I'm not actively pushing her away, it's been easier for me to accept the support she freely gives. I never realized how much I missed my mom and hearing her celebrate my success increases my own excitement.

"Come over tomorrow night for dinner, you and Jaxon. I'll tell Graham, too. It will be his last family dinner before his PCS. We should celebrate!"

"I'd like that, Mom."

"Good. We'll have that Bourbon Pecan Chicken dish you love."

I smile, happy she remembered. "Okay."

"I've got to go now. But I'll see you tomorrow, nineteen hundred hours?"

"Roger that."

Mom ends the call, and I turn toward Jax. He watches me from the steps, his feet crossed at the ankles. "What'd she say?"

"Dinner tomorrow, nineteen hundred hours."

"What're we having?" He narrows his gaze.

"Bourbon Pecan Chicken."

The left corner of his mouth ticks up. "Your favorite."

"Yeah."

"I can't wait." He holds his hand out toward me as he stands up. "Come on."

I lace my fingers through his as we climb the steps and walk into his house.

Denver and Carter are playing *War Cry*, both perched on the edge of the couch, their eyes glued to the TV as they toss barbs back and forth.

Daisy sits in the armchair in the corner, flipping through a magazine. She officially moved home after graduation but has seemed a bit lost lately. Even though the Kane boys sympathize with her current position and assure her it's only a matter of time before she lands an awesome job she loves, I think they're all secretly glad that she's home with them. At least for a little while.

"Guys, we have an announcement," Jax calls.

Denver and Carter don't move a muscle, but Daisy looks up from her magazine, watching us expectantly.

"We're moving to Texas!" Jax continues, as if he has the full attention of all in the room.

"You got in?" Daisy squeals, tossing down her magazine and jumping to her feet.

Carter pauses the game, and Denver turns to look at us, an actual smile working its way across his lips.

"Congratulations!" Daisy pulls me into a hug, her energy infectious as we pretty much jump up and down while clinging to each other.

"Ah, it was a given." Carter walks over, throwing an arm around my neck and pulling me into his side.

"Congratulations, Evie." Denver pulls on my ponytail, much like Graham.

"I'm moving too," Jax reminds them.

None of his siblings turn toward him, their attention all on me, as they ask questions about when we're leaving and where we're planning to live.

Jax tries again. "I got a job."

Daisy turns toward him and clucks her tongue, scolding. "Jax, this is Evie's moment. Stop trying to steal her thunder."

He snorts and steps back, letting the other Kane's wrap me up in their well wishes and warm hugs. I look at him over Carter's shoulder and note the pride that winks in his eyes, the smile that still hugs his mouth.

He loves that his family loves me.

And I love that they're all my family once more.

"I love you," he mouths at me.

I blow him a kiss as Daisy grabs my arm, pulling me toward the armchair to show me an image of home decor in her magazine that she thinks will work well in a home in San Antonio.

We spend the rest of the afternoon barbecuing and day drinking and being a family again.

And it's more than perfect.

TWO MONTHS LATER

EPILOGUE

Jax

"Got everything?" Carter asks, popping his head through the passenger window.

"I think so," Evie answers, turning her head to look at the backseat, which is piled high with our belongings.

"Make sure you check the oil halfway through your trip," Denver reminds me from my SUV window.

"Got it."

"Your snacks!" Daisy calls breathlessly, bounding down the porch steps and hurrying over, pushing a plastic bag filled with chips and other junk food and water bottles through the window. "There are some sandwiches and apples in there, too." She leans inside, pressing a kiss to Evie's cheek. "Don't let him eat too much greasy fast-food on the drive, or you'll die of asphyxiation before you reach San Antonio."

A stream of laughter erupts from Evie as I lean forward to scowl at my sister.

"What? It's the truth. I spent nearly three days in a car with you when we moved me back home, and I swear I questioned whether I'd survive the trip."

Carter pulls Daisy into a headlock and musses her hair while she smacks at his arms and yells for him to let her go.

"I'm going to miss you guys," Evie tells them.

"We're going to miss you," Daisy says, finally freeing herself from Carter. "Have a safe trip and call us when you get there."

"We will." I smile at my sister. "Y'all take care, ya hear?"

My three siblings nod as I pierce them with a look. My chest feels tight and even though I'm excited to start this next chapter of my life with Evie by my side, I'm really going to miss my family.

"We'll see you for Christmas," Denver reminds us, not mentioning that the reason we will be back so soon has more to do with Evie's testifying against Gary in January than it does with spreading holiday cheer. He raps his knuckles against the top of the SUV he pretty much rebuilt and gifted us for our new move, a signal that we need to get on the road.

"See you soon," I reply, pushing the gear stick into drive. Evie waves to my siblings as I pull out of the driveway and turn onto the road.

"You ready, Maywood?" I reach over the center console to place my palm on her thigh, squeezing her leg gently.

"Can we make one last stop?" She turns toward me, her eyes serious.

"Sure." I look at her questioningly. We already said goodbye to Graham last night via FaceTime. I know Evie is disappointed her mom couldn't see us off but General Maywood had to fly to Washington DC two days ago. We had dinner with her the night before she left and as we were saying our final good-byes, both she and Evie shed a few tears. It was good to see Evie open up to her family over the summer. She cried the whole way home from seeing Graham off but they talk nearly every day now. General Maywood and Evie are almost back to the close relationship I remember them having in high school. I know Evie is going to miss her family, just like I am, but having all of their blessings and support makes the move much easier.

The past few weeks have been pretty stressful as Evie learned about the court date to testify against Gary. She seemed simultaneously dazed, relieved, and terrified that the prosecutor is moving forward and although we're months away from an outcome, it all looks pretty favorable that Gary's going to serve time. That, coupled with the backlash he's receiving from the Army, is making his life hell right now. Not the degree of hell he deserves, but still, I'm grateful that some type of justice is being served. Paul took a plea and had to pay a hefty fine in addition to two years probation. Not even close to what he deserved to be charged with. However, after all the stories Evie and I learned about perpetrators squeezing past the criminal justice system without any punishment, the fact that Paul pleaded guilty and Gary is being prosecuted are both small victories.

On the bright side, both Gary and Paul received a beat down that left them bruised and bloody, although they're not offering up who doled out the punishment. The knowing glances and gentle pats on the shoulder Evie received from some of the active duty guys at Morris made it clear who'd taken care of the problem. I was proud as hell that my brothers-in-arms looked out for my girl the way they did. Evie seemed touched by their support and display of solidarity, too.

"Where're we stopping?"

She turns to me, "Can you pass by Gladys's house really quick?"

"Yeah, sure." I doubt Gladys will ever understand the importance she's played in both of our lives, but that doesn't mean we shouldn't try to show her. It's suddenly tough to be leaving since it seems that we both just got our families back. Sure, it's what we want to do, but the feeling is bittersweet all the same.

Five minutes later, I pull in front of Gladys's home and let the engine idle while Evie hops out of the car. I follow her up the steps to ring the doorbell.

Mindy pulls open the door, surprise crossing her features when she sees us.

"Hey, Mindy, your grandma home?" I ask.

She nods, her confusion receding as she holds the door open wider. "Yes, she'll be real glad to see y'all."

Gladys's face lights up when Evie steps into the living room. Her eyes are clear this morning, a knowing look passing between her and I easily. Evie drops to her knees beside Gladys's chair and envelops her in a warm hug.

"Thank you, Gladys. For everything," Evie whispers, even though Mindy and I hear her.

Gladys pulls back slowly and rests a hand on Evie's cheek. "I'm so happy for you, dear. So very happy. It's good to see you with some fire in your eyes again. You give them hell in Texas, ya hear? You'll be number one in your class, I'm sure."

"Yes ma'am."

"And don't let him step out of line." Her eyes cut to me, narrowing, even though a softness touches her lips.

"I won't."

"I know." She pats Evie's cheek.

"Now, y'all better get on the road and stop dawdling around here with an old lady like me."

We all laugh.

"I'm serious. Get going!"

Evie gives her one last squeeze, and I step forward to press a kiss to the thin, papery skin of her cheek. "I'll be checking up on you," I tell her.

She waves me away but her eyes shine. We say our last good-byes to Gladys and Mindy before climbing back in the SUV. I pull away from the curb, honking twice to no one and everyone in our little town.

Then we're on the road, our windows down, and fresh air

whipping against our faces. Evie reaches forward and fiddles with the radio, humming to herself as an old throwback from high school plays through the speakers. She leans back in her seat and turns toward me.

"You ready for this?"

"Yeah." I glance over at her before swinging my eyes back to the road. "I've been waiting for this for a long time, my Maywood."

"Me too."

The day is bright and beautiful as I pull onto the freeway and Evie and I literally drive off into our own type of sunset.

THANK YOU!

Thank you so much for reading Evie and Jax's story. I would love to hear your thoughts and feedback. Please show *Rescuing Broken* some love and consider leaving a review on Amazon and Goodreads!

RECOVERING BEAUTY

Stay tuned for *Recovering Beauty* (The Kane Brothers Series Book 2) coming August 30, 2018. To stay informed about Recovering Beauty updates, please subscribe to my newsletter. Thank you for reading!

Recovering Beauty

She saves him from himself. But he ruins her for anyone else.

He shouldn't smile at me. He shouldn't even look at me. He's cost me more than he'll ever know yet he's saved me in ways he'll never realize. Carter Kane is different. He sees past me and through me and into me all at the same time. He makes the damaged parts of me beautiful and the beautiful parts inconsequential.

She's the last person I expect to meet here. Wide blue eyes, full lips, and flowers in her hair, she looks like she could grace the cover of a magazine. Or dance at Coachella. But when Taylor Clarke unexpectedly catapults into my life, she flips it upside down, forcing me to see things differently. Forcing me to admit things I'd rather forget.

Sometimes life hands us a second chance. A fresh start. Sometimes life deals us a tragedy that we just manage to recover from. Sometimes, it's even beautiful.

RECOVERING BEAUTY

Chapter One - Taylor

"Lavender or lilac?" My friend, and I use the term loosely, Isabella asks, holding up two silk gowns that are very similar shades of purple.

"Lavender." I point to the dress on the right.

She sighs, dropping her arms, the silky material of the gowns sliding across the marble floor of her massive closet. "Taylor! This one," she raises the dress on the right, pushing it toward me, "is lilac!"

"Oh. Well, that one then. It's beautiful." I say seriously. The gown is gorgeous, but so is every dress in Isabella's closet. I run my fingers over the beading on the bodice, keeping my attention trained on the gown. I consider it thoughtfully as if this is the most important question I will ever answer.

Perhaps it is.

Isabella spins, catching her reflection in the trifold mirrors at the end of her closet. Dropping the lavender dress, she holds the lilac gown against her slender frame. "I think so, too. This shade just does more for my complexion, you know?"

"Absolutely." I bite the inside of my cheek to keep from laughing.

"So, what're you wearing?"

I look down at my tent summer dress. It's oversized and comfortable and doesn't show a hint of my outline. I love the bold colors of it though. Pairing it with some vintage boots and tassel earrings, it's cute enough to wear out but comfy enough to want to wear out.

Isabella sighs again and I look up, noting how she narrows her eyes at me in a flash of annoyance. "I don't mean right now, Tay. I mean to the gala."

Oh, that. I fight the urge to roll my eyes and prepare myself to pretend like the gala is the most exciting thing in the world. Because it should be; it's supposed to be. "Right. I have a new gown by a local designer. It's blue."

Isabella wrinkles her nose.

"Sapphire." I correct.

She considers this, tilting her head to the left, her eyes perusing my body. I know she's pretending to envision me in said blue dress but the way her eyes spend a beat too long on my thighs speaks to other motives. "Sapphire is a good choice. Especially with your hair."

I tug on the end of the fishtail braid that hangs over my left shoulder. My hair is sun-kissed and golden honey, with every shade of blonde running throughout. Reaching to the center of my back in wild waves, my hair is the one thing I won't negotiate on in my contracts. "Thanks."

"Is Barrington collecting you tonight?" Isabella turns away to the shoes that line one wall of her closet. She runs her fingers over them casually but her posture is too straight, too rigid and I know she's hanging onto every word I say.

"Yes, he's picking me up at seven." Collecting me is more accurate. Barrington Wade, and men like him, choose me, and women that look like me, to lightly clutch their arms, giggle appropriately at their jokes, and ultimately serve as props to attract attention to them. It doesn't matter that we've run in the same circles since birth. At some point, the boys in the group turned into men who were primed to conquer the world and the girls blossomed into women who were meant to shadow them.

Isabella nods, her fingers catching on the straps of soft cream heels.

"Anyway, I better head out now." I say, suddenly desperate to escape the closet that I can literally get lost in. "I'll see you tonight."

"Of course." She turns toward me and presses two air kisses to the space on either side of my cheeks. "I know it can take a while to get all dolled up. Especially when your date is Barrington."

I offer a small wave and walk out of her closet, across her enormous bedroom, and through the maze of the Kent family mansion before collapsing behind the wheel of my red Mini Cooper.

Releasing a deep breath, I spend several seconds staring at my hands against the steering wheel. My French manicure is perfect, my skin smooth and unblemished. The rose gold diamond band on the middle finger of my right hand scatters the sunlight. I have the hands of a woman whose never had to properly work a day in her life. Privileged hands that many yearn for and I would give anything to roughen up.

Starting the engine, I pull out of the horseshoe driveway and down the private road before turning onto the street, and breathing easy once more.

* * *

"You look stunning." Barrington greets me from the foyer of my parent's home. His eyes burn with satisfaction, his hair is perfectly styled, his tuxedo sharp. "As always."

My dad clasps him on the shoulder at his little afterthought. "Ah, Taylor knows how to light up a room."

Mom presses her hands together and smiles. Too bad it doesn't reach her eyes.

"Thank you, Barrington."

He nods before turning toward my father to exchange a few words as I stand as still as a statue, blending into the decor of the room like a piece of art. Something to be quietly admired but still, part of the backdrop. Just like my mom.

Turning my mind inwards, I let myself drift into other thoughts and memories. I hate galas and balls and all the high profile events that I frequently attend. Smiling for cameras and posing on red carpets. Sipping champagne out of delicate flutes and pressing a folded napkin to my lips. Never eating as consuming food would be viewed negatively. What would my peers think? Would the other ladies of high society zero in on my waistline and comment to my mom that I'm gaining? The entire charade is exhausting.

The only good thing about tonight is that it's one night closer to tomorrow. Tomorrow evening, I'm having dinner - pizza and Coke and fries - with Ria. I know she'll make me crack up until I snort soda from my nose and talk me into ice cream sundaes afterwards. She'll make me feel normal and grounded and like me once more.

"You ready to go, darling?" Barrington's hand is at the small of my back, an intense pressure that digs downward into my skin.

"Of course." I smile politely, leaning forward to gently kiss my mom and Daddy good-bye.

Barrington escorts me out of my family home to his waiting black Lamborghini. Not caring much for cars, I know that this sleek bad boy is expensive, exclusive, and an attention grabber. I fight the urge to roll my eyes as I place my hand gently in Barrington's to lower myself into his car.

He crosses around the back of the car, momentarily disappearing from view before settling behind the wheel. "Sorry about the car, doll," he offers me a wry grin, "my Bentley is in for routine maintenance."

"This is perfect." I say because I know it's what he wants to hear.

Barrington revs the engine and turns on some classical music. The space between us is tense and awkward, the way it always is. We ride to the gala in silence.

Just the way I prefer it.

* * *

The gala is beautiful. The decor, the flowers, the place settings, every single detail decided with careful attention and consideration. Ascending the stairs to the entrance, Paparazzi snap photos of Barrington and I. He angles our bodies to meet the cameras for a few moments, his grasp tight on my hip. Once we're inside, he places a hand on my shoulder, his fingers caressing my bare skin and causing a shiver to skate up my spine. "Remember, darling, we need to make a certain impression tonight. Don't forget your place." He whispers in my ear, his posture casual. To a passerby, it would look like a sweet moment between a couple in love. In reality, his tone holds a warning, his words hard and cold.

Turning, I place my open palm on his cheek and look into his eyes. "Of course."

He nods once before his eyes leave me, sweeping across the great ballroom and making a quick inventory of who's present. A calculated assessment of who needs to be approached and who should approach him, and the formation of a strategy for how the night will unfold.

"Champagne?" A waiter holding a small tray filled with champagne flutes stops next to us.

"Thank you." Barrington says to him, never making eye

contact, as he takes two flutes and places one between my fingers. "Don't drink too much." He growls at me under his breath.

I keep my features still, my smile in place, my face never slipping.

These interactions have become so predictable, they don't even surprise me anymore. Not enough to muster a reaction anyway.

"Dr. Hanover." Barrington's voice grows louder as Dr. and Mrs. Hanover turn toward us. We walk the few paces to form a circle with them and Dr. Hanover says hello to us, throwing a quick wink in my direction.

He's probably one of the only men in the room who I genuinely like. He's funny and thoughtful and so successful that he draws the jealousy of everyone present. Except he couldn't care less. Mrs. Hanover is a petite woman with sharp, observant eyes, a wide smile, and a contagious laugh. One that inspires you to laugh along with her. Even though it's not considered polite, it's always genuine, and that's something I admire about her.

"Taylor, dear, you look beautiful as always." She kisses my cheek. A real kiss she presses against my skin. "But you're too thin. Shall we stand closer to the kitchen so we can sample all the hor d'oeuvres on their way out?"

I fight the urge to giggle, instead glancing over my shoulder at Barrington. He dismisses me with the flick of his wrist and I wrap my hand around the crook of Mrs. Hanover's arm as we escape to a quiet corner of the room.

"Thank you." I tell her sincerely, once we are out of earshot of Barrington.

"No, dear, thank you. Poor Edward though." She references her husband, her eyes taking on a shimmer of glee, "he's going to be so bored talking to that stiff you walked in with. Really, dear, why Barrington?"

I laugh lightly, her words hitting their mark. Why Barrington? Because I don't have a choice. Suddenly embarrassed to admit aloud that my parents keep setting me up with him, I fib, "It's stated in my new contract that I make a certain amount of public appearances with high profile men."

"Oh," she nods, considering this, "well good. As long as you're getting something out of it too."

I make a noncommittal sound in my throat, feeling guilty for lying and also desperately wishing that my words rang true. That I was somehow in control over my own future, even tasked with something as simple as choosing my own date for a gala.

Mrs. Hanover snatches several crab puffs from a passing tray.

"These are divine." She pops one into her mouth and holds one out to me.

Doing a quick scan to make sure no one is watching, I eat the puff, a small moan escaping my throat.

"You really do need to eat more." Mrs. Hanover scolds. "I know models need to be thin to stay relevant but really the gaunt look went out in the nineties."

"Mrs. Hanover! I don't look gaunt, do I?"

Her eyes wash over me slowly before she shakes her head. "No. You don't. You look bored and uninspired. It has nothing to do with your physical appearance, which as you know, is absolutely stunning. But there's more to you than meets the eye, Taylor. I just wish you would let more people see you."

I lean forward to press a kiss against her smooth cheek. "I'm so grateful that you're here tonight, Mrs. Hanover."

She waves a hand at a waiter with the coconut shrimp. "You and me both dear. And please, call me Helen."

"Okay, Helen. Tell me when the coast is clear; I'm going to eat a shrimp."

Her eyes gleam again with that same mischievous sparkle. Several tables over, Barrington drones on as Dr. Hanover throws us SOS looks. Helen waves to him cheekily and then snags some coconut shrimp which we pop quickly into our mouths, washing them down with large gulps of expensive champagne.

* * *

After Helen is whisked away by Dr. Hanover, all the way to other side of the great room, the night drags. We take our seats for dinner and I spot Isabella at another table. I wave to her and she nods back, her eyes scanning my dress before she sinks into her seat.

The guests seated at our table greet each other, running through a quick round of introductions. When it's my turn, I open my mouth to say hello when Barrington cuts me off, "This is my date, Taylor Clarke. You probably know her father, Joseph, of Clarke Enterprises."

A few knowing looks and nods take place and I feel my cheeks redden at Barrington's obvious dismissal of me. I'm only of use to him because of my father and his company. I'm only of use to anyone because of the attention I can bring them through my father's name and my own good fortune of having a face that designers deem beautiful enough to market. Hence my career choice.

"You look very familiar." An older man to my right comments, peering at me.

"Oh, I volunteer a lot with the Little Sisters of Georgia. Perhaps you've come to one of our fundraisers?" I ask, using every opportunity I can to plug the organization responsible for keeping me sane.

The group titters and Barrington laughs boisterously, his large hand coming down to squeeze my thigh under the table.

"She recently landed the cover of *Vanity Fair*. She's the exclusive model for Adriana Rose's new campaign." Barrington explains, pride coloring his eyes as he watches the group for their reactions.

"Ohh, I love Adriana Rose! Do you get to keep the gowns?" The wife of the man to my right asks.

"No, but that would be nice." I grin at her, about to tell her about Adriana's new line when the comments start.

"No wonder you're so thin."

"That's it! I knew I knew you from somewhere."

"How exciting! The life of a model."

"Oh Barrington, you must be so proud."

"Do you have a strict diet and personal trainer?"

"How'd you land that job?"

The questions surge forth like an uncontrollable wave. I keep my expression neutral, my fingers digging into the satiny material of my gown. Answering each of their questions, I try to infuse excitement and enthusiasm into my voice. The entire time, I smile pleasantly, nod accordingly, and laugh when expected. Slowly, Barrington's hand releases me. We eat dinner. And I remember that no matter my passions or interests or skills, nothing will ever outshine my looks and the perception that accompanies them.

ACKNOWLEDGMENTS

Thank you so much for taking the time to read *Rescuing Broken*! I hope you enjoyed meeting the Kane and Maywood families and will stay tuned for Carter's and Denver's books (and maybe Daisy's and Graham's...).

I loved getting to know and understanding Evie and Jax. Although their circumstances were often difficult to write about, I think the issues they struggled to overcome are important to discuss - particularly in society today.

To my husband and Littles - thank you for your never-ending support, encouragement, and love. You guys are my world.

To my family and friends who continue to support me on my writing journey - I couldn't do it without you. Thank you!

To Regina Wamba at Mae I Design - I LOVE this cover *all the heart eyes*. Thank you for capturing the Evie and Jax I imagined.

To Rebecca Jaycox - THANK YOU for editing this project and for making me answer the tough questions. Your comments really took *Rescuing Broken* to the next level.

To all the Bloggers, members of my ARC Team, and author friends (shoutout to YAAR and the OP) - thank you x a million for all of the energy and time you poured into *Rescuing Broken* along with me. Your advice and support is invaluable and I think you all are awesome!

To you, the reader, thanks for giving me the opportunity to do something I love - write and create! I'm so grateful to you.

Happy Reading!

Gina

MORE BOOKS BY GINA AZZI

Corner of Ocean and Bay

The Senior Semester Series:

The Last First Game (Lila's Story)

Kiss Me Goodnight in Rome (Mia's Story)

All the While (Maura's Story)

Me + You (Emma's Story)

The Senior Semester Series Box Set (All 4 Books)

ABOUT THE AUTHOR

Gina Azzi loved every moment of college – especially her study abroad experiences, internships, and travel adventures. She draws from these experiences to create the storylines for her new adult and contemporary romance books.

A passionate reader, frequent globetrotter, and aspiring baker, Gina resides in Canada with her family. Her new series, the Kane Brothers, releases in 2018.

For more information, connect with Gina at:

Email: ginaazziauthor@gmail.com
Twitter: @gina_azzi
Instagram: @gina_azzi
Facebook: https://www.facebook.com/ginaazziauthor
Website: www.ginaazzi.com

Or subscribe to her newsletter to receive book updates, bonus content, and more!

SEXUAL ASSAULT & PTSD RESOURCES

Rescuing Broken touches on several sensitive subjects —including sexual assault and PTSD. If you or a loved one is struggling with these issues, please reach out for help.

If you or a loved one are dealing with the aftermath of sexual assault, or for more information, please visit RAINN.

For more information regarding PTSD and available resources, please see the National Institute of Mental Health.

Printed in the USA
CPSIA information can be obtained
at www.ICGtesting.com
LVHW090541091023
760531LV00003B/18